A CAPITOL
Affair

BOOK YOUR PLACE ON OUR WEBSITE AND MAKE THE ARABESQUE ROMANCE CONNECTION!

We've created a customized website just for our very special Arabesque readers, where you can get the inside scoop on everything that's going on with Arabesque romance novels.

When you come online, you'll have the exciting opportunity to:

- View covers of upcoming books

- Learn about our future publishing schedule (listed by publication month and author)

- Find out when your favorite authors will be visiting a city near you

- Search for and order backlist books

- Check out author bios and background information

- Send e-mail to your favorite authors

- Join us in weekly chats with authors, readers and other guests

- Get writing guidelines

- AND MUCH MORE!

Visit our website at
http://www.arabesquebooks.com

A CAPITOL
Affair

ANGELA
WINTERS

ARABESQUE

BET★
BOOKS

BET Publications, LLC
http://www.bet.com
http://www.arabesquebooks.com

ARABESQUE BOOKS are published by

BET Publications, LLC
c/o BET BOOKS
One BET Plaza
1900 W Place NE
Washington, DC 20018-1211

All Kensington Titles, Imprints, and Distributed Lines are available at special quantity discounts for bulk purchases for sales promotions, premiums, fund-raising, and educational or institutional use. Special book excerpts or customized printings can also be created to fit specific needs. For details, write or phone the office of the Kensington special sales manager: Kensington Publishing Corp., 850 Third Avenue, New York, NY 10022, attn: Special Sales Department, Phone: 1-800-221-2647.

BET Books is a trademark of Black Entertainment Television, Inc. ARABESQUE, the ARABESQUE logo, and the BET BOOKS logo are trademarks and registered trademarks.

First Printing: October 2005

10 9 8 7 6 5 4 3 2 1

Printed in the United States of America

Chapter 1

Skye Crawford was beginning to come back to earth, and that wasn't necessarily a good thing. As she opened the door to her small apartment in the Lincoln Park section of Chicago, the silence that met her was deafening. There was no one to reward her for sticking to her principles, no one there to commend her for taking a stand. She was feeling a sense of doubt and she hated that.

Always an optimist, Skye wasn't used to what she was feeling now. Was it fear or dread or . . . the reality of life that her sister warned her would come once she turned thirty? Whatever it was, she wasn't about to let it get her down. Things were going to turn around and that was all there was to it.

She tossed her keys on the console table and headed straight for the kitchen. She grabbed a pint of ice cream from the freezer and a spoon from the drawer.

"Come to Mama," she whispered as she licked the spoon. She let the ice cream melt in her mouth and relished the moment. This was what life was all about, wasn't it? Living in the moment and savoring every second of it.

Skye had let that get away from her these past few months. She had become afraid of uncertainty and comfortable with security. She had betrayed all the values she had come to live by. She had become one of those people who came home and went straight for the mail even though there was nothing more than bills or junk mail.

She had gotten into a routine, even though she'd promised herself life would always be an adventure. Daddy and Mama would be ashamed of how quickly their daughter had conformed to society. Free-spirited hippies, they had taught Skye and her older sister, Naomi, to ride the wind and go with their hearts. Never let society force you to play it safe. Skye had embraced that mantra more than Naomi, but now she was turning into Naomi. What next, a husband and kids in the suburbs? God forbid.

As she sat on the stool, Skye reached over and pulled her easel toward her. This painting, which she had named *Smile*, had been left in her living room untouched for months. She had preferred to come home and mindlessly watch television instead of indulging her mind. After a day at Outreach Chicago, there wasn't any creativity left to lift the brush.

Not anymore. She had quit and Outreach Chicago was no longer in her way. Skye was going to get her life back.

How she was going to pay for it was another thing. There had never been a lot of money in nonprofit public relations. But the satisfaction of doing good paid tenfold, and Skye had never been a materialistic person. She had seen herself as a nonconformist in a capitalist world even though she knew she really wasn't.

Her position as manager of public relations for Outreach, the leading charitable organization serving children in the city, paid just enough for a small one-bedroom apartment in Lincoln Park and a monthly pass on the L train. Not enough for a savings account, God forbid, investing for the future. She hadn't thought that was important during her twenties, believing instead that the future would take care of itself. This move was long overdue. It was time she got out. Doing good deeds was one thing, but growing old without a retirement plan was another.

Skye could have done like Naomi and married money and played it safe. There had been a couple of opportunities, but she wanted to make it on her own. Being dependent on a man was out of the question, or so she told herself when she was making money. Now it didn't sound so bad.

"Stop it," she said out loud, reaching for her palette. "You'll be fine and you know it."

She had taken a stand. Jason Banks, executive director of Outreach Chicago, hadn't given her a choice. When he joined the organization from a highly respected fund-raising firm six months ago, Skye had high hopes. Then, on his second day, the married father of four made a pass at her. She pretended it hadn't happened, but when he did it a second time she couldn't ignore it. She was a woman who always believed in exploring her sexuality, but some things were just wrong and downright disgusting.

Skye acted swiftly to cut short Jason's continued advances. And although he said he understood, he had quickly turned cold, unconcerned that it was affecting their ability to get work done.

She could have handled that. Skye was a tough girl. She had spent summers in Africa teaching writing in the Peace Corps and volunteered for the Red Cross during the tsunami disaster. A middle-aged crisis was nothing.

Only, Jason didn't leave it at that. When he began taking the nonprofit in the wrong direction, Skye Crawford reached the end of her rope. Instead of helping those children really in need, Jason wanted Outreach to focus on the "safer" issues. He didn't want to deal with anything that would be seen as promoting the wrong values, although he never seemed able to articulate what the wrong values were. He made it clear that certain subjects such as race or sex would scare away the more conservative donors. The people with big money would give millions for books in schools, but teaching teenaged single mothers parenting skills was promoting the wrong values.

Skye had had enough and drew a line in the sand. Apparently that line hadn't been strong enough, because Jason, along with several new board members, ignored it and her voice disappeared. Outreach was going to have to go on without her and she had made that clear today.

So now what?

She wasn't going to think about that now. She was going to relax and paint. She was going to eat an entire pint of ice cream, go to sleep early, and wake up late. She was going to face a cold March morning in Chicago with her eye on the future, and nothing could stop her.

"The world is yours," she told herself in a voice less convincing than she had expected.

The phone rang and Skye at first considered not answering, but changed her mind. If she was determined not to let today's turn of events get her down, she couldn't retreat. Who knew? This call could be her first reward for reclaiming a life lived in the moment.

"Skye?" The male voice over the phone sounded a little reserved.

"Yes?"

"It's me," he said with a deep laugh.

Skye was racking her brain, but nothing came to her. "I'm sorry . . . I . . ."

"Today was a hard day for you," he said. "I understand. I would just think that since we were engaged, you would recognize—"

"Jeff?" Skye wasn't sure how to react.

Jeff hadn't called in six months and she wasn't in the mood for the usual *Why couldn't we work it out?* talk, which really meant *I'm coming to Chicago. Can we have sex?*

"Yes, baby. It's been a while, but I'm hurt that you didn't recognize the voice that whispered dirty come-ons to you for almost two years."

"I'm sorry." She settled into her sofa. Jeff liked to talk, or rather he liked to hear himself talk. "It's been a . . . Hey, how did you know it's been a hard day?"

"You quit, right?"

Skye rolled her eyes. "You've been speaking to Tammy."

Tammy Breslin was the receptionist at Outreach Chicago, the daughter of a major contributor who couldn't seem to do anything for more than ten minutes without getting bored or messing up. She'd had a crush on Jeff for years.

"She still calls me sometimes. You know it can be lonely in D.C."

"I sincerely doubt that," Skye said. "You, a young, handsome, single, rich black lawyer in Chocolate City? Those sisters are crawling up and down you."

That had been part of the problem in Chicago. There had been love between Skye and Jeff, but she wasn't sure what it turned into. She had been so impressed with the boy who rejected his bourgeois Westchester, New York, upbringing to roll up his sleeves and work for the state for next to nothing. She had been somewhat naïve at the beginning, but quickly became aware that Jeff's choice wasn't about the people. It was all about him.

He became obsessed with being a hotshot lawyer in the district attorney's office, and his high-profile image attracted all types of women. Jeff was a flirt and he knew he was a catch. He had pursued Skye and had to ask twice before she agreed to marry him.

Skye knew she was beautiful and smart, but she let doubts and suspicion take her over. Suspicion that was confirmed when she found out Jeff had been unfaithful to her three months into the engagement. There was no going back, although Jeff did the proper begging and pleading. It had all been a waste of time. Skye knew the difference between being sorry and being sorry you got caught.

There was no hate between them. Four years had passed and Skye had come to realize that she knew he wasn't the faithful type all along. It was her optimistic spirit that made her think she could change him, made her think her love would keep him home. Some men just don't stay home and those men need a different type of woman than Skye was ever willing to be.

"I get to play," Jeff agreed, "but that doesn't mean it isn't lonely. I haven't found a girl like you."

"Woman," she corrected, "and what can I do for you?"

Jeff huffed at her correction. "It's about what I can do for you."

"I'm listening." She was open to any ideas right now.

"I'm running for Congress."

There was a short pause while Skye let it sink in. "This is . . . I thought you had gone into the private sector."

"I had, Skye. I know you don't approve, but damn, a brother has to make some dough."

"I'm just surprised." She wasn't sure that was the response he was hoping for, but she had to be honest. "You live in the district. Are you running—"

"I want to represent District Eighteen in New York," he answered. "Westchester is my hometown, remember?"

"You don't have to live there?"

"I do live there, technically. My parents' home is my address there and I'm getting an apartment in a couple of weeks. I announced last week. You should watch television every now and then."

"I watch it enough, thank you." Skye sighed. "I'm sorry, Jeff. I don't mean to be a drag. I'm happy for you. I really am. I know you'll win."

"That's what I'm calling you about." There was hesitation in his voice. "I need your help, Skye. I'm running against a hotshot and I need all the firepower I can get."

"What can I do?"

"You're looking for a job, aren't you?"

Skye caught on right away. "Jeff, no. I'm not moving to D.C. Chicago is my home."

"You've lived in Chicago for thirty years. Let it go for a while at least. You don't have to stay here. I just need your help. You're the best PR person I know when it comes to reaching people's hearts."

"Thanks, but that's in Chicago. I'm good at what I do because I know this city and everyone in it. I don't know D.C. or Westchester."

"It's not the place, Skye. It's you. You connect and you write like a genius. I need someone to help get my name out, get my campaign funded, and I need a speechwriter. That speech you wrote for Alex Ramires was great."

Jeff's knowledge of Skye's life was somewhere between flattering and eerie. "How did you—"

"Don't worry how I know," he said. "I know and you're the best. I need you. You don't have anything to do right now. You're not seeing anyone."

"Excuse me. You don't know that."

"Yes, I do. You kicked that Eric guy to the curb three months ago. Weed-smoking musician didn't have a chance with a staunch feminist like you."

"I'm not moving to D.C."

"I gotta beat this guy, Skye. He's a brother and he's a conservative Republican."

"Interesting."

"His name is Darren Birch. You familiar?"

"No, but you know better than to ask me that."

"He's a minor celebrity here. You know, young, rich black rising star in the party."

"I'll bet."

"He's good too. He's smooth and charming, with money and a family name."

"You've got all that and you're on the right side of the issues. You'll beat him."

"Westchester, sister. Remember?"

"Just don't toe the party line, Jeff. Say it in words

they'll understand. Just because they have money doesn't mean they don't care."

"See, you're helping me already."

Skye couldn't help but smile. She was most excited when starting a new fund-raising campaign, but this was out of the question. "No, Jeff."

"Just do me a favor and look over some stuff."

"What stuff?"

"My platform and my attack."

"Attack?" she asked. "Jeff, please don't tell me you're going to be dirty."

"I'm going to tell the truth and it's going to be dirty. Trust me, I have some stuff on this guy and his—"

"I don't want to be a part of that."

"Just look at it and call me tomorrow. I'll send it overnight."

"Just e-mail me."

"I don't want it on the computer. It can be traced."

Something was wrong. "Jeff, what are you up to? Why can't you send this via e-mail?"

"The Internet isn't safe and I've got some things boiling in the pot."

"I'm getting more and more skeptical by the moment."

"I love hearing your voice," he said.

Skye was touched by the sudden tender tone in his voice even though she knew it wasn't genuine. "You aren't my weakness anymore, Jeff."

"You have that raspy, hoarse kind of sexy voice thang going on. Very hot stuff."

Skye rolled her eyes. "If I agree to look at this stuff will you stop the player monologue?"

"I'll send it tonight. Just make sure you keep it private."

"Because I'm sure someone is after it," she said sarcastically.

"You'd be surprised what I got on this guy."

"I'd give you my address, but I have a feeling you've already got it."

"I'm on top of everything, baby."

After saying good-bye, Skye hung up and sat silently on the sofa for a while. She was thinking of better days when she loved Jeff and darker days after she broke off with him and he left for D.C. A girl had to stick with her principles.

"There's no way I'm going to D.C.," she said before returning to her easel.

"Good afternoon, Congressman Birch." The host of The Grill at the Capitol Hill Club on First Street greeted Darren with a smile wide enough to make it seem as if Darren was the highlight of his day.

"How are you, Charlie?" Darren smiled his signature effortless charming smile and grabbed hold of the much older man's hand, shaking it firmly. "I'm here to—"

"Mr. Cramer." Charlie, a man in his late fifties with the spry step of someone twenty years younger, was already leading him into The Grill. "He's been waiting for you. I'll show you to your table."

Located just one block from the nation's capitol, the five-level Capitol Hill Club was one of D.C.'s premiere exclusive Republican meeting places where movers and shakers came to work, attend meetings, network, party, and eat lunch paid for by lobbyists and political action groups while negotiating power and bill sponsorship.

Second-term Congressman Darren Birch, now a regular at the club, waved and nodded hellos to the men and women holding the reins of power as he passed. The smiles on their faces used to make him uncomfortable, but not any longer. They spoke to him, saying *we're depending on you* and *make us proud*. He was used to such expectations, having heard them his entire life. At thirty-five, he was the promise and the world was his.

The reason the messages were sent to him in smiles instead of actual words was that, compared to them all, he was a pup. Only in his second term, Darren had to earn his keep before the accolades came out loud and strong. Capitol Hill, referred to as the Hill, was all about the game. And if you didn't learn how to play quick, you didn't stay long.

Grant Cramer was a millionaire and one of the most influential men in all of Washington. A former military hero with a slew of medals, he was now a powerful political consultant and lobbyist for the real estate industry, and his time spent on the Hill had paid off well. At sixty years old, Grant Cramer looked like J.R. Ewing and would have fit better in the oil industry than real estate. He was an aggressive man who found a way to charm even those who hated him.

Grant had welcomed Darren with open arms since the day he moved to D.C. four years ago after winning his first election. Darren had kept his distance from the lobbying world in his first term, choosing instead to stay chained to his desk doing as much work as possible. He had been excited about the opportunity to help the "little guy" and be a voice for the people, but in Darren's case that was easier said than done.

Being that his constituents were from Westchester and Rockland Counties, two of the wealthiest areas in the country, there weren't a lot of "little people" that came to him. Things weren't perfect in the place where he was born and raised, but far from the need in other areas of New York. So Darren found the best way to help the little guys was to get on as many committees as possible and work toward legislation that promoted American values, personality responsibility, and opportunity for everyone. Darren made the unusual leap to the extremely powerful Appropriations Committee's subcommittee on Housing and Development after his reelection, and Grant Cramer quickly became his shadow.

"Congressman!" Leaning back in the booth against the window, his favorite in The Grill Room, Grant held his hand out to Darren as he grinned from ear to ear. "It's about time, man."

"Grant." Darren shook his hand before sitting across from him. He looked up at the waiter who was eagerly waiting for his drink order. "I'll have a water."

The waiter looked disappointed before leaving.

Grant was disappointed as well. "Let me look under this table for a skirt. Water? You want a lemon wedge with that?"

Darren smiled, pointing to the glass of scotch in front of Grant. "That stuff will kill you. It's only one in the afternoon."

"Hell, man. I've been drinking since age ten. It's been a long day." Grant sighed in that way that made one think he had the weight of the world on his shoulders.

"Am I about to make it longer?" Darren asked.

"I hope not. You got the documents I sent you?"

Darren nodded. "I haven't read them. I gave them to Lonnie, one of my legislative assistants. . . . Talk to me."

Grant's eyes lit up the way they always did when he talked real estate.

"This bill has got to pass," he said. "It's been standing around for four years now, ever since the Adrian family willed it to the state. There are millions to be made in housing development in that area. It's just perfect. Do you have any idea how much money can be made on this?"

"You just said millions," Darren responded. "But who is going to make it? From what I hear, this project is going to make the people who are already rich richer. There might be better uses for that land than more million-dollar homes."

"And businesses," Grant added. "You can't be against that."

Darren shrugged.

"Not to mention all the jobs it will create to build." Grant smiled. "Let's not talk about that now. We'll just enjoy lunch. You have time, don't you?"

Darren heard the talk about life after you've made it in D.C. It was all parties and lunches from then on. The members schmoozed and socialized while their staff did all the hard work.

Darren straightened his tie and looked down at his watch. "We might have some bills in the next hour, so I can't lunch long."

Grant shook his head. "I've been in D.C. for almost as long as you've been wiping your own butt and I've never seen a black man as uptight as you."

Darren sent Grant a stern look, but he wasn't offended. If there was anything Darren knew about Grant it was that he wasn't a bigot. He had worked hard to get more minorities in leadership positions in the lobbying and political consulting industries. He played a major role in creating industry measurements for hiring minority-owned contractors, and his firm, Cramer and Associates, gave minority law students several thousands of dollars a year in scholarships. Not to mention the fact that he was married to a black woman.

Besides, Darren was uptight.

"Can I count on you?" Grant asked.

"You can count on me to look at it, Grant." Darren opened his menu. "I respect you and myself too much to make a promise I might not be able to keep."

"All I'm saying is with you on my side, I know I'll win. You're a winner, Congressman, and I . . ."

Darren looked up from his window, wondering what in the world could make Grant speechless. He turned his head in the direction Grant was looking and saw the subject at hand.

Jeff Preston, raisin brown, six feet tall, and the image of a *GQ* model, entered the Grill Room with a cocky stride and a chin held high. He had a lot of nerve written all over him.

"Let it alone," Darren said.

"Can you believe him?" Grant asked. "I want to know who in the hell invited him into this club."

"He knows a lot of people on the Hill. He's represented a lot of them."

Grant laughed. "Yeah, he's gotten a lot of people out of a bind, which is the only reason they tolerate him. But he's not running in D.C. He's running in Westchester and he has no idea he isn't going to win."

"Confidence is a good thing," Darren said, trying not to smile at the anticipation of beating the pants off Jeff. "I'm up for a challenge. I ran unopposed in my last election."

"That's because you beat the guy by eighty percent in the election before that. Prince Preston over there seems to have forgotten that."

"I need to keep fresh," Darren said.

Grant frowned as if wondering whether or not to

take Darren seriously. "You can't really consider this guy competition."

Darren smiled, returning his attention to his menu. "I'm not worried about Jeff Preston."

"You know he's been asking around," Grant said, "trying to get dirt on you."

Darren immediately thought about his brother, Franklin. He loved his older sibling, but he was clearly the weak link in the family. Sometimes Darren thought he was purposefully trying to make his life hell, but knew that was selfish thinking.

"He won't get far on that."

"What about your brother?" Grant reacted to Darren's glare. "Sorry. I just think you should have your guys looking under Preston's bedsheets as well."

Darren shook his head. "I'm not opening that Pandora's box. He's got nothing on me and he won't be in this race long."

"You know something I don't?" Grant asked.

Darren winked. "Trust me."

He had spoken to enough people in Westchester to know that Jeff barely had the signatures to get on the ballot, and he knew enough people on the Hill who had no intention of backing him from this end.

After they gave the waiter their lunch order, Grant leaned over the table and just above a whisper said, "You know what you need to do."

Darren looked toward the dining room entrance and noticed Jeff was staring in his direction. He nodded a polite hello and Jeff nodded back. He would enjoy beating this guy, but he wanted to do it fair and square. Clean was his style.

"Don't start with that getting married rant." Darren

had heard enough of that from everyone this past year. "Settle down, get a wife, and make it a package."

"It's a wise choice," Grant said.

"Not if it's made for the wrong reasons."

"You're a great-looking guy, Darren. Tall, dark, handsome, fit, and you've got a lot money."

"I'm a public servant."

"You know what I mean," Grant said. "Your family has money. Everyone knows who your father is."

Darren didn't respond. He wasn't interested in getting into the topic of women today. The entire female species was a cross to bear for Darren. Although he had never had a problem attracting the most beautiful and connected women, turning that attraction into a successful relationship was an entirely different issue.

During his twenties he had played the field. He could remember only one real relationship that lasted two and half years, which he ended because she kept bringing up the M word and he wasn't ready.

A few years ago, Darren had found himself ready for that commitment, but his search for something real kept coming up empty. So he gave up, choosing instead to focus on his career. He had needs and didn't believe in casual sex. He had Elizabeth, a woman that was more than a friend but not a lover. They were convenient for each other and there were no lies. She had a busy, demanding career and social life. She knew the deal and the deal suited them both fine.

"It figures."

Skye had just sat down at her laptop, ready to do some serious job searching, when the doorbell rang.

The last thing she needed was a distraction to keep her from something she didn't want to do anyway.

She had forgotten about Jeff's package until the deliveryman appeared on the other side of her door. Skye was under the impression she was getting a few memos and reports. This felt more like an entire campaign strategy.

"Something from a secret admirer?"

Skye's head shot up from the form she was signing at the sound of her best friend's voice. Monica Guillen, 100 percent Puerto Rican spice, sashayed up the hallway with that eternal smile on her face.

"Hey." Skye thanked the deliveryman and took the package. "What are you doing here, girl?"

"My upstairs neighbor is playing his damn piano." Monica pointed to the package. "What is that?"

"Something from Jeff."

Monica grabbed it from her and walked into the apartment with Skye following behind. Skye had met Monica at a rally for raising the minimum wage in the state about five years ago. Both women went for deep-dish pizza and beer at Gino's East and had been tied at the hip ever since. Skye liked her attitude and respected her brain. She was a counselor at Planned Parenthood, one of the many organizations that Jason had decided was no longer an acceptable partner for Outreach Chicago.

Monica lived in a studio apartment just two floors down, but arguably spent more time in Skye's only slightly bigger place than her own.

"You have to tell me everything he said to you," Monica ordered. "Wait, let's do it over margaritas. I feel like getting drunk."

"Can't." Skye hadn't thought it was the best idea to tell Monica about Jeff, but she had to tell someone. She should have known Monica wouldn't be satisfied with a summary. "I have to get on the Net."

Sitting down on the sofa, Monica started ripping open the package, but Skye grabbed it from her and placed it on the coffee table. "You can't look at it."

"What difference would it make? It's not like I care. I'm not in New York or D.C."

"He was very serious about it being kept secret." Skye returned to the computer, although she knew there wasn't a chance of her getting any work done now that party girl was here. "It was all pretty weird."

"And you certainly know weird." Monica leaned forward, her hand reaching out. "All the more reason—"

"Moni!"

Monica threw her hands up in the air in surrender. "Okay, okay. I'll leave it alone, but you have to tell me if you're going to do it."

"Are you nuts?"

"Yes, but the question still remains." Monica reached for the remote and flipped the television on. "It sounds like a lot of fun and it's not like you have anything keeping you here."

"You sound like Jeff."

Monica turned to her, her nose squinching. "That was weird, wasn't it? That he knows so much about you. He's still in love with you."

Skye wanted to laugh at the thought, but couldn't for some reason. "I'm not devious and underhanded enough for the world of politics."

"You've got it in you, girl. I've seen it." She joined Skye at the computer, standing behind her. "You still addicted to that porn?"

Skye jabbed her with her elbow. "You're sick. I was going to look for a job."

"I got a better idea." Monica grabbed a chair and pulled up to the computer table. "Let's order pizza and find out who this Derrick Birch is."

"Darren Birch." The thought had occurred to Skye to Google him, but not seriously. "I think I pretty much got his number from what Jeff told me."

"Ah yes, the reliable rose-colored glasses of a man who thinks of no one but himself. It might fire you up if you knew more about him. I know you don't like conservatives."

"I never said that." Skye was already sliding her rolling chair aside as Monica attacked the keyboard.

"Oh yeah," she answered, laughing. "That was me."

Monica hit the Search button. "Wow. He's a popular guy. Look at all these hits."

Skye was curious. "Click on News About."

Monica did as told. "This one is the most recent. It was in the *Washington Post* just last week." She clicked on the article titled Charity for District Schools Raises $25,000.

The District Reading Society hosted a fund-raiser at a swanky hotel and the attendees were a who's who list of D.C., none of whom Skye knew.

"Here we go." Monica scrolled down to a group of pictures from the event. "Let's see which one of these pretty people is our soon-to-be ex-congressman."

Skye could tell who he was right away. She didn't need to see the caption reading HOST EMMA DRIER AND PHILANTHROPIST AMY MOORE FLANK CONGRESSMAN DARREN BIRCH. He had a presence about him that told anyone he was important the second they looked at him. The way he held himself, the self-assured smile, and the charming good looks introduced to the world a man that was about something.

"Hello, Papi." Monica leaned in. "I thought all the hot politicos were Democrats."

A little unnerved by her own reaction to him, Skye was eager to move on. "What else you got?"

Returning to the search results, Monica selected his official page in the House of Representatives. Another handsome, winning picture of the young congressman popped up in the corner of the page with a few text-book politician pictures beneath it. Holding a baby and shaking the hand of a working-class man.

"Go to his issues page." Sky pointed to the link. "This is where it'll get good."

"Screw the issues." Monica clicked on his biography. "I want to know if this man is single."

"All politicians are married," Skye said. "I think it's a requirement."

"Jeff isn't." Monica scrolled down to the extensive biography and blurted out keywords. "Political science at Howard, MBA from Brown, and a law degree from Yale. That's serious stuff."

"Jeff is Ivy League as well," Skye offered. "And look, he worked at his daddy's law firm after Yale. He couldn't make it on his own like Jeff did."

Monica made a smacking sound with her lips. "You trying to say Jeff didn't use his family connections to get in with the D.A.'s office? You're reaching, honey. Our Mr. Birch is Episcopalian. That's close to Catholic, right?"

"Says who?"

"Close enough to your type of Catholic at least. It's not like you're at Mass every Sunday like me."

Skye rolled her eyes and turned her attention to the

screen. "Member of the Main Street Republicans, where conservatives meet the center. Yeah, right."

Monica didn't seem fazed by Skye's skepticism. "The interesting thing is that he's not married. Check it out. This is where all the personal stuff is. They mention his mother, father, and older brother. That's it."

"What's your point?" Skye thought this was at least good for Jeff. It was hard for single politicians to run against a candidate with a family. "Jeff can beat him. He's too . . . too perfect. He can't be real."

"Nothing is real in Washington," Monica said. "That's why the country is in such a mess."

"Don't be so pessimistic." Skye gently slapped her on the back. "There are a lot of committed people in D.C."

Monica looked at her and smiled. "You sound like you're interested."

With a hint of annoyance, Skye said, "Would you click on the issues, please?"

After she did, Skye read through the list of Darren Birch's stances on major issues and her blood began to boil. "Centrist, my ass. This guy is way on the right."

Monica was laughing as she scrolled the list. "Lower taxes, smaller government, school vouchers, welfare reform, pro-life, cut spending, no embryonic stem-cell research, and end affirmative action."

"Enough." Skye's arms folded over her chest. "What does a man born with a silver spoon in Westchester know about welfare, inner city schools, women's health care, or . . ." Skye noticed the widening smile on Monica's face. "What?"

"Nothing," she answered. "Just that I want your apartment when you leave."

Chapter 2

Darren barely remembered a day when he could count on a moment of peace. He hadn't had one in a long time. His cell phone, which had been buzzing in his pocket during the half-hour voting session at the Capitol, was still going strong as he made his way back to his office at the Cannon House office building across the street.

"Yes." His tone was sharp.

"It's me." *Me* was Mia Barozza, his office manager. "You need to call Valerie Salvatores ASAP."

"Who?"

"Who . . ." She made a smacking sound with her lips. "She's executive director of Barrio Futuro. You've met her several times and you're speaking at her charity function next month."

It had completely slipped his mind. "What does she want?"

"She wants to talk to you about your speech," she answered impatiently.

"Remind me when I . . ." Darren wasn't sure what to make of what he saw, but it didn't look good.

"Congressman?"

"I'll call you back."

Darren hung up and quickly made his way into the building's famous Rotunda Room where his twenty-one-year-old legislative assistant, Lonnie, was standing with Jeff Preston. Darren couldn't tell what Jeff was saying, but from the look on Lonnie's face, he wasn't giving a compliment.

"You know something," Jeff asserted. He was leaning into Lonnie, who looked utterly intimidated. "I know you do."

"What in hell is going on?" Darren asked sternly as he approached.

Initial alarm on Jeff's face turned quickly to contempt. "Congressman—"

"What do you think you're doing?"

"We're having a conversation," Jeff said, sneering. "He is allowed to speak without you around, isn't he?"

"That didn't look like a conversation to me." Etiquette aside, Darren wasn't going to take any crap from this guy. "You're going about this wrong, Jeff. This is not how you run for office."

"You're telling me about ethics?" Jeff laughed loud enough to garner stares from others passing through the Rotunda. "I know what you're up to and you're not getting away with it."

Darren's first instinct was to ask him what he was talking about, but he decided against it. He didn't know what Jeff meant, but he wouldn't let him know that. He wouldn't give him the satisfaction of being vulnerable to something Jeff thought he had over him. He had seen this game before.

A loud clearing of his throat was followed by "Jeff?"

All three men turned to a young, dark woman with cornrows and an angelic face staring uncertainly at them. "We're . . . going to . . ."

She pointed to her watch, seeming unable to finish her sentence.

Jeff's posture took ownership of her presence and without further comment he stiffly turned and walked over to her.

Darren's anger was tempered by those standing around, but he could tell it would take more than on-lookers to calm Lonnie down. Lonnie didn't look easily intimidated. He had an athlete's body, but the disposition of a pacifist. It took a lot to make him lose his temper, and his flaring nostrils and brooding glare made Darren curious.

Darren reached out to Lonnie, placing his hand firmly on the young man's shoulder. "Calm down, man. Just tell me what's going on."

"He was threatening me." Lonnie slowly pulled himself together. "He said he knew what we were up to and he wasn't going to be scared out of this race."

"He's seeing the inevitable and becoming a little un-hinged," Darren said. "We haven't made any attempt at—"

"Forget it." Lonnie smiled as if nothing had happened. "He's just being a jerk to me because he's too afraid of you."

"What else did he say?"

Lonnie just shook his head. "He just asked me what I knew. What do you know? What do you know? If this is how he acts in March, I don't want to be around him in November."

"He won't make it to November," Darren said.

He had a handle on his campaign and there weren't any immediate plans to go after Jeff. Darren had planned to give him a few weeks' grace period before showing up his inadequacies as a leader. "Not if this is how he operates. I'm going to talk to him. I think this is about more than the race."

"Like what?"

Darren waved to an approaching senator and her aide. "I'm not sure, but either he's paranoid as hell or he thinks we're doing something we aren't."

Skye could sense the tension in Jeff's voice the second he answered the phone. "If this isn't a good time, I—"

"It's just . . ." There was a heavy sigh on the other end of the line. "I'm going to handle Darren Birch."

Skye didn't like the sound of that. "You mean defeat him in November, right?"

"I won't have to beat him in November. He'll be in jail by then."

"What are you talking about?" Skye had done all the surface research she could on Darren Birch and hadn't found any dirt.

"He's been here, but I can't prove it."

"Are you trying to say Darren Birch broke into your apartment?"

"He had someone do it."

Skye could hear odd noises in the background. It sounded as if Jeff was tearing the place apart. "Why would he do that? What—"

"I had a disk and now it's gone. I kept it right here on my desk. I should have hidden it considering what was on it."

"What was on it?"

"The information I needed to bring Darren Birch down. Jessica Rancer is never going to—"

He was talking so fast between short breaths that Skye was having a hard time following him. "Are you sure you didn't put it away?"

"No. It was right here at my desk. I was going to copy it right after I sent you your package, but I got a call from . . ."

Skye smiled, reaching for the envelope Jeff had sent her the day before. "You thinking what I'm thinking?"

She reached for the blue disk that fell out. It was titled *Orveko Inc.*

"Please tell me you have it."

"Orveko Inc.," she answered. "Is it blue?"

A long sigh was followed by a laugh. "You just saved my life."

Skye doubted it was that important. "You must have slipped it in by accident."

"I was rushed because the pickup guy came early. Whew! That disk is my life insurance."

"You're very forgetful." Skye placed the disk back in the envelope. "Now tell me what you have on Darren Birch that would make you think he'd break into your apartment."

"Oh my God," he said. "I made such a fool of myself today."

"I hope you didn't accuse him of breaking and entering." Skye could just imagine the public relations battles in front of her if that was true.

"Not exactly, but it doesn't matter. He's guilty of worse and he's not getting away with it. Can you send it to me overnight?"

Skye felt that tinge of excitement that had been missing from her life for some time. "How about I give it to you tomorrow instead?"

It took him just a second to catch her drift. "You're coming? You're moving here?"

"Whoa, buddy. Nobody is moving anywhere. I'm coming for a visit. I'm coming for a talk."

"I knew I could count on you, Skye."

After she hung up, Skye was thinking of too many things to count. She was thinking of her relationship with Jeff, wondering if they could be friends and work together.

She was excited about being a part of the Beltway power center.

She was already thinking of how she could shape Jeff's campaign to appeal to the people he needed to sway away from the favored son.

Most of all, she was wondering why Jeff had said Darren Birch would be in jail by November.

The last time Skye had visited the nation's capitol, she was twelve years old. A trip with her parents who were protesting some injustice the government was committing against the impoverished. She hadn't remembered, having been there at least once a year with them for some cause or another. After that it had always been her choice to come or not and she chose not to. She was more a local activist and the capitol was old stuff to her by then.

It was different now and as she made her way up the hill toward the lines, it saddened her. Security had tarnished the appeal and accessibility of the place. Now, instead of walking up the white steps of the west front, one had to walk around barriers to a tented receiving facility with tickets, ID, and a guide.

Skye's guide was waiting for her at the top of the Hill, waving his arm in the air. Seeing Jeff after so many years did spark a little flicker in her belly. He was an incredibly handsome man. Then there was the fact that she had loved him once and a part of her heart would always be with him. She had no desire to get involved with him temporarily or otherwise, but had made certain she looked her best when he saw her. Even though she had gotten over his betrayal, there would always be that little part of her that wanted him to know what he had lost by his stupid mistake.

When she reached him, she hugged him tight and felt no need to be nervous about an awkward situation. Everything was going to be fine.

"It's so nice to see you," he said, taking her in.

Skye knew she looked great in a cream rayon and linen pantsuit with wide legs underneath a petal-pink thigh-length suede blazer that matched her shoes. Her V-neck, buttoned top was low enough to be a little inappropriate but not too much.

He hugged her tightly again. "You're just . . . you're beautiful."

"Thank you." She placed a tender hand on his cleanly shaven cheek. "You look great too."

"Yeah, right." He took her by the hand, leading her past the crowds standing in line. "I look like hell. I haven't gotten a lot of sleep lately, but now that you're here . . ."

He stopped, turning back to her. "We're gonna work great together."

Skye could see that his eyes were red, and that sense

of being just a step off, unusual for Jeff, concerned her. "Are you okay?"

"I'll be fine," he said unconvincingly. "Now that you're here. Look at it, Skye."

She followed his outstretched arm looking up at the Capitol and was touched by its beauty and significance. It was an incredible building: beautiful, almost regal in the way it stood out and above.

"You know," he said, "no building in D.C. is taller than the Capitol except the Washington Monument. It's a law. Nothing can surpass the tip of the dome."

"How are we getting in without standing in line?"

"Oh." Jeff reached into his pocket and pulled out a SPECIAL VISITOR ID. "Take this. It'll get you inside. I have enough connections to avoid that line, but we still have to go through security at the door. Just stick with me and you'll be fine."

"Sounds like a plan." She reached out and squeezed his arm. "You're really excited about this."

"Power." Jeff had a spark in his eyes. "This is the power center of the world and I'm gonna be a part of it."

"So that you can help people, right?" She laughed at his guilty smile. "Keep your eyes on the prize here."

"That's what I have you for."

Darren cleared his throat loud enough for both Jeff and his pretty friend to notice. He had been reluctant to interrupt them considering the scene yesterday, but he was compelled to come over, catching sight of Skye.

Darren found her incredibly attractive. She had a careless look about her, with hair several shades of brown going every direction in natural curls. She wore no makeup, but her face, a rich caramel, glowed like sunshine, her dark brown eyes sparkled, and her tiny lips had a colorful tint. She had a healthy, curvaceous body that told him he would regret it if he had kept on walking.

Skye recognized the dashing congressman immediately. He had that winning smile, that charm that made men and women stare. But no . . . she wasn't going to be fooled. She didn't have to see him as the enemy, but she couldn't fall under his spell either if she was going to do her job effectively.

"Jeff," Darren said, never taking his eyes off the woman at Jeff's side. The little twist in her small lips made it clear she was someone to deal with. A little hell-raiser. "Come by to see some debate?"

"No." Jeff's response was flat and his stare was undeniably cold.

Skye, the public relations professional in her kicking in, squeezed the hand she still had on his arm. Jeff reacted immediately with a pasted smile.

"Just showing a friend around," he answered. "You must be coming from some afternoon votes."

Darren held his hand out to Skye. "I'm Darren, Darren Birch."

"I know who you are, Congressman." She accepted his hand. His firm grip and shake seemed to alert a sixth sense inside her. She retrieved her hand from him as soon as possible. Her job was going to be harder than she imagined.

"Then you're one up on me," Darren said.

Jeff rolled his eyes before acquiescing. "Congressman Birch, this is Skye Crawford."

"Skye?" Darren's brow rose. He was eager to hear her speak again; he liked the raspy tone of her voice. "That's a beautiful, unique name."

Skye could only smile, not trusting she wouldn't say something embarrassing in response to his charm's effect on her. This guy had to be no good; he was too perfect not to be. She reminded herself of his stand on the issues. Yes, that would be her cold shower to fight off his appeal.

"You must not be from D.C.," Darren continued. "I would know you if you were."

"What makes you think that?" Skye asked.

"I just would," he said. "I couldn't help but know you."

"It was nice talking to you, Congressman." Jeff took Skye by the arm, pulling her to his side, away from Darren. "I'm sure you have some lobbyist to serve."

Darren frowned, but for only a second before his smile came clearly through. "Funny, Jeff. Real funny. I'm right, aren't I, Ms. Crawford?"

Skye nodded. "I'm visiting Jeff from Chicago."

Darren leaned back. "Ah, the Windy City."

"You know," Jeff said, leaning in, "the city gets that name from its windbag politicians, not the weather like everyone thinks. You'd be happy there."

Skye took Jeff's hand and squeezed tight. Darren Birch didn't come across as a guy who took well to being insulted in front of women.

Darren nodded, ignoring the lesser man's attempts at attention. "I hope you enjoy D.C., Ms. Crawford. Chicago is a great city, but we actually have a spring."

Darren stepped closer to Skye, surprising himself at his forwardness. He was usually more reserved with women he was attracted to, but this woman had a flame in her eyes and he was like a moth. "How long will you be here?"

Skye was taken aback by his forward approach. It went against everything she had assumed about him based on her research and intuition. She liked his quiet, assertive style. She liked it too much.

"I'm not sure," she said, her voice sounding weaker than she had expected. "As long as Jeff needs me."

Darren looked at Jeff, relishing the look of jealousy on his face. Darren enjoyed the opportunity to put Jeff in his place. The man was no match for him on any level, including the attention of beautiful women.

"Jeff certainly is a lucky man," Darren said, backing away.

"In more ways than you know," Jeff added.

"Enjoy D.C., Ms. Crawford." Darren smiled one last time before turning and walking away.

As Jeff let off a litany of curse words, Skye watched Darren walk away. His every stride was confident and in control. Power, success, and adoration were natural to him. He wore them so well it was hard to believe any of it could be faked.

"Skye." Jeff waved his hands in front of her face to get her attention.

"Sorry." She returned from her trance.

"Yeah, he's good looking, but don't be fooled."

"I'm not—"

"Don't lie. You're only human." Jeff stuffed his hands in his pockets, scowling like a little boy. "He's a great-looking brother, but he's got a girlfriend."

"I don't doubt," Skye said. "I'm surprised he isn't married."

"Elizabeth? She's a barracuda, not the marrying type."

"Whatever that means," Skye said. "He's going to be

a tough one to beat, and being a jerk to him isn't going to make it any easier."

"I can't be civil to someone who is so crooked." Jeff pulled Skye to him, leaning in to whisper, "Do you have the disk?"

"I'm sorry, Jeff. I left it in the hotel." Skye hadn't remembered it until she was in the cab on the way here. "We can go get it anytime."

"No." Jeff looked around suspiciously. "It's better that it stay with you. No one knows you have it and I know they're looking for it."

"What in the world are you talking about?"

"I think my apartment is being bugged."

Skye had thought he was being paranoid on the phone, but standing this close to Jeff, knowing him as well as she did, she could see he was serious. "Why would he be doing that?"

"If I can tie him to . . ." Jeff stopped talking as a group of women passed by. "Darren Birch thinks if he can get me out of this race, I'm not a threat to him. He doesn't know I know his secret."

"What secret? Another family, a gay lover, what?"

Jeff shook his head. "Did you look at the disk?"

"No. I haven't had time."

"Good. I don't want you to know yet. I need to confirm some things first. The less people know, the better." He took a deep breath as if getting his second wind. "How about lunch?"

Skye wondered what she had just gotten herself into.

Darren was trying to concentrate on his work in his office on the second floor. He only had an hour between the last votes and the next set of votes at the Capitol and had hoped to spend it returning calls. Instead he was looking out the window across New Jersey Avenue at the Longworth Office Building thinking about a beautiful woman named Skye. That keen look in her eyes gave notice of her intelligence to anyone who thought she was just good-looking, but it was those soft, light brown eyes that told him she was tender and that was what attracted him. That, and of course that flirtatious cleavage that anticipated the rest of her body.

Darren smiled at the wicked thoughts that jumped to mind, but the smile only lasted a minute before he thought of Elizabeth. That itch he was feeling about their relationship wouldn't go away. It had been agreed between them that there would be no commitment, that what they did was for comfort and mutual satisfaction. They had something to offer each other and there had been a real physical attraction at one time. That attraction had gone away for Darren and he was getting the sense that Elizabeth was walking away from the agreement.

It would be presumptuous and cocky of him to think she was falling in love with him, but she was demanding more and more when he wanted less and less. He was counting on their agreement to keep them both honest. He was beginning to believe that his lapse in moral judgment was going to bite him in the butt. He couldn't believe any longer that Elizabeth knew this wasn't going to last; knew that she had promised to keep her end of the bargain.

There was a knock on the door before Lonnie stuck his head inside. "You wanted me?"

Darren waved him in. "Yeah, do you know a woman by the name of Skye Crawford?"

Lonnie thought for a moment. "Nope, I . . . Not off-hand. Who is she?"

"She was with Preston this morning. Beautiful sister." Darren noticed Lonnie's smile. "No, I'm not thinking anything, I'm just curious. She's from Chicago. You've done your research on Jeff. Find out who she is."

"I'm on it."

Lonnie slipped out just as Mia entered with an annoyed look on her face.

"Michelle Parks is on line four for you." She placed her hands on her ample hips.

"No press right now," Darren said. "She annoys me anyway."

"Tell me about it." Mia paused, looking at the floor for a moment. "She wants to talk about Franklin."

Darren went on alert. Something was wrong. Something was always wrong when the press wanted to talk about Franklin. What had he done now?

"I'm busy, Mia." He reached for the phone, waiting for her to leave before dialing his father.

"I know what you're calling for." The flat tone of the usually upbeat voice of Gary Birch gave it away. "I'm sorry it reached you, Son."

"What now?" Darren asked.

"Who is asking?"

"The *Washington Post.*"

"Why would they care about . . ." There was a short pause. "Your brother was arrested last night for disorderly conduct."

Darren felt his chest sinking as abjection washed over him. It wasn't just Franklin's antics that were taking a toll on him; it was the unpredictability of them that kept him on edge. "He's drinking again. Where is he now?"

"I bailed him out of jail this morning. He said he was going back to his place in Manhattan, but I called him an hour ago and no one answered."

"He's probably coming out to me." Darren wasn't looking forward to another conversation about money with his brother. Although Franklin was three years older than him, Darren had reluctantly taken on the role of older brother and Franklin never let him forget how offended he was about it.

"You don't have to take him in, Darren. You're running for reelection. You have to distance yourself from Franklin's antics this year."

"The more I try to do that, the worse he gets." Darren was resigned to the coming nightmare. "I'll have to deal with him sooner or later. Better in March than October. I can handle it."

"You're going to give him money?"

"Hell no," Darren said. "I'm going to send him to rehab."

"That's what you just did," Gary responded. "It's all we always do."

"I'll send him some place better this time."

"It's your choice, Son. Just know that your mother and I won't fault you if you don't."

"How is Mom?" Darren inquired.

"She's beside herself as usual. She could really use your comfort. You'll be home this weekend, right?"

Darren agreed to come home before hanging up. He was feeling a bit of the weight of the world on his shoulders, but he had to stop feeling sorry for himself. It was Franklin who had the real problems. He had to fight the lesser man in himself that resented his older brother, the one who had failed to live up to his potential.

When they were young, life was great. They were two privileged boys, best friends who relied on each other. Frank and D, the Birch boys of New York. Then came high school and their differences were becoming more and more apparent. Darren had always been quicker, smarter, and more charming. Franklin was handsome with more of a rough edge that the girls liked, but he was also short tempered with a tendency to screw up. As Darren's strengths grew, so did Franklin's weaknesses. The animosity, which began in small doses, grew to a general constant, and although the love remained, the friendship had died over a decade ago.

It had died because every girl that Franklin liked preferred Darren. Every dream their father had, Darren fulfilled with ease before Franklin could even get a chance to. A failed marriage and dependency on drugs and alcohol had estranged Franklin from the entire family, while Darren's academic, legal, and political success had made him the pride of joy of the Westchester Birches and everyone they knew.

It was the talk around society in New York and Washington, D.C. The more Darren impressed, the greater Franklin's shortcomings seemed to be. Interactions between the brothers were limited to arguments and ultimatums. Franklin had even resorted to threats, although he never followed up on any of them. Darren had tried to show deference to his older brother for as long as possible, but he'd had enough.

Lonnie knocked on the office door before sticking his head in again. "You okay?"

Darren was slow to look up. The answer was no, but what good would it serve to worry Lonnie? He was a good kid and Darren knew he looked up to him. "What is it, Lonnie?"

"Skye Crawford?" Lonnie looked down at the notepad in his hand. "Preston lived in Chicago for five years,
working for the D.A.'s office. As far as I can get, Skye
Crawford was his girlfriend. She's a PR chick with a spe-
cialty in speechwriting."

Darren nodded. "Thanks, Lonnie. That's all."

Jeff's reemerging girlfriend was going to have to take
a backseat for now. Darren had a bigger problem to deal
with, and his heart was hardening at the thought of it.

As she rode up the elevator to Jeff's luxury apartment, Skye was sure she knew what the wink the doorman had given her meant. She had thought to take a
second to make it clear to him that she was not one of
the many women she was sure he'd seen taking the ride
to Jeff's corner of the Metropolitan Premiere Apartments. That whole thing was going to have to stop anyway. If Jeff wanted her to be his PR consultant, he would
have to listen to her and stop playing the player. It
wouldn't be an easy conversation, but she was going to
put her foot down. Voters liked their leaders to show
commitment and responsibility. Jeff was going to need
all the help he could get competing with Congressman
Birch, a man that had been on Skye's mind too much
that afternoon.

The elevator opened onto the twelfth floor decorated in a hospital disinfectant type of white that made
Skye feel cold and uncomfortable. There was a light
pine bench in the center between the two apartments
and an abstract rectangular painting in red, black, and
green. Skye had a feeling that there was no African significance to it. She was probably certain the landlord
didn't even know what colors he had chosen.

When she reached Jeff's door, Skye could see it was slightly open and wasn't surprised. Jeff was expecting her to come by to deliver the disk before they left for dinner. She was sure he wasn't ready yet, as was the case most of the time when they were dating. With all the complaints that men had about women taking forever, Jeff and Skye had played opposites of the stereotypes. Her natural look made it easy for Skye to be ultra-low-maintenance, but Jeff was a primper. Getting ready to go out was just as much an event as going out itself.

After knocking, Skye entered the apartment and saw the essence of the man she once loved everywhere. As cynical as he could be at times, Jeff loved light and color. His apartment was full of expensive furniture that didn't match but somehow went together. He had paintings and sculptures throughout and large windows everywhere so the light from the sun could stream through.

"Jeff?" Skye peeked into the large, modern kitchen trying to speak loud enough to be heard above the stereo playing Mary J. Blige a little too loud. It was empty so she started down the hallway.

"Jeff?" The light at the end of the hallway was likely the bathroom and she was certain to find Jeff in there or in the bedroom not anywhere near ready.

Skye didn't mind, thinking as she reached into her purse and pulled out the disk that they would have some time to take a look at the mysterious blue disk before dinner at eight.

The bedroom door was wide open and Skye walked in without caution, which she immediately regretted. She was so terror-stricken by what she saw that she fell back, hitting the floor with a force. She didn't feel the pain. She could only feel shock and horror at the sight of Jeff hanging from his ceiling fan with a noose around his neck.

Darren felt a sense of dread come over him as he slowly, quietly slid out of bed. He looked to his left and was grateful that Elizabeth hadn't moved. He made his way to the bathroom, deciding against turning the light on.

Standing in the dimness in front of the mirror, he looked at himself and knew that he had to be a better man than he was at this moment. He had needs and yes, it was nice to have someone to sleep with, but the pleasure ended as soon as the sex did. It wasn't enough anymore and he had to be man enough to admit that to himself. He had to be man enough to end this and put what was right ahead of what felt good for now. Hell, it didn't even feel that good anymore.

He believed in the value of a committed relationship, and just because he hadn't found the time to have one in the past few years didn't make it okay for him to settle for this.

He faced the facts as he knew them as a man: sex and love weren't the same thing. It was just that they could be, and when they were, nothing was better. There couldn't be anything in his life that kept him from having what truly mattered: a woman that loved him and a family. If Jeff Preston could recapture something with a woman like Skye Crawford, then Darren could find a real relationship. And he knew Elizabeth deserved to be free to find the same for herself.

"What are you doing?" Elizabeth flipped the switch and the bright light illuminated the room. "Why are you walking around in the dark?"

Darren blinked as his eyes adjusted. He turned to her standing in the doorway like a woman in need of a cigarette.

Elizabeth Sandon was a beautiful woman; there was no denying that. She was five eleven with long legs that turned into round hips, smooth chocolate skin, almond-shaped green eyes, and jet-black hair that traveled to her small breasts, which were still firm and pert at her age of thirty-five. She stood out in a crowd and knew it. From her modeling days she had met and married and divorced a rich California real estate mogul in a five-year time span. Although she wasn't a rich wife anymore she had taken her settlement and last name into the world of philanthropy and made a name for herself as the executive director of the Jack and Evelyn Barry Foundation, one of the largest in Washington, D.C. That position had also gotten her on the board of the Washington Ballet and the very influential Corcoran Gallery.

Darren had met her at a fund-raiser at the National Gallery, and although he was intrigued, she was the one who pursued a date, which had taken forever to make because of their schedules. Darren found her sexy and worldly and he liked that, but never took to her icy edge and careless attitude toward real issues. Besides the parties and fund-raisers, Elizabeth cared very little about the charities she worked so hard for.

Their difficult lives allowed them to come to their agreement, which they had both considered very cosmopolitan at the time.

"I didn't want to disturb you," he said, turning away.

She laughed a cold, careless laugh. "Darren. Always the considerate one, but I wasn't asleep. Since you're being so nice, can—"

"No, you can't smoke." Darren splashed his face with water. "Go out on the balcony."

"It's too cold," she said. "If you're finished, I need to use the . . . you know."

"Liz," he said, "we need to talk."

"Not now." She was looking down at her nightgown, pressing against the wrinkles. "I have to get out of here. I'm meeting the girls for drinks at H2O at ten. It's almost nine. I told you I was just stopping by for a quickie."

With her head still down, she started past him, but Darren stepped up to block her way. Her eyes widened as she looked at him, and her expression quickly became annoyed.

"What?"

"We can't keep doing this, Liz."

"Not this again." Elizabeth rolled her eyes, backing up a little. "Listen, Darren. I understand what you're feeling, but we're both realists. We live in a different world than most people. Love . . . Well, love isn't really in the cards for us."

"How can you believe that?"

"Love can make you make wrong decisions," she said. "How many promising futures have been destroyed or, even worse, never realized because love allowed them to make bad decisions that came back to bite them?"

"If it's real love," Darren said, "it's not wrong."

"Tell that to Javier Guzman," she responded. "He had all the promise in the world. He was going to be the future mayor of Baltimore, governor of Maryland, and then God knows what else. He married that girl he loved even though he knew she used to have a drug problem."

"She had kicked her habit before she met him."

Darren didn't want to go over that story again. In his last election for mayor, his good friend Javier was caught off guard when his opponent paraded former drug addict buddies of his wife and destroyed his campaign.

"But he knew about it before he married her," Elizabeth argued. "Love gets in the way of politics, Congressman. You and I have plans and our futures require choices and sacrifices."

"Your sacrifices are too big," he said. "And they're sacrifices I never agreed to. What we're doing isn't making either of us happy and—"

"Then let's get married."

It was Darren's turn to step back. "What . . . Where did that come from?"

"It only makes sense."

"It actually makes no sense." Darren didn't need this mess. First, he had come home to a nasty message from Franklin demanding money, and now this.

"We are people who have chosen our careers as our lives." Elizabeth's tone and mannerism would make one think she was explaining a simple situation. "Our decisions are based on what is best for our careers. We'd both benefit from getting married and neither of us has the time to actually devote to a real relationship. God knows how long that would take."

Darren was only shaking his head.

"If you're afraid of being stuck with me," she said, "don't be. You can have other women as long as you choose them wisely and stay discreet. I'll do the same."

"Woman, you sound crazy." Darren stormed out of the bathroom in need of a stiff drink.

"Darren!"

The harsh tone of her voice made him turn around,

and the serious look on her face made him stay at attention.

"I have plans," she said. "This wasn't just for you. Being with you has opened doors for me, and I need your name to get what I want."

"Not a chance," Darren said. "I'm sorry, Liz, but not a chance in the world."

"Please, Detective." Skye wished she could be more helpful to the hard-edged Detective Alice Ross, but she was in pieces. It had been a couple of hours since she phoned the police, but the reality still hadn't sunk in. She was still expecting someone to say it was a joke or that they felt a pulse and everything was going to be fine because she had caught him just in time.

When she arrived, Detective Ross had taken the initiative with Skye, who was in complete shock. When the paramedics left, declaring Jeff dead, Detective Ross held Skye back as she yelled at them and ordered them to try again. They hadn't seemed fazed by her reaction and just left.

"I can't," Skye continued. She had tried to call someone, but every time she picked up the phone, her hands were shaking too much to dial. "I don't even know anyone in his life anymore. Our dinner . . . tonight, he was supposed to tell me about . . . We spent all of lunch talking about me."

"He didn't seem in an unusual mood at all?" Detective Alice Ross, a middle-aged, raisin-brown woman with a hard look and a wide girth, stared intently at her.

Skye shook her head. "I can't think. I'm sorry, but I can't help you."

"I know this is hard for you." Detective Ross leaned

against the back of the sofa alongside Skye, looking down at the floor. "There's nothing I can tell you to make you feel better, but I really do need your help."

"I've . . ." Skye had to catch her breath through tears. "I've told you everything I know. I came here and—"

"Not about that," Detective Ross said. "About Mr. Preston. What might make him want to kill himself?"

"Nothing," Skye insisted. "There is no way Jeff killed himself. He wasn't that kind of person."

"You've only been back for one day," Detective Ross said. "Not even that. How would you—"

"I know this man. I was in love with him for two years. We were engaged."

"That was some time ago."

Skye wanted to explode. "Jeff was not a depressed person. Everyone who knew him will tell you that he was an optimist. He was too cocky and self-centered to be suicidal."

Detective Ross gestured for her partner, an older white man with an eternal scowl. Skye watched through sore, red eyes as he handed Detective Ross a plastic baggie with a sheet of paper in it.

"What is that?" Skye asked.

Detective Ross handed it to her. "It's a suicide note, Ms. Crawford."

Skye tossed the letter back at her. "No."

"It says that he's ashamed of what he's done."

Skye stood up straight, her hands clenched in fists. "No."

"It says that he would rather die than have to face the music." Detective Ross handed the baggie back to her partner, who walked away. "Ms. Crawford, something was going to come out about him, and with his entire future planned in the public eye, maybe he couldn't take it."

None of this made sense. Jeff wouldn't have done this to her. He wouldn't have asked her to come out here for nothing. He would never ask her to come over here and see this.

"The doorman said no one has visited Mr. Preston since he came home, which was around four."

"What if they were waiting for him?" Skye asked, trying to clear her mind to think.

"We're checking the tapes, but the doorman said it's only been you. The front lobby and delivery area are the only way visitors can get in, and they're both monitored."

"He asked me out here to help him on his campaign," Skye said. "He was excited about his future. He said he had . . ."

Detective Ross seemed curious. "He had what?"

Skye thought better of mentioning Jeff's secrets about Darren Birch. There was no proof to anything and she knew better than to bring it up. If she was wrong, she could be bringing hell on herself. "It's nothing."

"Ms. Crawford, if you don't give me a reason to believe there is anything else, then this is a suicide."

Skye wrapped her arms tightly around herself, feeling cold, alone, and afraid. "Someone killed him, Detective. I don't know if it's on purpose or just a random act of violence, but Jeff Preston did not kill himself."

"Did he have any problems with anyone?"

"Not that he told me." Skye turned away, eager to get out of the apartment as she was feeling the walls begin to close in on her. "You'll have to ask his friends here in D.C. He worked at—"

"We know all that," Detective Ross interrupted. "I'm asking you about his campaign."

"The campaign doesn't even exist yet."

"You're out here, aren't you?" Detective Ross sighed, nodding to her partner, who was calling her down the hallway. "You know this is going to be very public."

Skye felt a quell in her stomach. If it was in the paper, then she couldn't keep denying it.

"We'll try as much as we can to keep you out of it, but my men are telling me that the press is already downstairs."

Skye could only shake her head, thinking of his mother. *Oh God, Jocelyn.* "Can't you send them away?"

"No, but I can make sure you get out of here without them seeing you. I just need a guarantee that you'll stay in town."

"Why?" Skye couldn't get out of Washington soon enough. "You don't think I—"

"Until I can rule his death a definite suicide, I need you to stay in the district." She offered Skye her card, placing it on the end table after Skye wouldn't accept it.

Skye nodded, looking up as two men with MORGUE written on the back of their black jackets entered the apartment with a mobile stretcher. She felt a wave of nausea wash over her and rushed for the bathroom.

Chapter 3

"You owe me!"

Darren tried to keep calm despite his brother almost breaking his eardrum over the phone. "I don't owe you anything, Franklin. I'm trying to help—"

"Don't patronize me, you little bastard."

Darren was tempted to hang up. This was the second threat he had received today and it was only 8:30 in the morning.

"This isn't up for discussion," he said shortly. "You either go to rehab or—"

"Go to hell?" Franklin asked, laughing angrily. "That's my only other choice, right? You think I'm gonna let my little brother, the boy I've protected and stood up for his whole life, give me orders and tell me how to live? You've let your fame get away with you. Maybe it's good that you lose it."

There was the threat again. Franklin had shown up at his apartment at midnight last night, dirty, smelling like bourbon, and sweating like a hog. In between slurs and mumblings, he demanded five thousand dollars. Darren refused but agreed to let Franklin sleep there that night. After about an hour of yelling obscenities and accusations at the world for his messed-up life, Franklin passed out on the living room sofa.

Darren had hoped to get out the next morning without any more drama, but Franklin woke up in enough time to demand the five thousand again. Darren's refusal had resulted in a threat to destroy his life before Franklin's hangover had him rushing to the bathroom to throw up.

"There are some clinics better than the last one," Darren said. "I can send you—"

"To hell with the clinics, Darren. I need the money, and if you don't—"

"You threaten me one more time," Darren warned.

Darren held the phone away to avoid the slamming sound when Franklin hung up. He imagined everything in his apartment either destroyed or gone when he came home, which was why he had taken efforts to secure everything of real value and importance that morning. He was certain Franklin, who had to have the hangover from hell, wouldn't be able to find the safe inside the wall of his bathroom.

The intercom buzzed and Darren reluctantly pressed it.

"Is it Franklin again?" he asked Mia.

"No," she answered and after a long pause, said, "It's her."

"I'm busy," Darren said flatly.

"She said she didn't care."

"Then hang up." Darren shut the speaker off.

Before his ever-pleasant morning battle with Franklin, Darren had been awoken by a call from Elizabeth, threatening to ruin his reputation if he didn't marry her. She hadn't decided if she was going to say he was gay or that he had a myriad of fetishes that she couldn't satisfy, which was why she had to end things. Darren thought the world had gone crazy. Who were these people in his life?

Darren hadn't given in to her, more determined than ever to reject her. In the public eye with political aspirations, he was a target. He should have chosen more wisely, but that was done now. Elizabeth could hurt him, but if he let her know he believed that, she would go to town. Instead, he played hardball and let her know she was playing with fire by trying to back a man like him into a corner.

It seemed to make her hesitate, but Darren got the distinct feeling he hadn't heard the last of her and he felt bad for what he had done. He was smart enough to know the reality of life on the Hill. One had to use one's power to get things done and not always in a good way, but he didn't want to become a bad guy. He didn't want to become like some of the men he worked with who had threatened to derail his career if he hadn't backed this bill or that. He wanted to do things the right way, but he knew that wasn't always possible when the other person was determined to do things the wrong way.

Darren could recognize Lonnie's knock and wondered why he hadn't just walked in like he usually did, but when he came in after Darren's prompting, the look on his face said everything. Lonnie hadn't been eager to enter Darren's office because he had bad news.

What else was new?

"Just come out with it," Darren said. Franklin had set

his apartment on fire. The press wanted to know the name of his gay lover. "What?"

Lonnie took a deep breath and with a pained looked said, "Mia . . . Mia wanted me to remind you that, uh, you haven't given her a draft of your speech for the Barrio Futuro event in two weeks."

"Yeah, and?"

He bit his lower lip. "Yeah, uh . . . it's Jeff Preston."

"What does he want?"

"He doesn't want anything," Lonnie said. "He's dead."

Darren was sure he had heard him wrong. "Lonnie."

"It's on the news, Congressman. Jeff Preston killed himself last night in his apartment. The rumor is he hanged himself."

Darren's head fell back in his chair and he was speechless. Whether or not it was appropriate, the only thing that came to mind was the false pervading theory that blacks didn't do the suicide thing. They did, but what wasn't false was that those who did make the tragic choice did not hang themselves.

The knock on the door of her hotel room broke Skye from the silent trance she was in. She was weak and barely had the strength to cry. She certainly wasn't in the mood for a visitor, especially one she didn't recognize through the peephole.

The girl couldn't have been more than eighteen with glowing skin, large brown eyes, and dark cornrows in her hair. From her red eyes, Skye perceived her to be a fellow griever and opened the door.

"Skye Crawford?" the girl asked through a cracked, weak voice.

Skye nodded, but wasn't at all expecting what happened next. The girl threw herself at Skye, arms wide. She squeezed her tight and began sobbing uncontrollably. After the shock wore off, Skye guided her into the room and sat her down on the sofa and handed her a tissue. She sat silent as the girl cried for a few moments more.

"I apologize for my directness," Skye said in the nicest way she could manage. "But who are you?"

"I'm Sierra," she sniffled. "Sierra Jackson."

"You're Jeff's assistant." Jeff had mentioned his invaluable administrative assistant at the law firm who was going to be his right hand during the campaign.

Skye reached for her, touching her just for comfort. The gesture brought on another few minutes of uncontrollable sobbing.

"I can't believe . . ." Sierra blew into her tissue. "I can't believe he's dead."

"I know." Skye felt a stab in her stomach that wouldn't go away.

Sierra's attention moved beyond Skye to the open suitcase on the bed and a confused expression took over her face. "You're leaving?"

Skye nodded. "There's no reason for me to stay here now. I only came for Jeff and . . . I've spoken to his parents and I'll be in New York for the funeral, but I can't stay here anymore."

"You can't leave, Skye." Sierra reached out, grabbing Skye's hands in hers. "You have to help me."

"I know this is hard for you, but there isn't going to be a campaign."

"Not the campaign, Skye. The murder."

Skye wasn't sure how to respond, but the eager look on Sierra's face told her she had to say something. "The detectives believe it was a suicide."

"But you don't, do you? You can't."

"I don't want to," Skye said, "but there isn't anything I can do. I don't know anything about Jeff's life."

"He was so excited about you coming. He . . . he's still kind of in love with you." Sierra looked away. "He was at least."

Skye was touched and her heart ached for the man she had thought she knew. "When I was leaving his apartment building, I heard the detective mention that the security cameras showed no one was admitted to the twelfth floor at all yesterday. They made it sound like that was definitive proof."

Sierra sighed. "It isn't possible for anyone to get on the floor without the doorman pressing the elevator release, and the other apartment on the floor is empty."

"Maybe it was an accident," Skye said, although she didn't believe that.

"You can't accidentally hang yourself. I can't explain the evidence, but I know Jeff was killed and Congressman Birch has something to do with it."

"Whoa." Skye had put forth an effort to wipe these thoughts from her mind. "You can't go around accusing a powerful politician of murder without proof."

Sierra stood up and began pacing the room. "Whoever killed him must have taken the disk." Skye's gasp got her attention. "What?"

"The disk." Skye stood up, trying to rack her rattled brain. "He sent it to me by accident."

Sierra threw her hands in the air. "You have it? Okay, now we've got something. That disk has to have something on Congressman Birch and we can take it to—"

"I dropped it." The scene played itself over in Skye's mind and her hand went to the wall to steady herself. "I dropped it when I . . . when I saw him . . . in the bedroom."

Sierra just looked at her for a while with a pained expression on her face before asking, "Do you think the detective has it?"

Skye shrugged. "I didn't mention it and I don't think she would have told me either way."

"And she won't now." Sierra reached inside her pocket, pulled out a set of keys, and offered it to Skye. "There's a chance it's still there. We've got to get it before we hand it over to them."

"Jeff's apartment?" Skye asked. "It'll look suspicious."

"No one will see you if go this secret way." Sierra rushed to the desk against the wall and grabbed a pen and paper. "Only select residents have access to this door via the top level of the garage."

Sierra went into great detail on what Skye had to do to get into the garage, on the VIP top floor, and into the elevator. She gave instructions and yet another code for turning off Jeff's security alarm if by some chance someone had turned it back on.

Sierra ripped the sheet from the pad and handed it to a reluctant Skye.

"What exactly is on that disk?" Skye asked.

Sierra bit her lower lip. "That's the million-dollar question, Skye. All I know is that Jeff was trying to get dirt on Congressman Birch's relationships and he found something that guaranteed he could beat him. It was better than a sex scandal, better than money under the table from a lobbyist."

Skye had always relied on her intuition, but she was second-guessing herself big time now. She didn't want to believe that Jeff could have killed himself, but the evidence was suggesting otherwise. That disk might prove that her intuition about Jeff was right, but that meant her intuition about Darren Birch was wrong. Despite her opposition to his views, he hadn't seemed capable of murder. He was too confident to feel so threatened. He seemed like a man who prided himself on his moral character, one willing to stick with his principles no matter what the price.

Sierra spoke as if sensing Skye's thoughts. "This is Washington, D.C. Power is like crack to these people. The ones who have it will do whatever it takes to keep it."

The thought sent a chill down Skye's spine, but anger proved a stronger pill than fear. If Jeff had been murdered, she didn't care if she had to go against a powerful and popular politician in his own territory. She was going to do whatever she had to in order to make the guilty pay.

After the news about Jeff's suicide hit him, Darren was taking some time to come back down. The last thing he wanted to do was entertain Westchester socialites, but a promise was a promise. That was part of being a public servant: whenever someone from your district made their way to the nation's capitol, they paid their representative a visit.

As the two sixty-year-old women, decked out in age-appropriate socialite casual pantsuits, sat in his office chatting between themselves with the occasional complimentary interruption from Grant, Darren moved in and out of the present. The women seemed to be satisfied with a smile, nod, and random "isn't that something?" dropped in every now and then. It wasn't until a knock on the door came that Darren really came to attention.

Mia opened the door with a worried look on her face. "It's for you, Congressman."

Darren knew it had to be serious considering that Mia never interrupted him while he was with visiting constituents unless it was an emergency or a vote, and there weren't going to be votes until 6:30 that evening.

Darren stood up and walked to Mia, blocking her from the rest of the group.

"What is it?" he whispered.

"Detective Ross," she said, tilting her head behind her. "She's investigating Jeff Preston's death."

Darren frowned. Investigating a suicide? When he turned back to the eager group, only Grant seemed to have an idea that something was up, and Darren was confident he would do what he could to make this easier.

"Ladies." Darren flashed that winning smile that made older women wish he was their son. "I'm so sorry, but I have an impromptu meeting I can't pass up."

"Oh dear," one of the women said. "It must be important."

When Detective Grant appeared in the doorway, Grant quickly stood up and said, "Everything the congressman does is important and it's all for you ladies."

These women melted to even the cheesiest of flattery and both stood up as Grant held his hand out to them.

"If you'll both come with me," he added, "I will show you the Rotunda and the building's beautiful Caucus Room. Later, Representative Birch will join us for pictures on the Capitol steps."

Darren winked a thank-you to Grant, who ushered the two women, clutching their tiny Chanel purses tightly, out of the room. The three of them gave Detective Alice Ross, who looked nothing less than daunting, a curious once-over as they passed her on their way out. She was unfazed and Darren could tell right away she was a formidable woman. He would be careful not to underestimate her, which was why, the second Mia closed the door behind her, he got right to the chase. This woman wasn't interested in the political small talk.

"Detective Ross," he said, holding out his hand.

"Congressman." She ignored his hand, nodding instead.

"What can I help you with today?" He gestured for her to join him on the leather sofa against the wall, but her stance made it clear she was the standing-up kind.

"You've heard about Jeff Preston's death?" she asked with a poker voice to match her face.

"His suicide, you mean?"

Alice raised a curious brow. "No, I mean his death."

Darren nodded. "I was saddened when my staff informed me of this tragedy earlier today, but I was under the impression it was considered a suicide."

"That's what it looks like, but it hasn't been decided yet."

"So, you're interested in knowing where I was last night?"

She seemed pleased that he wasn't going to make this a show. "Around seven in the evening."

Darren took a quick breath, deciding on the best way to handle this. "I'm a public figure, Detective. You understand it's important that—"

"I only understand how to investigate a suspicious death," she said. "I'm not concerned with anything else."

"Fair enough." He studied her. "I was with a friend of mine, a lady friend."

Detective Ross flipped open the top of her pad and clicked her pen. "Name, please."

Grant returned, sans socialites, only a few moments after Detective Ross made her exit. "Tell me that wasn't about what I think it was."

Darren nodded. Grant had called him only seconds after Lonnie broke the news, but Darren had been too shocked to talk at the time.

"I thought it was a suicide." Grant threw his hands in the air. "That's just great."

"What?"

"Don't you get it? If he didn't . . . if someone killed him, you're a suspect."

Darren wasn't even going to venture into that territory. "There is no way, Grant. First of all, we don't know it wasn't suicide. They're just dotting their Is."

Grant didn't seem at all satisfied. "I knew something was wrong."

"Who would kill him?" Darren held up his hand to stop Grant from answering. "No, forget it. I'm sure it's suicide. If it's not, my alibi clears me."

"That's not the point," Grant said, running a harried hand through his salt-and-pepper hair. "All that has to happen is for someone to suggest it wasn't suicide and you're tainted. You've got to start covering your tracks."

Darren was getting angry now. "I told you I'm not guilty of anything. There's no reason for me to act as if I am."

Grant was unrelenting. "Cover your ass, man."

Darren nodded. "I've got Lonnie tracking down his girlfriend to show my concern."

"He's got a girlfriend?" Grant smiled. "I was hoping we could catch him with a—"

"Grant, the man is dead, for Pete's sake."

Darren felt hypocritical. He had tried to convince himself he was doing the gentlemanly thing in trying to find Skye Crawford, but he knew there was a little voice in the back of his head eager for a chance to see her again. It was wrong of him and he wouldn't admit it to anyone.

Grant's expression said he couldn't care less about Jeff's demise. Patting Darren on the back, he said, "You're always on top of things."

If you only knew, Darren thought. He might be on top of things now, but Franklin, Elizabeth, and now Jeff Preston's death threatened to topple him over.

Sitting in the Washington, D.C. police headquarters on Indiana Street, Skye was beginning to lose patience after waiting for Detective Ross for a long time. She was nervous, mostly because she knew she was being deceitful and wasn't any good at it. She was trying to work up the nerve to go back to Jeff's apartment, but the idea of being there again made her ill. There was still a part of her that wanted to believe she was having one of those dreams that seemed to last for days, but really only existed for a night and was gone when she woke up. If she went back there, that possibility was done with.

"Ms. Crawford?"

Skye shot up from the bench and turned to face Detective Ross. The woman already looked as if her time was being wasted, but Skye didn't care. She had waited too long for that.

"Detective, I wanted to get an update on Jeff's . . . death."

"I'm sorry, hon." She handed a file to a passing officer. "You're not next of kin."

"I'm the one who found him. I'm the one you asked to stay in town."

"I can't tell you how the investigation is going." She looked around before gesturing Skye to follow her into a more private corner.

"What can you tell me?" Skye asked.

"I've spoken to his parents. Why don't you ask them?"

Skye sighed, unwilling to admit she didn't have the emotional strength to talk about Jeff with someone who cared about him. That one, quick conversation she'd had with Jocelyn set off an hour of crying.

"What about Darren Birch?" Skye asked.

Alice leaned back, folding her arms across her chest. "What about him?"

"Is he a suspect?"

"I haven't said Mr. Preston was murdered."

Skye tried to keep calm. "Look, Detective, I know you're doing your job, but . . . I was engaged to him once. We were going to be married."

"Even if you were married," she said, "I couldn't tell you the specifics about an investigation."

Skye stared the detective down and thought she might have earned a little respect as the other woman sighed deeply, rolling her eyes.

"Congressman Birch," Alice said, "has an alibi."

For some reason that piece of news made Skye feel a hundred times better. "So he isn't a suspect."

"We haven't confirmed the alibi yet, but I'm not telling

you any more." Alice cocked her head to one side with a smirk on her face. "Ms. Crawford, you need to understand something about the district. People think the capitol is supposed to represent the ideal of America. It does, but not the America in the Constitution. It represents the real America. Here, certain people count more than others and if you cross them, you'll pay."

"Are you afraid of Congressman Birch?" Skye didn't need to be schooled on power. She was somewhat naïve to the game, but she wasn't stupid.

"I'm not afraid of anyone," Alice protested with conviction. "But there are rules and there are ways to play this game. Mr. Preston was an emerging person of importance in D.C., but Congressman Birch's power reaches very far."

Skye believed her and knew she was going to have to play it safe as well.

Detective Ross started to walk away, but stopped midstride and turned back. "I don't want to hear you're doing anything stupid, Ms. Crawford. You're not doing your friend a favor by making yourself look suspicious."

"What could I do?" Skye asked with an offhanded shrug. "But I have one more question."

"Which I'm probably not going to answer."

"Did you find anything at the apartment?"

She tried to hide her curiosity, but it revealed itself, laced with a little suspicion. "Like what?"

"I don't know," Skye said. "Maybe a clue that could lead to evidence of an enemy of some kind."

"What I have is a suicide letter, Ms. Crawford." She leaned in. "If you know of something else I should have, I suggest you give it to me. Otherwise, I can't help you. And if it turns out this was a murder and I find out you've held something from me, you're going to be in trouble."

Outside the precinct, Skye hoped she had made the right decision in not telling Detective Ross about the disk. There was a part of her that didn't trust the police to do anything with it. After all, it had been made clear to her in so many words that Darren Birch was close to untouchable.

Skye didn't want to become paranoid. She needed to hold on to what little wits she had about her to compensate for the lack of reason her emotion was causing. She made her way to the curb and was ready to raise her arm for a cab when she noticed the silver compact across the street. She didn't so much notice the car as she noticed the young man sitting in the front seat. He stood out because he looked to be half the size of the entire car itself and he was staring directly at her.

Skye didn't like it. She was used to being looked at by men, but this wasn't a check-out-the-hot-girl type of stare. It was an I-know-who-you-are type of stare and Skye was frozen in place. She had enough of a mind to stare him down. First lesson of self-defense: *let him know you know he's there.* It seemed to be effective, as he quickly sped off, an unusual choice for being in front of a police department.

So much for not becoming paranoid.

Still shaking off the prying driver outside the police department, Skye wasn't at all prepared for what she saw when she entered her hotel. She loved surprises, but had had enough for one week.

Darren hadn't seen her yet. Standing in the lobby with an eye-catching bouquet of deep purple moonshadow carnations, bloodred roses, and white December lilies in his hand, he was speaking to the bellman in a posture indicating that he was giving orders or directions.

Skye thought of slipping into the nearby café, but was afraid any slight move would get his attention. She decided to try it anyway and he didn't notice; the bellman did notice her and he began waving his arms wildly in the air, leaving Skye no choice.

"That will be all," Darren said to the bellman. "Thank you."

He smiled and waited patiently as Skye approached cautiously. There was a tender, uncertain smile on her face that made her seem girlish, and he liked it. The wide mineral-blue V-neck cashmere top and white tuxedo pants with a satin waistband she was wearing were fitted, revealing more of her figure, and Darren felt a charge as his eyes caught her firm breasts and the rounding curve of her hips.

"Ms. Crawford, I'm glad I caught you."

"What are you doing here?" Skye hadn't meant to sound as rude as she did. But if Darren had been offended, he certainly didn't show it. He was cool and collected and she found it very appealing.

Darren offered her the bouquet. "I was bringing these for you."

"Thank you." When she accepted the bouquet, their fingers touched, sliding against each other softly. Their eyes met as if by instinct and Skye felt a tingling sensation run through her. Feeling suddenly exposed, she looked down at the colorful bouquet. "How did you know where I was?"

"I didn't." All Darren wanted was to touch her again. No matter how inappropriate it might seem at the moment, he would give anything to feel his senses leaping to life as they had a second ago. "I was just planning on leaving them with the bell—"

"No," she said, looking up at him and wondering if it was possible he was getting more and more attractive as time went on. "I mean, here. How did you know I was staying at this hotel?"

Darren liked that she wasn't one to get over on, but he never had the idea that she was. "How are you handling things, Ms. Crawford?"

"As well as could be expected," she answered, feeling herself soften to the tender look in his eyes. "It's still a shock."

"I can only imagine." He wondered if she knew about the investigation as a smile ruffled his full lips. "I've lost a loved one before and it seems like the world just stops."

Skye was touched by his attempt at compassion, but tried to remind herself of who she was dealing with. "I look around and wonder how people can just go about their day as if nothing has changed."

"If there is anything that death teaches us," he noted sympathetically, "it's that life goes on despite it."

Her long lashes sweeping over eyes that looked as if as a storm was brewing behind them attracted Darren and he couldn't look away. He wanted to touch her, hold her, and console her as if they were close. He was stricken with attraction and felt like a cold, heartless bastard for wanting the woman of a man who had died just a couple of days ago.

"Skye." He took one step closer to her as if shortening the distance would help him find the right words.

"How . . ." Skye was finding it hard to speak or think through her confusion. She was entertaining thoughts that had no place right now. "How did you know I was here?"

"Why would he do it?" Darren asked. "Why would Jeff kill himself?"

"I don't think he did."

"What do you mean?" Darren engaged.

"I don't think Jeff killed himself." Skye could only hope he wouldn't come closer, because she knew she wouldn't push him away. She had always been in tune with her body, and it was trying to talk to her, warn her. "I'm sure the police have mentioned this to you."

Darren stepped back, analyzing her words and her tone. "I'm not surprised you feel that way. It wouldn't make sense that a man with so much ahead of him would give up. He had the campaign and he had you."

"Me?" Skye realized what Darren was suggesting. "Wait, I . . . Jeff and I weren't together in that way."

Darren's mind was moving a million times a second. He had no right to be pleased, but he had already passed that and was wondering how he could find himself in this woman's life. "I'm sorry. I thought you had come here because you were with him again."

"No, I came here to work for him. Or, I was considering it." Skye caught on late, but was on alert once it came to her. "Again, how did you know we were together?"

"You were engaged, right?" Darren mumbled under his breath as he reached for his ringing cell phone. He smiled apologetically before saying, "I have to answer. It could be a vote."

As she kept a curious eye on him, Skye was growing more uncomfortable with every passing second. She felt at a clear disadvantage wondering what all this man knew about her.

Darren quickly dismissed Lonnie and put the phone back in his pocket. "Skye, I was hoping I could—"

"I have to get going." She wanted him to leave because she wasn't sure she could move. "I have plans."

"Are you leaving?" he asked. Sensing her confusion, he elaborated. "D.C. Are you leaving D.C.?"

"Eventually," she answered. "Why?"

"I want to see you." Propriety aside, he couldn't pass up this chance.

"What?"

Darren shook his head, feeling ashamed. "I'm sorry. I'm really not usually this rude. I . . . I just would like to see you before you leave."

He reached into his pocket, pulling out his card. "Despite our situation, Jeff and I weren't enemies."

Skye took his card, making sure their fingers did not touch this time. Either he had no idea how much Jeff had despised him or he was a complete liar. "I can't make any promises."

"I don't expect you to," Darren said, although he had no intention of leaving it up to her. "If you feel like it."

"Thank you, Congressman."

"Call me Darren." He stepped aside, still owning her gaze. "If I don't see you before you leave, I'll see you in New York."

"New York?"

"At Jeff's funeral." He smiled again, never losing sight of her tentative posture. "I'll see you there. After all, it's just politics."

Skye couldn't take her eyes off him as he walked away. She had to believe he was innocent, because she couldn't imagine him being so deceptive. If he even suspected for a second that she knew something, he would be pushing his luck. Maybe that was the kind of man he really was. Maybe the conservative image was just that, an image. Jeff had seemed to think so.

Feeling the flutter in her belly begin to subside, Skye looked down at his card and saw he had written his home number down. Why had he affected her so much? The last thing on her mind was getting herself tangled up with a man, especially one that could have a hand in murder.

As she made her way to the elevators, Skye held the flowers to her nose and let the fresh scent breeze through her senses. Foremost on her mind was her hope that the honorable gentleman from New York's alibi panned out.

As he tossed the last pillow back on his living room sofa, Darren made his way to the bar against the windows overlooking Eighteenth Street. He needed another stiff drink.

After coming home to a loft in shambles, he made the decision to change his locks. He hated it because he could only imagine the reaction Franklin would have when he tried to get in and couldn't, and Darren couldn't bring himself to tell the desk man, Sam, to turn him away.

Darren had been lulled into a sense of complacency when he'd come home Wednesday and things were just fine. With Jeff's death and the visit from Detective Ross, he hadn't needed any more surprises and was grateful that Franklin was nowhere to be found. He needed a good night's rest.

Legislation ended early Thursday and he was free to go home to New York. He alternated weekends in Westchester and D.C., and this weekend was one reserved for staying in the district and having a good time, but he was going back home. It wasn't just to console his mother over Franklin's latest escapade.

There was the funeral Sunday and then there was Skye Crawford. She hadn't called him, but Darren hadn't expected her to. It was okay. He would see her in New York and find a more tasteful way than before of getting her interest.

Now with his place torn apart, Darren was reminded of Franklin's desperation. He had to be looking for money, and upon not finding any, decided to make Darren pay. Glass was broken, furniture was dented and turned over, and the expensive Stickley sofa he had just ordered from New York was ripped apart, its pillows destroyed with goose feathers all over the place.

Darren pushed his flight back a day and did his best to make his place look like less of a disaster area.

There was a knock on the door just as he poured himself a glass of premium scotch. Expecting to see the locksmith, Darren was dismayed by the sight of Detective Alice Ross. She seemed to sense that and was clearly pleased.

"Congressman Birch." She gestured toward the half-empty glass in his hand. "Having a party?"

"Having a drink, Detective." He opened the door just enough to fit himself outside. "It's Friday evening. I hate to think you have to work tonight."

"As long as people are dying," she answered, "I'll be working. Can I come in?"

Darren frowned, knowing this wasn't going to look good. "I'm sorry, but what can I help you with?"

A suspicious expression draped her face. "I'm not allowed in? Do you have female company?"

"What can I help you with, Detective Ross?" He didn't have the patience for her Columbo impersonation.

"You've got something to hide obviously."

Darren suppressed a sigh, realizing this woman wasn't going to give up. She could go on all night with this because she got a kick out of it. So he stepped aside and let her in, studying her reaction to his apartment. Although it looked ten times better than two hours ago, it was still clear that some mischief had ensued.

"Was there a . . . problem here?" she asked, turning back to him.

"No problem." He didn't have to tell her anything.

Alice laughed. "Fine, Congressman. If you want me to believe that this is how you keep your apartment, I will. But I have to tell you, it doesn't fit your image."

Darren went to the bar to get more ice. "Are you here on behalf of the realty assessment's office? Because if you are, I've really got better things to do."

"I came," she offered sarcastically, "to discuss your so-called alibi."

Darren placed the glass down. "Elizabeth?"

"I spoke with Ms. Sandon today." Alice laughed to herself, raising her hand with a pointed finger. "She's something else."

"That she is."

"And a hard woman to get a hold of."

"She's busy," Darren said. "She travels for her charities. Is everything clear?"

"Actually it isn't." Alice made her way across the room

to him. "Because when I spoke with her, she couldn't corroborate your story."

Darren paused, keeping up with the detective's manipulative stare. "Is this a joke?"

"I don't have a sense of humor," she answered. "If you haven't figured that out yet."

"I was with Elizabeth in this apartment Tuesday evening from six to about eight-thirty."

"She says you weren't."

Darren pressed his lips together to prevent himself from saying something he'd regret.

"Congressman?" Alice was egging him on.

"Let me speak to her," he said.

"I don't think that's a good idea, Congress—"

"I don't care what you think." Darren retrieved his phone and started dialing. When he put the receiver to his ear, he realized there was no dial tone. Looking behind him, he watched as Alice reached down and picked up the broken phone cord.

"Damn it!"

"What in the heck has been going on here?" she asked.

Darren's eyes darkened as he replied sharply, "Detective, Ms. Sandon and I are in the difficult process of ending our relationship and I believe she is speaking out of emotion."

"Did she do this?" Detective Ross walked farther into the living room surveying the damage.

"No," he asserted. He had never been stupid enough to give Elizabeth the keys to his place. "I'm certain after I speak to her, she—"

"That's no good," she said. "It doesn't work like that. Now, you told me at your office you're going home this weekend, so we need to talk about a time for you to come down to the precinct."

Darren hid the insult from his expression. "So, I am a suspect."

"There is some physical evidence suggesting Mr. Preston engaged in a struggle before he died."

"What type of evidence?" Darren grew annoyed with her constant smile. "Fine, you won't tell me, then we're done talking. I'll get back to you next week."

"You'll get back to me on Monday."

"I'll be calling my lawyer first," Darren said. There was no point in pretending here. He was a suspect and he had to start protecting himself.

There was another knock on the door and Darren, knowing who it would be, dreaded opening it. When the blacksmith announced himself, the expression on Detective Ross's face was one of delighted regard.

"Changing locks?" She started for the door Darren was holding open for her. "Interesting."

Darren stared expressionless at her and said, "I'll be calling my lawyer as soon you leave."

"Better use your cell." With that, she winked and walked out.

"Wow."

Darren turned to the blacksmith, who was looking around the apartment. He whistled before saying, "Whoever did this, you need to keep out of here and out of your life period."

Darren groaned. He could do without the commentary.

Chapter 4

Skye looked out over the expansive backyard of the Prestons' stone Colonial estate in Armonk. She had been to this house several times in her life, but couldn't remember noticing the dense trees just thirty yards from the back of the house. There had seemed to be more room before.

As she stood alone leaning against the railing of the wooden deck, Skye tried to drown out the voices of all the others who had come to the reception after the somber funeral. Whispering mourners in black dresses and suits blurred around her as she tried to clear her heart of sadness so she could be of some use to Jocelyn.

Jeff was gone and the pain presented itself as a kind of hypocrisy because, although Skye hadn't forgotten about Jeff, he had ceased to be a factor in her life some time ago. He had become an afterthought, a reminder of a past that she neither regretted nor needed to hold on to. Suddenly, he was thrown back into her life and then ripped away in the most awful way. Whether it was suicide or murder, the image of him hanging from the ceiling would be with her forever and filled her with regret, for what she didn't know.

Skye jumped at the touch of a hand firmly planted on her shoulder. Without turning around, she smiled and covered the hand tenderly with her own. The familiar jasmine scent of her older sister, Naomi, comforted Skye's soul.

"Thank you for coming with me," Skye said.

Naomi leaned in, her long straight hair brushing against Skye's shoulder. She whispered in that fluid, nurturing voice of hers, "Don't even say that. I cared about him too."

That wasn't true, but Skye loved her for saying it. Naomi, two years older, had always been the more responsible sister. In a family of free spirits, she was the conservative one. She was the traditional at heart, seeing preventable risk as unnecessary. While everyone else in the Crawford family saw life as a terrain waiting to be explored, Naomi saw it as a course to be carefully planned and made as safe and stable as possible. Skye couldn't understand why a girl who had mounds of encouragement to take the world by the horns wanted none of it.

While Skye traveled Europe and Africa to join groups with a cause and explore her artistic nature while falling in and out of love too many times to count, Naomi married her high school boyfriend one month after graduating from college and proceeded to have three kids in five years. She stayed at home, baked up a storm, and coached a girls' soccer team. The highlight of her life was the annual weeklong trip to Disneyland.

She was one of the happiest people Skye had ever known.

Naomi never liked Jeff and made that clear to Skye. She had warned her he was untrustworthy and would never settle down. When Skye flashed the engagement ring at her, Naomi told her nothing had changed. "Marriage doesn't mean anything to men like Jeff. It was just something else to do."

The protective one, Naomi had planned a torture ritual for Jeff after the breakup, but Skye held back. Life was a series of lessons, some painful and some joyful with most fitting somewhere in between. She would be okay.

"These people are something, aren't they?" Naomi leaned against the railing with a smirk on her face. She was wearing a black and white flower dress over her generous figure with sleeves down to her wrists looking more like a Mormon than a Methodist. "They even make a class statement out of their grieving. A catered reception?"

"It was more a time thing," Skye said, although she didn't doubt the Prestons would have catered the wake had they had weeks to plan. That was how they did things in Westchester, and Reggie and Jocelyn Preston were all Westchester.

"Still," Naomi said, "this would never have gone over in my neighborhood. In Harlem, it would be an insult. The labor you put into making the food is part of the grief, part of the love."

Naomi reached up, pinching Skye on the arm. "If you smile, I'll leave you alone."

Skye obliged. "I don't want you to leave me alone."

"I didn't know you still loved him."

"I didn't." Skye shook her head. "I guess I just . . . I don't feel complete about this. I think—"

"You're not gonna suggest he was murdered again?"

Skye bent her head, studying her arms. "I don't know, but thinking that he killed himself just doesn't close it for me."

"Suicide is like that," Naomi said. "It's inherently a selfish act, leaving your loved ones to wonder if they're to blame. Leaving them with regret."

Skye thought of the letter that Detective Ross had given her in Jeff's apartment. The one she refused to read. She would give anything to have it back now.

"It's emotion," Naomi said. "It's clouding your mind, halting your reason. Although reason was never your strong point."

Skye was about to agree with Naomi when she noticed that her sister's attention was elsewhere. When she turned around, Skye spotted him immediately. It was as if she had an internal magnet that could sense him.

Darren Birch was standing in the middle of the great room with a small crowd surrounding him with admiration.

"What is that?" Naomi asked.

Skye looked at her, confused. "What is what?"

"That wicked little smile on your face," she answered. "Who is he?"

The tenseness of her jaw betrayed Skye's own words. "I don't know what you're—"

"I know who that is." Naomi's eyes squinted tight as if seeing better could help her remember. "He's, uh . . . he's the . . ."

"Congressman Birch," Skye offered. "Darren Birch."

Naomi's mouth opened in a wide circle. "That's the guy Jeff was running against. I'm surprised he's here."

"Why wouldn't he be here?" Skye asked. "It's just politics. It doesn't matter at times like this."

"I guess." Naomi shrugged. "He's pretty hot. No wonder you like him."

"Who says I like him?" Skye had gone over the previous week's events with Naomi in very brief detail and was certain she hadn't mentioned anything about her attraction to Darren.

"Says the fact that I've known you for thirty years."

Skye turned away, feeling guilty for even acknowledging the effect seeing him had on her. She felt compelled to go to him and entice that winning smile of his. "He is very attractive and he has a way about him."

"I'll bet he does, girl." Naomi made a smacking sound with her lips. "You be careful with him. He's the kind that you never know until you know too much, if you know what I mean."

"No, not at all. Besides . . ." Skye stopped midsentence as Darren spotted her. The penetrating look in his eyes lit a flame inside her. His attention was like a drug and she felt childish for wanting more of it.

"Besides what?" Naomi asked.

"Besides." Skye was unable to tear her eyes away from him. "He might be involved in Jeff's death."

Darren was responding to the people around him, but wasn't sure what he was saying. He couldn't take his eyes off Skye. She looked tired and pained and it affected him. He wondered if she had been telling the truth when she said she and Jeff weren't involved anymore.

"Darren."

The fact that she hadn't called meant nothing. Darren wasn't easily deterred in most things, but especially those he really wanted. Seeing her now, still somehow looking free despite her somber expression, he was all the more encouraged to pursue her. The intense emotion in her eyes and the promise of those full lips pressed tightly together gave him no other choice.

"Darren. Darren!"

Darren blinked as his father grabbed his arm to get his attention. "What?"

"Who is that woman?" Gary asked.

"That's her," Darren answered. "Skye Crawford."

Scratching his salt-and-pepper hair, Gary studied her for a while, nodding as if confirming something for himself. "I haven't decided what to do with her yet."

Darren cocked his head to one side. "Excuse me?"

"For you," he said. "I'm thinking about your career."

Gary Birch was always thinking about Darren's career even when Darren wanted him to leave well enough alone. He was thirty-five years old, but his father still wanted him to fulfill his dreams for him. It came and went in waves, but with Jeff's death, he was in Super Dad mode.

"On the one hand," Gary offered, "you should get close to her to show you're a friend. It would weaken a political motive if you can show you were friends despite the competition. It might soften you to their side if any of this should get out."

"We don't know anything is going to get out." Even before calling his lawyer, Darren made sure his parents were aware of what was going on, that he was possibly a suspect in Jeff's as yet unexplained death. "All they know is that my alibi didn't check out. They still have no cause for murder, nor do they even have proof it was murder."

"It's not about Preston," Gary said. "It's about you. Can you take your eyes off that woman for one second?"

Darren turned and with a still expression said, "Dad, I know you're worried, but I have it under control."

"On the other hand." Gary's brows flickered a little. "If this does get out it can look like you have a motive for killing Jeff. It wouldn't be a stretch to think a man would kill over that woman."

Darren couldn't argue that. "I know exactly how to deal with Skye."

"Will you marry her?"

Darren frowned, his eyes narrowing. "Have you been in the scotch? I don't even know her."

"You should check into her background," Gary said nonchalantly. "See if she would make a good wife and get to it."

"Not this again." Darren started away, but his father took hold of his arm.

"I'm only doing this for your own good, for your career."

Darren knew that a stable, photogenic family was a plus for his political career and image. He also knew that Westchester was full of marriages based on something other than love that were working just fine for everyone involved. None of that mattered to him.

"When I get married it will be because of love and nothing else." Darren leaned in, speaking just above a whisper. "That's what you did."

"I was lucky," Gary said. "And I was never running for public office. It makes you a target for something untoward."

"English, please."

"It's safe being married," Gary insisted. "It would have saved you from this debacle with Elizabeth. Now, I know you hardly know . . . Skye now, but looking at her, I can't imagine it would be at all hard to love her."

Darren didn't imagine that either, but he wasn't comfortable with his father getting involved. What he knew about Skye was that she would probably turn and run when sensibility, his father's middle name, reared its head.

"Worry less about me," Darren admonished, "and figure out how to help Franklin."

Gary's head tilted back slightly as he rolled his eyes. "Marrying you off to a stranger would be much easier a task."

While engaging in conversation with distant family friends, Darren was keen not to give away that he was following Skye's every move. Part of his hesitation was that he didn't believe he could act appropriate for a reception and keep his attraction under control. He wanted to wait until she was alone, and when she escaped to the kitchen, he saw his chance.

When he entered, the only other person there was a catering waitress who smiled nervously at him on her way out. Skye's back was to him and he imagined the look on her soft face as she perused the dessert selections that had yet to make it outside. Her black dress was an A-line and she wore a conservative blue blazer. Her self-willed hair was pulled back in a wavy, unruly bun.

The way she moved along the counter confused and excited him. She moved slowly, but there was no sense of restraint in this woman, and Darren's unfamiliarity with this intrigued him. He had always been a restrained person, willingly fitting within a certain expectation of responsible behavior. The way Skye moved made one believe there was no telling what she would do next. She moved only for that moment. It was both dangerous and exhilarating.

"Skye."

She swung around and felt an unexpected warm glow rush through her body at the sight of Darren walking toward her. Her mood was brightened just by the sight of him, and watching the purpose of his movement she was somehow reassured. Skye wasn't going to lie to herself and pretend this was just a casual flirtation or an overactive emotion. The look in his eyes told her that he wanted her, and Skye was disconcerted with the fact that she liked it.

"Congressman—"

"Please call me Darren." He kept his distance from her. Not because she was cautious, but because she was so open. She stared up at him with large eyes, her arms at her side with the audacity of refusing to brace herself for anything that was to come. He had never been intimidated by a woman before, but his novel curiosity with her told him he was outgunned before even starting.

"How are you coping, Skye?"

She intended to offer a smile, but realized she was already doing so. "Well, you know . . . in general. It's just that today hasn't been so good."

"Seeing a young black man with so much ahead of him, so much to offer . . ." Darren sighed. "It's such a waste."

Inside, Skye was waging a war with herself between her attraction to this man and her questions about him.

She didn't ignore her mind, but she had always been one to choose her heart above anything else since that was where her intuition lived. Love was worth the risk, wasn't it?

Observing Skye's pressed lips, he wondered if she was holding her tongue. "You still believe he was murdered?"

"Yes," she answered. "I've had time to separate myself, and the more I think about it, the more I refuse to believe that he killed himself. Jeff was looking forward to life. He was looking forward to beating you."

Darren smiled. "That wouldn't have happened, but I'm glad he was enthusiastic. I enjoy competition."

"Do you?" she asked, ready for whatever response she would get.

Darren stood firm to the challenge. There wasn't any reason to play games and he didn't want to risk it with this woman. "Is that really what you want to ask me?"

"It's what I asked, isn't it?" Skye felt like he was trying to handle her and she didn't like it.

"Yes, but I know your type."

Skye gave him a hostile glare. "I sincerely doubt you know me."

"I didn't say I knew you," he answered. "I said I know your type. You don't like to offend people, but you don't want to appear weak. You ask one million circling questions to avoid being assigned the confrontation that might come with asking the one and only question you really want an answer to."

Skye was angry, but more with herself than Darren. He was right. The old Skye wouldn't have played this game, wouldn't have been so cautious. Despite that, she wouldn't give in to his judgment. "Then I guess I'll cut to the chase."

"I would appreciate it," he said curtly.

Skye's hands went to her hips and she leaned forward. "How in the hell did you know what hotel I was staying at in D.C.? I hadn't told anyone except Jeff and his assistant and I know they wouldn't tell you anything because neither of them can stand you."

Darren opened his mouth to speak, but Skye interrupted and didn't offer the chance. "And how did you know about my engagement to Jeff? That was over well before he came to D.C."

Darren was amazed at the thrill she gave him and at least proud he was able to bring out the spice that had been hidden under grief. "That was much better, Skye."

"Thank you." With a second wind, Skye was now feeling electrified and could feel a pulsing knot within her wanting more. "Your turn."

"Lesson one in politics," Darren prompted, "is to know everything about your competition. Or in my case, so-called competition."

"So-called?" Skye was feeling her flesh heat up with anger. "What is that supposed to mean?"

"You're looking for honesty," he said harshly. "Here it is. As good a man as he may have been, Jeff Preston had absolutely no chance of beating me. His only understanding of politics is networking on the Hill, and that means nothing in Westchester and Rockland. When he entered the race, his entire speech was laced with liberal ideology, which has no place in the real world."

His contempt sparked her anger. "I love this real world you Republicans always talk about. The one where there are no real problems that a tax cut and teaching abstinence in high schools can't solve."

Darren's response was firm and crisp. "At least we try

to solve the problems instead of stuffing more money into them, which was what your former fiancé wanted. He didn't have a chance in Westchester and that's all there was to it."

"That still doesn't explain—"

"Despite that fact," he interrupted, "I had to do my due diligence and look into my opponent's background. In finding out everything about him, I found out about you."

"Looking for dirt? What a surprise."

"Haven't you heard the saying? All's fair in love, war, and politics." He grinned as she leaned back. "It isn't like Preston didn't do the same."

"Is that what you were afraid of?" she asked. "Jeff finding evidence to prove that you aren't the squeaky-clean conservative you pretend to be?"

He met her accusing eyes with unflinching defiance. "I've never pretended to be anything other than what I am. I've never been squeaky clean and I'm not ashamed of it."

"Apparently." Skye felt her composure was under attack, and this only worked to fuel her resistance.

Darren's voice had never faltered from its cool, even tone despite her affect on him, but as he looked into her fiery eyes, something inside him threatened to show emotion. He worked at getting past it.

"There is nothing," he added, "that Jeff Preston could have found out that would have frightened me."

"Don't be so sure of that," Skye warned.

His eyes sharpened and he felt himself harden to her as she flashed him a quick, knowing smile. She was good, but he wasn't falling for it. She was bluffing and as he slowly looked her over, Darren found himself feeling pleasure at the prospect of calling her on it one day very soon.

"Your defense of your lover is impressive," he said harshly. "But you won't shake me. Until the police can prove otherwise, he killed himself. He had skeletons and there might have been one or two he'd thought were hidden forever that came back to bite him."

"Jeff was not my lover," Skye corrected, "but he was a fighter and he wouldn't have given up. Not because of a little skeleton in his closet or you."

"You're naïve, Skye." Darren was turned on by her angry stare, but he wouldn't let that distract him from the truth. "Skeletons in closets are never little. They're big and noisy and no matter what you do about them, they'll come back at you. They never go away. They . . ."

Darren was stopped by his own words. If it hadn't hurt so much, he would laugh at the irony.

Skye was bewildered by the conflicting emotions she felt. He wasn't talking about Jeff anymore and she felt as if she had awakened something too close to him to venture into. After all he had said about Jeff, she would think it would please her, but it didn't.

Still, she had to wonder if Jeff was right. Was there something in Darren's background, a skeleton so big and noisy it could send him to jail?

Darren took a quick breath, feeling guilty in response to the anticipating look on Skye's face. As exciting as sparring with her was, thinking of his brother had taken the fight out of him.

"Is there anything else?" he asked.

"Congress . . . Darren, you came to me, so I should be the one asking that question."

"You wanted to know how I knew where you were

staying while you were in D.C." His tone softened, his
voice lowered. "I wanted to send you flowers, so I had
my staff track you down. It isn't hard to find out what
you want about a new face on the Hill. It's like Hollywood when it comes to gossip."

"And you expect me to believe that you, Mr. Future
of the Party, had to deliver the flowers yourself?"

For a second, Darren wondered if this woman had
ever been put over her father's knee, but he didn't want
to take his mind in that direction. "I delivered the flowers myself because I wanted to see you. I didn't expect
you to be too dense to figure that out."

"Insults mixed with flattery. How clever." To Skye's
dismay, her voice cracked a bit in response. "No, Congressman, I'm not dense at all. I just don't trust you."

Darren leaned back, soaking up her self-righteous
defiance. The creased brow, the tense jaw and stirring
eyes did something perilous to his libido.

"I've deduced that," he noted smartly, "but despite
that fact, I'm disappointed you didn't contact me before you left."

"I left that evening."

Darren sent her a thoughtful and easy smile.
"Somehow I get the feeling I wouldn't have heard from
you whether you had stayed another day or another
month."

Skye spread her hands in the air regretfully and
shrugged.

"I'm disappointed."

Her eyes traveled up his body, settling on his face.
"Don't tell me the handsome young bachelor is having
a hard time getting a date?"

She was cute, but she wasn't going to get away with

that. "I can get a date any time I want, and I think you know that."

Skye's lips parted slightly with the intent of tossing a comeback she couldn't muster. He was an arrogant one and she had to admit she liked it even though all she wanted to do was slap him.

"And thank you," Darren added. "For the compliment."

"Compliment?"

"You said I was handsome."

Skye huffed before asking, "Would you like to hear everything I think you are?"

Darren had to resist the urge to grab her right now and kiss that smart mouth. "When will you be back in D.C.?"

Skye was taken off guard by his insistent tone and urgent expression. She felt a pull at her gut that threatened to show itself. She was never really good at hiding emotions because she didn't believe in it. Only this time, her feelings made no sense considering their very recent exchange.

Skye swallowed hard, took a step back, and offered her words slowly. "I won't. There's nothing in D.C. for me now."

"I would like a chance to prove you wrong." He had been contemplating the dangers of flirting with propriety, but they had passed that point some time ago.

Despite everything, Skye found herself drawn to him, his tone captivating and authoritative. "I have to get back to Chicago."

"To what?" he asked. "You don't have a job."

Skye's hands formed in fists at her sides as she fumed. "You—"

"So," Darren continued, ignoring her anger even though it kindled his fire. "So who is in Chicago?"

"I am," she spat back defiantly.

He appreciated her quick wit. "Then no one will be jealous if I make a trip there."

Sarcasm and disbelief laced every bit of Skye's laughter.

"You find me amusing?" he asked, feeling more confident as every second passed. She liked him despite her desire not to.

"Among other things," she answered. "Mostly I find you obscenely presumptuous."

"I prefer optimistic."

"I bet you do."

Darren had to stifle his laugh. "Is that a yes or a no?"

"What was the question again?" Skye didn't protest as he took a step closer to her, although his forwardness was unexpected.

Captivated by the intensity of his gaze, she was powerless to resist as he reached his hand out to hers. Tenderly but deliberately, he wrapped a few of his fingers through a few of her own. Skye's senses exploded and a tingling impression surged through her entire body.

"You heard me," he said smartly, curious as to his own developing thirst for this woman he barely knew. Her feminine scent was seductive and the tender touch of her soft skin made him want to kiss her badly.

"You're incredibly fresh, Congressman." Skye was shamelessly flirting now and didn't care. It felt good and Skye hadn't felt this kind of good in a long time. "I get the impression this is not your usual style."

"What's wrong?" he asked, his voice deepening as his breath caught it. "Am I bad at it?"

"I wouldn't say that."

"Then just say yes."

Before Skye could get out the word *yes*, which she had every intention of doing, her attention turned to Sierra, who busted into the kitchen with a tear-stricken face of anger.

"How could you come here?"

Releasing Skye's fingers, Darren turned to face a girl clearly on edge. They had exchanged tense glances a couple of times since he'd arrived, but she looked in a rage now. He searched a second for her name. "Sierra, politics are put aside at times like this."

Sierra let out a choked, bitter laugh. "You can cut the poli-speak, Congressman. There aren't any news camera crews here. I know you had something to do with it."

"You're angry," Darren said. "I understand that, but it's not a good idea to accuse—"

"Why not?" she asked. "Will it mysteriously cause me to commit suicide soon?"

"Sierra." Skye walked over to her. "Why don't you and I go get some air?"

"How could you be in here flirting with him?" Sierra wiped the tears from her face. "After everything I've told you."

"What exactly did you tell her?" Darren asked.

Skye turned to Darren. "Please, don't make it worse."

She reached out to Sierra, but the young woman backed away.

"No wonder you never went to his place again," Sierra accused. "You don't want to find that disk because you know it would hurt this . . . this murderer!"

Skye looked back at Darren, and the dark expression on his face unsettled her.

"Sierra," she said, "that's enough."

Sierra was having none of it. "You've fallen for his manufactured charm because you don't know the truth."

"Neither do you apparently," Darren asserted. "Where is this disk and—"

"That's where you're wrong." Sierra was rolling her neck with a hateful stare. "I may not be a powerful politician, but I have connections and I know that your alibi fell through."

Darren turned to Skye, who was looking back at him with wide, wondering eyes. "It's not—"

"Yes, it is what you think," Sierra interjected. "His alibi busted him up and now he's lawyered up. I know for a fact that he refused to go down to the station with the cops. He's not talking."

Skye was hit with the inner turmoil of disappointment, confusion, and anger. She was struggling to comprehend Darren's expression, which was a mask of stone.

Darren knew there would be no rush to making those flight arrangements to Chicago. "This can easily be explained, Skye."

Skye turned away as Sierra began sobbing uncontrollably and threw herself into Skye's arms.

"He killed Jeff," she stammered. "He did it."

Skye had her arms around Sierra and rubbed her back while feeling somewhat numb to the situation.

When Darren approached them, Skye looked up at him and could tell he was angry as well as hurt, but she couldn't care right now. Without a word she looked away. As he stormed out of the kitchen, Skye sighed in relief. She had always believed in living in the moment, but the rapid swing of her emotions these past few minutes had taken its toll on her. She didn't know what to want or who to believe and it mattered more now than it had ever before.

Darren noticed the stares sent his way as he walked through the Capitol Club to his table where Grant was waiting. The first thing he noticed was that Grant's usual smile was missing and he wondered if it was because of him or Grant's own problems at home. Whatever the problems were, Grant hadn't wanted to talk about them when Darren asked why his caller ID gave his call from the Capitol Hill Hyatt away.

After a mumbled hello, Grant gazed out the window as Darren placed his breakfast order even though he didn't have much of an appetite.

"If you don't want to talk business," Grant finally said, "I'll understand."

"I have to apologize, Grant. I haven't even hooked up with Lonnie about the research on your bill."

"It's working its way through the process." Grant waited until the waitress poured their coffee and left. "It'll be there waiting for you next session."

Darren huffed sarcastically. "You might want to rethink pinning your hopes on me."

"You've never let me down, Darren."

"We both know how things are in Washington. If I'm going to be poison, it could hurt your bill."

Grant's furrowed brow and deep sigh told Darren he had been thinking of just that for some time. Grant was his friend, but he had tunnel vision when it came to his lobbying efforts and he had never been as aggressive as he had with this bill. He stood to make a great deal of money if the bill was passed and the land sold.

Darren appreciated Grant's loyalty, but there was loyalty and there was career suicide. "I wouldn't be angry with you if you distanced yourself from me while this gets settled out."

"You've been honest with me since I've met you," Grant said. "So I'll do the same. I was thinking about it. I have to consider the promises I made and the money at stake. My investors . . ." He looked away again and his shoulders slumped. "My marriage."

"What are you talking about?" Darren asked.

Grant gestured with his hand. "It's nothing, really. We're having a spat about money and stuff, but . . ."

Darren sighed. "Grant, you're not gambling again, are you?"

When Darren first met Grant four years ago, he had gotten on the road to recovery from a sports betting addiction that had cost him countless dollars and his wife's respect. Darren was confident it was a thing of the past.

Grant laughed. "It's just marriage, Darren. Things will be fine. I'm moving back home today, but that's not for you to worry about. It's this bill. Getting this bill passed at the beginning of the next session is crucial. It means more than I can put in words. You have to get it in there so it can go the Rules Committee."

"I just have to be cautious right now," Darren said. "I don't like it any more than you do, but pushing through a new bill is a complicated thing."

"That's why you're going to get support and cosponsors," Grant said. "I've already got Grinn lined up and—"

"Grant." Darren held his hand up to stop him. "Do you understand what I'm dealing with right now? It isn't fair or right, but any legislation pushed by me right now will be tabled no matter how much support it has."

"But it's just a few rumors here or there. They're wrong, aren't they?"

"Depends on which rumors you're talking about." Darren shook his head. "Elizabeth has decided to ruin my life by saying we weren't together that night."

"You can straighten her out," Grant said. "She's just scorned. The woman is cold, but she won't go that far. That's got to be some of kind of breaking of the law, isn't it?"

"My lawyer has ordered me to stay away from Elizabeth," Darren said. "Any attempt I make to contact her will be seen as intimidation. He's working on getting proof we were together that night. She met with some friends afterward and maybe she mentioned me."

"She always mentions you. You're her claim to fame. She was a philanthropist socialite until she was seen on your arm around town."

"I ended that and she's going to make me pay." Darren had gone over and over better ways to have handled his breakup with Elizabeth, but how could he have perceived this situation? He hoped he wouldn't regret this forever.

"Those casual relationships never work," Grant said. "You need to get . . . Ah, hell, never mind."

The waitress brought their breakfast to the table and both men played with their food in silence until Grant decided to break it.

"Cheer up," he said. "You'll come through. You always do."

"I'm not worried about this," Darren said. "I know I'll be proven right again. It's just the damage done in the meantime."

"To your reputation?"

"Among other things." Darren gave Grant an overview of the weekend's kitchen encounter ruined by Jeff's assistant.

"Sounds bad," Grant said, "but you made an impression."

"I had hoped so, but . . . no. She doesn't want anything to do with me."

Grant leaned back in his chair, seeming disappointed by what he inferred. "That might be a blessing in disguise. She was your dead opponent's girlfriend."

"She isn't . . . wasn't his girlfriend," Darren insisted. "They were going to work together on his campaign. There was nothing going on between them."

"Whatever you say." Grant shrugged, dipping his toast until it was too soggy to eat.

"I was so close too." Darren poked his fork at his omelet so hard, it made a loud scratching sound against his plate. "She was just a second from inviting me to Chicago."

"Then?"

"Then that . . ." Darren sighed. "It's not her fault. She's just upset, but going half-cocked turned Skye against me. Apparently she made several calls to D.C., because the rumor mongers here have picked up too."

"Skye doubts you now?" Grant pushed his plate away, reached into the seat to get his copy of the *Hill,* a daily congressional newspaper, and began flipping through the pages.

"That's putting it nicely."

"And she didn't before?"

"That's the thing." Darren put his fork down, leaning into Grant. "It has to do with this disk Sierra mentioned. It has something bad Jeff supposedly had on me."

"What's on it?"

"I don't know," Darren said. "But whatever it was, that woman seems to think it would prove motive for murder. Apparently, Skye was supposed to go to Jeff's place and get it, but she didn't and Sierra thought it was because she didn't want to hurt me."

"Then she does like you," Grant said, smiling for the first time. "Or maybe she doesn't doubt suicide as the cause of death as much as she says she does."

Darren shook his head. "She isn't like that. Skye says what she means."

"Well, ain't that a . . ." Grant looked up from the paper, grinning ear to ear. "Don't fret, buddy. If she had any doubt before, I think this will quell it."

Darren reached for the paper, opened to the fifth page with Jeff Preston's picture front and center.

Darren read the title out loud. "Former Congressional Candidate's Skeletons Make Their Way Out."

Chapter 5

Sitting at her home computer, Skye was too shocked for words. She read the article Sierra had forwarded to her along with the message *This is all lies!* written five times above it.

The article revealed the contents of the rumored suicide letter just as Detective Ross had read them to her, but went on to share breaking news speculating on what Jeff must have been talking about.

A young woman, going only by the first name of Wanda, claimed that she had been Jeff's lover for three years. Their relationship was a secret, not just because she was living in the projects in southeast Washington, D.C., but because she was only sixteen when the illegal relationship began. Last year, Wanda said, Jeff had gotten her pregnant and forced her to have an abortion. She hadn't wanted the abortion but promised to do it if he would marry her when she turned eighteen.

After the procedure, which Jeff paid for, was performed, Jeff told Wanda about his plans to run for

Congress and ended their relationship. Despite ending things, Jeff promised to give Wanda enough money to get out of the projects and move to Arizona where her favorite aunt lived, but never followed through.

He avoided Wanda for weeks until she confronted him outside his apartment and threatened to expose him whether he gave her money or not. He would be arrested for statutory rape and his reputation would be destroyed after the public heard he had forced an innocent project girl to have an abortion.

That confrontation had been only days before his suicide.

The only thing that kept Skye from exploding was that the story was weak and she knew no one was going to buy it. It wasn't the far-fetched and suspect nature of it that made Skye not believe a word. She knew something this writer didn't. After coming against brick walls in the form of voice mails at the paper, Skye decided to call Detective Ross.

"Ms. Crawford?" Detective Ross's voice came over impatiently.

"Detective, I take it you've read this article about Jeff in *The Hill*."

"Yes, the reporter contacted me before printing it."

"You can't possibly believe it," Skye said. "It's got so many holes and unverifiable—"

"The journalist covered all her tracks," Alice said. "She used all the legal, right words to get it out."

"And you told her what was in the letter?"

"No, I didn't. We're investigating how that information got out."

"Maybe the person who left it there after they killed Jeff told the reporter. Did she give her source for the letter's contents?"

"She's a credible journalist. She's won awards."

"I'm very impressed," Skye said sarcastically. "Well, this award-winning journalist has been duped."

"Look, Ms. Crawford—"

"No, you look. You should never have let her print this article."

"Have you ever heard of freedom of the press, Ms. Crawford? Now, I have murders to investigate, so—"

"I'm talking about one of those murders!"

"Your tone," Alice warned.

"I was engaged to Jeff. I knew him in ways—"

"*Knew* being the operative word," Alice argued. "It's been years and I can tell you after fifteen years in this business, you can never really know anyone. I know wives and husbands who knew nothing about their dead spouses' other lives, so don't assume because you were engaged to someone four years ago, you know every little secret today."

Skye wasn't daunted. "I know enough to know that Jeff wouldn't mess around with a sixteen-year-old."

Detective Ross laughed. "He's a man, isn't he? Now you're going to tell me he would never have unprotected sex."

"He was smarter than that."

"No man is smarter than that, Ms. Crawford."

Skye would concede to a human mistake, but not a criminal act. "When he was with the D.A.'s office, he prosecuted statutory rapists. He thought they were sick to prey on these young girls and seduce them. Not to add to it, Detective, as much as I loved Jeff, the man was a snob. He required at least one college degree and professional business card even for his one-night stands. He wasn't going to—"

"You're naïve, Ms. Crawford. The richest, most educated society men do this kind of thing. Women of good breeding like you don't want to believe their men would be attracted to an uneducated poor girl, but you need to wake up."

"I'll give you all that," Skye answered back. "But don't put words in my mouth. I didn't suggest that she was beneath him. I said he thought that way, not me."

"Is that all?"

Skye was saving the best for last. "One thing you can't argue is that Jeff didn't get that girl pregnant. He couldn't get anyone pregnant. He's . . . he was impotent. We talked about it at great length and agreed we would adopt."

There was silence on the other end of the line and Skye felt somewhat victorious.

"That doesn't change the story, Ms. Crawford. The fact is he didn't want the information to get out and that's why he killed himself."

"You've been doing this for what, fifteen years, you said? Then tell me exactly why he would demand a woman abort a kid that he knew wasn't his? How many men with a future like Jeff had would rather kill themselves than pay off some ex-girlfriend? Jeff made several hundred thousand dollars a year at his firm and his parents had money as well."

"You can never tell what a man backed in a corner will do, Ms. Crawford."

"Have you spoken to this . . . Wanda?"

"I'm not going to tell you that."

"Why not? You're apparently convinced this was not a murder."

"The young woman showed us her bank accounts with unexplainably large cash deposits that coincide with weekend rentals at a downtown hotel in her name.

Her abortion has been verified with her permission by the clinic. Most of all, she gave intimate details of Mr. Preston's . . . well, she's seen him naked. I'll leave it at that."

Skye felt her stomach sinking at the news. Why would Jeff be so stupid and irresponsible? "Detective, I still don't see how any of it leads to suicide. How do we know she didn't—"

"She has a firm alibi for the night of the murder. And remember, we've already discussed the tape at Mr. Preston's apartment. No one visited him."

Skye thought about the key Sierra had given her and wondered if she could prove someone with a similar key, which a lover would have, could get in undetected by cameras. Especially someone that Jeff certainly didn't want to be seen visiting him.

"Thank you for your time, Detective."

After hanging up, Skye got up and headed for her purse just as the phone rang.

"Hello, Skye."

Her emotional reaction to his voice, which she recognized as if she'd known him forever, made Skye uneasy.

Skye had been thinking about Darren Birch more than she should have in the past few days. After their encounter in New York, she was torn by her own emotions. The guilt feelings she had over her attraction to him after what Sierra had told her conflicted with the flutter in her belly at the sound of his voice. It seemed her body at least was intent on defying everything her mind was telling her.

"How did you get my number?" she asked bluntly.

"I can sense from your tone, you aren't too happy to hear from me."

"Just answer my question."

"You're in the phone book, Skye."

"Oh." She felt like an idiot.

"Have you heard the latest on Jeff?" he asked.

"Yes, I've read the article. Is that why you're calling? You think all my suspicions about Jeff's death have been allayed by these lies?"

"Lies?" After returning to his office, Darren had used every resource he had to confirm the story and its facts. It was unsettling and suspicious in every way, but there was a part of him that desperately wanted to believe it if only to make things easier for himself.

He hadn't gotten what he wanted in confirmation, but was relieved to hear from his lawyer that a trip to the station was no longer in order.

Most of all he was sad for Jeff, but optimistic about his chances with Skye.

"The story is lies," Skye answered, "and it only convinces me more that he was murdered. Someone was getting worried that the truth was coming out."

"What truth would that be?" Darren asked.

Skye was an emotional mess, but she wasn't stupid. "I have to go, Congressman."

"Wait." Darren sat up in his chair and leaned over his desk. "These things can be hard to accept. Trust me, I've had to accept ugly truths about those I love as well. Accepting what is in your face is the first step to moving on."

"Trust you?" Skye knew she was being cruel, but she felt like he was playing her again, and knowing that she was very vulnerable to him she had to strike first. "I don't even know you."

"I've been trying to change that."

"Don't bother."

Skye hung up, but found herself unable to let go of the phone. She tried to trust her intuition, but a hint of regret bit at her. She had looked into his eyes and seen someone who was honest and trustworthy, but wasn't sure if it was her physical attraction to him that made her want to believe that. Maybe she had seen someone she just wanted to have sex with and convinced herself it was more. Maybe she had let him fool her into believing whatever he wanted her to.

After all, he was a politician and he was a good one.

Skye didn't want to think of what she had just passed on if she was wrong. Instead, she focused on what she could do to get the truth either way, and that meant going back to Washington, D.C.

The meeting of the Congressional Black Caucus, a group of African-American House and Senate members, had come to an end and the forty-plus members began gathering their items to make their way back to their offices with their staff members straggling behind. Darren had been grateful this week's meeting was in the Cannon House, because the less he had to walk around the less he had to deal with people asking him questions or giving him looks. He wasn't going to let this controversy shake him; he was a better man than that. He wouldn't be so callous as to be grateful Jeff's supposed motive for suicide had come to light. Besides, most of the talk on the Hill centered on how implausible the story was.

Still, politics was about survival day to day and one couldn't know if one would or not, depending on the way the whispers went. So although suicide was again the leading cause, Darren knew he would be connected to the story as long as it lasted. He would have to ride it out.

He smiled appreciatively for Marcus Hart, the very powerful and commanding senator from Maryland. He was approaching with an understanding look Darren assumed was based on his own experience with family skeletons. Coming from a major East Coast society family, Marcus was a few years older than Darren and the two had known each other in a casual way for a couple of decades, and Darren had a great deal of respect for him. Marcus was a private man and Darren figured it was due to the glare under which his family had always lived.

"Hello, Senator," Darren said. Unlike some other members of the black caucus, Marcus had never seemed to have a problem with Darren's decision to take the right side of the aisle.

Marcus reached across and squeezed Darren's arm briefly. "You can't fool me with that confident look on your face."

"This has been some kind of month, brother." Darren followed Marcus's lead out of the Caucus Room, knowing that Lonnie was close behind.

"This too shall pass," Marcus said, the whites of his eyes sparkling against his very dark skin. "It's all a damn shame, but you're a stronger man than any of it. I know you'll make it through."

"Thank you," Darren said thoughtfully. "I appreciate that."

"I've got your back, brother." Marcus held out a hand and leaned in with a smile. "Family. What the hell you gonna do?"

At first Darren thought Marcus might be referring to

his own situation. That was until Marcus nodded to his left.

Darren felt a brick in his gut at the sight of Franklin, looking disheveled and angry in an intense discussion with a security guard outside his office.

"This too shall pass," Marcus repeated before walking away.

Darren took a deep breath and made his way toward his office. Franklin turned to him with a dark smirk on his face to show how he was relishing the embarrassment he was causing as members of the black caucus made their way down the hallway.

Darren took hold of Lonnie by the arm. "Show my brother in, please."

Lonnie nodded, quickly rushing to the door and ushering Franklin, who was reluctant to give up the spotlight, inside.

"Can I help you gentlemen?" Darren asked the frustrated guards.

"Sorry, sir," said the younger, bald one. His face was bloodred from either embarrassment or anger. "We didn't know he was your brother. I mean he said he was, but—"

"He passed the detectors, didn't he?" Darren asked. "So why are you bothering with him?"

"Congressman Birch." The older, larger guard nudged his younger partner aside. "We're sorry about this. We just heard some loud noises and he was on his cell phone, so—"

"Well, he's off now," Darren said.

Both men nodded as they turned and walked briskly down the hallway.

Lonnie slipped out of Darren's office the second he

showed up. Darren knew that Lonnie didn't like Franklin; no one in his office liked Franklin.

Truth be told, Darren didn't like Franklin either. He loved him and his heart ached every time he saw him, but he hadn't liked Franklin for some time and he knew he was wrong for it. He tried to understand his brother's choices and appreciate how hard these last few years had been on him with his wife leaving him for another man and cleaning him out. He was fired from his job as an investment banker when he lost two major clients and had been pushed away by the society set he had come to rely on as part of his identity.

"What are you doing here?" Darren asked, sitting down at his desk.

Franklin was standing by the window, looking through books on the bookcase as if he were interested. "I'm a constituent of Westchester and I've come to pay a complaint to my representative."

"You live in Manhattan, Franklin." Darren wasn't going to play his games.

Franklin laughed, pointing decidedly. "You got me there, bro."

"If you don't . . ." Darren was stopped in the middle of his sentence as he watched his brother's shoulders fall and his body begin to shiver with tears. "Franklin?"

Franklin fell back into the leather sofa against the wall and lowered his face into his hands. He sobbed for about a minute with no interjection from Darren before lifting his tearstained face.

"I'm so . . . I'm sorry, man."

Darren sighed, wanting so badly to believe this but knowing better. He needed a third hand to count how many times this crying apology scene played itself. The request for money was soon to follow.

"I know you're sorry." Darren spoke softly. "That's not the problem. It cost me a few grand to make up for the damage you did to my apartment."

"A pretty penny to change the locks."

"So you've tried to get back in?" Darren asked. "You should have known better."

Franklin's humble expression turned to fury. "Don't talk to me like I'm a little boy! I'm your bigger brother."

"Then act like it!" Darren gripped the edges of his desk, trying to control his temper. "You have to stop this."

"What's the matter?" Franklin's tone was teasing. "A little too much heat on your neck? Are you a murderer or aren't you?"

Darren's dark eyebrows slanted in a frown that made Franklin swallow hard. "I can make it so you can't get into this building again."

"I'm only responding to the rumors. Your alibi isn't—"

"Elizabeth is just pissed because I ended things between us, but it doesn't matter anymore. The case is closed."

"That worked out well for you." Franklin leaned back into the sofa casually, as if the crying scene had never happened. "At least somewhat. You've still got a little stink on you because of it all. I can't make it better, but I can make it worse."

"Are you threatening me?"

Franklin shot up and came to the desk. Leaning forward, he stared menacingly at his younger brother. "I need some money."

"You need rehab." Darren didn't blink. It had been two decades since Franklin had been able to intimidate him. "You'll get nothing else from me."

"You underestimate me," Franklin said. "I've already—"

"Enough!" Darren slammed his hands on the desk and Franklin stepped back. "It's rehab or get the hell out. Everyone has had it with you. You don't even care what you're doing to Mom. You're almost forty years old, for Pete's sake. Aren't you even getting sick of yourself?"

The words, harsher than Darren had meant them to be, seemed to hit Franklin hard and he let go of any pretense that he had an upper hand. With his having no fortitude to stand up to the truth, his somber expression returned.

"If you decide you want to go," Darren said, "let me know. If not, we have nothing to talk about. I'm on the people's time."

There was a knock on the door and Lonnie stuck his head in. "Congressman?"

Franklin threw his hands in the air and laughed. "The servant boy is right on time! Might as well come in 'cause I believe I have been dismissed."

Lonnie stepped slowly into the office, keeping his focus on Darren. "You said you wanted to be interrupted no matter what."

"Go ahead," Darren said.

Lonnie's eyes quickly glanced at Franklin with a critical squint. "It's about Skye Crawford."

Darren's eyes widened. "Go ahead. Franklin doesn't care."

"Yes, please," Franklin urged. "Let's hear about Skye Crawford."

Lonnie rolled his eyes. "Well, she's here. She's in D.C."

"Ohhhh!" Franklin feigned excitement. "Who in the hell is Skye Crawford?"

Darren felt a little shiver at the news. "Where?"

"She's back at the George Hotel."

"Thanks, Lonnie." Darren was already reaching for his Blackberry to see when he would have a moment to get away. "That will be all."

"Not fair," Franklin said after Lonnie left. "He got a much more civilized dismissal than I did."

Darren looked up at his brother, his entire posture giving away his impatience.

Franklin bit his lower lip and his shoulders fell as if he was surrendering. "Look, little brother. I'll make you a deal."

"No deals. Rehab or nothing."

"I'll go," he said angrily. "If you tell me who Skye is."

"Skye is none of your business."

Franklin smiled wickedly. "So she's why you kicked Elizabeth to the curb?"

"No, she isn't," Darren said. "It's nothing like that. Skye isn't a part of my life."

"But you want her to be."

Darren wouldn't let him move away from the issue at hand. "What I want is for you to get into rehab."

Franklin backed away, leaning against the wall and folding his arms over his chest. He seemed to have all the time in the world.

"She's a woman that I care about," Darren said. "A friend of Jeff Preston."

"How incestuous of you."

"That's enough." Darren reached for his phone. "Now am I calling the rehab center or are you getting out of my office?"

Franklin lowered his eyes to the floor and mumbled, "Just make sure the food doesn't stink this time."

Skye's hands were shaking so hard, the piece of paper with the security code to Jeff's apartment fell out. She was running out of time as she knelt down and snatched it back. She had been so preoccupied with her covert actions to get this far that she hadn't prepared herself for the emotion overload she got when she finally entered his apartment for the first time since the night she'd found him dead. If she didn't turn off the security code in time, it would all be for nothing. The last thing she wanted was to get arrested for breaking and entering.

Finally the code box beeped and the green light assured her that she had passed the final test. Closing the door behind her, she treaded lightly into the apartment. It was cold and silent and . . . a mess.

Her first thought was that his parents had decided to start packing. She knew they had been halted when the detective decided the suicide scene might be a murder scene. That was over now and they would be returning to get the rest of his things. Still, it seemed a little messy for packing.

Her stomach wound tighter and tighter with every step she took toward the bedroom. She was glad that she hadn't taken the time to think through her choice to return to D.C. and investigate Jeff's murder, because she had been second-guessing herself ever since landing at Washington Reagan National Airport. She had no plan, no idea of what to do, and no confidence that she could follow through if she had. It took every bit of strength she had to plant her feet firmly one at a time.

Which was why she didn't have a second to brace herself before a body came out of nowhere and slammed her against the wall. Skye let out a scream as her body made impact with the wall, and she felt herself falling to the floor as light and darkness traded seconds in her head. On the ground, she looked up dazed at a man in sweats stumbling over her and rushing down the hallway.

Skye moaned in pain as she tried to pull herself up. Her body was shooting with pain everywhere, her surroundings were still circling, and her mind was trying to still itself enough to deal with what had just happened.

Finally up, she found her knees wobbly as she moved down the hallway that was swinging from left to right. She was clear enough to know that someone had broken into Jeff's apartment before she had and they were probably after the same thing she was.

Holding on to the wall, Skye reached Jeff's bedroom. The flashback of seeing him hanging from the ceiling, compounded by everything else, made her too weak to stand and she quickly fell to her knees. She was right where she needed to be.

It hadn't occurred to her she was kneeling in the same place she had been standing when she saw Jeff hanging from the ceiling. Whoever that was, he moved all of Jeff's furniture around and emptied his dressers, but the disk wasn't in the dressers and it hadn't reached the floor. There was only one other place to look.

On the door next to her hung two tailored Armani dress shirts on one high hook and a dark blue Ralph Lauren sport jacket on a low hook. Rummaging through the pockets she found what she was looking for. The disk had fallen from her hands safely and quietly into the jacket pocket.

Now that she had it, Skye did the only other thing she could do. She called the police to report a break-in.

"Are you going to talk to her?" Mia asked, hands on hips.

"Yes," Darren said, appeasing her. "I'm going to call her today. I'm not canceling the event. Why would she think that?"

"The charity is in less than two weeks. Valerie wants a copy of your speech and you have nothing to give her unless you've got the staff working on it and haven't told me."

"I think I do," Darren said, not sure at all.

"Lonnie doesn't have it," she answered with a short tone.

"Ask him who does. I'm sure I gave Nikki or Donna the talking points."

"Neither of them knows how to write." Mia rolled her eyes. "Fine, I'll ask but if you don't . . . then what?"

"Then get one of them on it." Darren was shuffling through papers on his desk, which was unusually cluttered. He was orderly and efficient, no fuss or muss, but had been distracted and embarrassingly absentminded from the moment he'd heard Skye was back in town. "Have you rearranged my schedule like I asked?"

Mia nodded. "You have the afternoon free, but there are going to be four votes at six-thirty."

"Fine."

"Is this about her?"

Darren looked cautiously at Mia. He didn't have many secrets from her, but something about his feelings for Skye, whatever they were, was too delicate at this moment. "That will be all, Mia."

"That's a yes." She turned to leave, but stopped as she looked up at the wall-mounted television set always running. It was turned to the news local station 8. "Speak of the devil."

Darren looked up, shocked at what he saw. The video was of Skye at the top of the police station steps with Sierra at her side. Press was all around her asking a flurry of questions. The caption underneath read APART- MENT ATTACK MIGHT REOPEN CASE.

Attack! Darren tossed and slid papers aside as he searched for the remote on his desk. Finding it in his in- box, he pressed the Mute button to hear the reporter's voice.

"What is interesting about the attack on Ms. Crawford is that it happened while she was in Mr. Preston's apart- ment illegally. Reasons why weren't given, but sources say Ms. Crawford believes Preston's suicide was a staged murder cover-up. This brings up the question, is there a reason for the police department to reconsider this case?"

Darren reached back for his keys and rushed out the door. Mia jumped aside just in time to avoid being run over.

Outside his office, he hit the brakes as Lonnie stood in his path.

"Did you know—" Lonnie began.

"Skye was attacked." Darren nodded. "I'm going to see her now."

"Is that a good idea?" Lonnie asked. "I mean, we're already getting press calls now that there are rumors the case might be reopened."

"I don't give a damn about that." Darren pushed Lonnie aside.

* * *

Detective Ross was gone and the security guard, on loan by the hotel for the rest of the day, was outside the door. Finally alone, Skye searched frantically through her purse. She had been frightened that it would be searched even though she said she had been unable to find anything. Her heart was beating wildly, a sensation the old Skye would have enjoyed, but this one was grateful when it was over.

Just in case, she had hidden the disk underneath the bottom panel of her purse, which was wide enough to keep from breaking it. She was grateful Darren hadn't used a CD, because she would have had no way of hiding that.

As she waited for her computer to come on, Skye erased any regret she felt about keeping the disk from Detective Ross. Her attitude had been horrible from the beginning. She was rightly angry; after all, Skye shouldn't have been there, but that hadn't seemed to be what she was most upset about. Skye had proven that someone could get into the apartment without being noticed by the cameras, and that meant she might have to reopen a case she had closed.

When the computer was on, Skye slipped the disk in and waited for the system to pick it up. She clicked on the first option, a profile of Orevko Industries, a holding company involved in several businesses in Russia and the U.S. The clickable notes made no sense to her. Someone had typed the words DEAD END at the bottom of the page.

There were dates and names and Internet links. Skye clicked on the first link, which led to Orevko's Web site, which was entirely in Russian. Going back, she selected the second link, which led to a *New York Times* article and the title ALLEGATIONS OF RUSSIAN MOB TIES THREATEN CORPORATE MERGER.

Raised male voices outside her hotel room startled Skye. She was still frightened and felt at a complete disadvantage when it came to her attacker knowing who she was. Slowly, she crept to the door and peeked out the peephole. There was no denying the excitement that ripped through her at the sight of Darren Birch arguing with her security guard, but she wanted an explanation. Why would her emotions disconnect so decidedly from her mind? Part of it frightened her, but the uncertainty of it excited her enough to want to explore.

When she opened the door, Darren stopped yelling and turned to her. A smoldering flame hit him at the sight of her. Her eyes were wide like a vulnerable child's and her lips were pressed tightly together like an obstinate woman's. He wanted to console her fears and reprimand her rash behavior at the same time. Mostly he wanted to touch her, seeing her glowing, youthful flesh underneath a slim tank top and shorts.

"Skye." He gestured to the guard. "Would you?"

"It's okay," she said, stepping aside as Darren made his way into her room. She nodded a thank-you to the guard, who shrugged and returned to his chair and magazine.

Closing the door behind her, Skye felt her body on alert at his closeness. She was suddenly aware that she had changed into a more comfortable gray tank top and cotton low-ride shorts, revealing a considerable amount of her belly and making it clear she wasn't wearing a bra.

When she turned around, Darren wasn't hiding the

distraction her state of dress was causing him. He was looking her over with a frustrated, irritated look as if her body was an inconvenience at the moment. Skye didn't know how to react to it, but she knew she liked his eyes on her.

"Are you all right?" he asked, reaching out to her.

Skye winced as his hand connected with her bruised shoulder. The bruise hurt like hell and she used that as an excuse to create some distance between them.

"I'm sorry." Darren didn't lean on her attempt to make room between them. He looked down and saw that her hands were shaking. She had to be frightened, and that made him angry. "What did he do?"

"He just knocked me down." The compassion in his voice melted whatever resolve she was pretending to have simply out of pride, but she kept herself in check. "I'm fine."

"You're not." Forgetting his own mind, he stepped to her and took her left hand in his. There was a threat inside him, something on the verge of making him act a fool with this woman. He squeezed her hand tight, grateful that she didn't pull away. "Your hands are freezing and they're shaking."

"It's just jitters."

As Skye looked up at his wanting eyes, a thick silence enveloped the room. Skye couldn't divert her eyes away from his dark, emotional expression and she felt her pulse quicken as the warmth of his hand reached beyond her hand, up her arms, and into her chest. His eyes moved from hers down her chest, and looking down, Skye realized how clearly he could see her nipples hardening.

"My hand, please," she said in a husky whisper.

"I'm sorry." Darren let her hand go, embarrassed by his evident vexation at such an inappropriate time. His blood was pounding and his mind, as well as his eyes, had wandered in the wrong direction. She was reacting to him, but it was clear she wasn't going to give an inch.

"I know I'm probably the last person you want to see," he said in a deeper voice than expected. "But when I heard about—"

"I appreciate your concern, Congressman, but I'm fine, thank you."

"I believe you," he said.

Skye frowned in confusion, taking a second before understanding that he wasn't responding to her last comment. He was responding to her whole reason for being here. She felt an unexpected relief wash over her.

"Thank you," was all she could say.

She was grateful and happy, so much so that she didn't feel safe saying more. She was also hit with the reality that this man's approval meant so much to her because she wanted him, and that was like a brick to her stomach.

"I'll put pressure on the police to catch this guy," Darren said.

"Don't feel like you have to . . ." Skye searched for the right words. "This isn't about you, Darren."

"I know." He was offended that this would be her first thought, but he understood. He was a politician and he wouldn't be the first to take advantage of someone's misfortune to save his own butt, or make himself look heroic and concerned for the people. "I'll stay behind the scenes."

"I don't know if that's possible even if you tried."

"I hope that's a compliment," he replied, "but either

way, don't worry. I'll talk to the congresswoman from D.C. She is incredibly close to the chief of police."

"It's appreciated," she said honestly, "but it won't make a difference. I didn't see anything. Only a man about six feet tall who could have been white or Hispanic wearing sweats."

"Any insignia?"

She nodded. "Red letters . . . Moscow State U was on the front of his shirt. I saw it as he stepped over me. Before things went black for a second."

"That will be noticeable from the video cameras."

"That's just it." Skye's exasperated tone gave away her emotion. "It would be if he ever showed up on the camera. It's just like the first time. There is no record of him entering the building, using the elevator, or anything. I wasn't on camera, but the elevator records the exact time my trip to Jeff's apartment happened. This guy used the stairs and took that same entrance to avoid cameras."

Darren wasn't sure what to make of that news, but his first thought was that someone in the building might have had a hand in this. "How did you get in?"

As Skye explained her plan to prove that someone could get into the building without being seen on camera, she noticed Darren inching toward the computer. Her body tensed and her nerves tightened. Because of the physical affect he had on her and the compelling emotion in his eyes, she was already telling him more than she should, but he was about to see what she had been there for and she couldn't risk that.

"Darren." She lunged toward him, grabbing his arm and turning him to her, away from the computer. "Thank you."

Darren was surprised but pleased by the action. "For what?"

"For coming by." Skye wanted to trust him, but knew she couldn't do that yet. Not completely at least. She looked into his eyes seeing a sense of confidence and calm she could only hope to have. "I know you're very busy and I haven't been kind to you."

Darren softened to her touch, her sweet gaze. "I know you've been through a lot. It's a horrible way to get to know someone, but I can't seem to stay away."

"You don't give up," she answered, trying to stay focused. It was hard. She could feel his muscles beneath her hand and he smelled clean and strong. "That's how you've gotten as far as you have."

"That and a lot of campaign donations."

She smiled at him like an angel, her eyes lighting up with promise and honesty. Darren couldn't resist any longer. When his mouth came down on hers, the softness of her lips set him on fire. He reached out and grabbed her by the waist, pulling her to him as his mouth pressed harder wanting more and more.

Skye let out a tortured moan as desire sent both relief and insanity through her at the touch of his forceful lips. Wanting to always be in control, she was assaulted by a desire to be taken and responded by melting into the arms of this man whose aggressiveness threatened to consume her. She opened her mouth at the urging of his own and felt his tongue tease at hers. She met him, wrapping her arms around his neck, gently caressing the back of his head and neck with her fingers.

His breathing was out of control as his mouth went to her ear. He whispered her name, but it could barely be heard as he felt a wave of hot lava rushing through his body. His hand was touching her smooth, silky skin as it slid higher and higher. When his fingers brushed against the bottom of her breast, he groaned at the titillating temptation she offered.

His touch to her sensitive breasts made Skye's body shiver all over. When he cupped her breasts with his hands, gently caressing and rubbing them, they were both moaning and breathing heavy and loud. Skye felt her knees get weak, so she held tighter.

Her mouth went to his chin, then his neck where she left hot, wet kisses everywhere. He smelled so good and held her with such demand, she felt more like a woman than she had in any man's arms. Skye wanted him so badly there was a part of her that felt as if he were already inside her, and she ached to make that real.

When Darren returned his hungry, starving lips to hers, he felt Skye's hands lower to his waist and she began pulling his shirt out of his pants. He knew what was going to happen and he wanted it, but had to be sure she did as well. He separated his lips from hers and looked into her eyes, dark with passion that matched his own.

"Do you want this?" His words barely came through between heavy breaths. "Because it's going to happen unless you—"

Skye pushed away and backed up, shocked to her bones at the power this man had over her. What had started as a simple diversion had almost led to her bed, and then where would she be? In love with a man whom she couldn't trust? A man who could have a hand in murder? She had to get a grip on herself.

"I'm sorry." She held up her hand to stop him as he took a step toward her. "No, I'm—"

"I'm the one who should be sorry." Darren tried to compose himself, but his body still held power over his mind and all he could do was stand there, staring at the woman he knew he had to have. After a moment of tortured silence between them, he offered, "I didn't mean to do that."

"Is that true?" Skye asked, wanting to hit herself on the head for such a stupid question. "No, don't answer that."

"You're right," he answered, wanting to grab her again. He stepped a little farther back, not sure he could trust reason to win a fight with his body. "I did mean to do that, but that shouldn't come as a surprise to you."

"It didn't." As he backed up closer to the computer, Skye's rattled mind remembered why she had started this in the first place. She walked briskly past him and lowered the laptop screen.

Darren noticed. It was just a second, but he caught the quick move and he was smart. She was hiding something from him and the grab and kiss had been a part of that. It didn't matter. For whatever reason she kissed him, he knew the vibe he was getting from her wasn't fake. Still, he was curious about what she had on that computer and why she felt she had to hide it from him even after their passionate encounter.

"That's good to hear," he said, pretending as if he hadn't seen. He didn't want to mess with the moment. He would deal with whatever was on that computer another time. "I hope it also doesn't come as too much of a surprise that I don't want you to leave D.C."

"I don't plan on leaving any time soon." Despite her distance from him, Skye felt his presence all over her body as if he had left his mark on her with just a kiss and touch.

"Can I make you an offer?" he asked with a smoother, calmer voice now that he had caught his breath.

The danger inherent in those words absorbed Skye and, still coming down from tasting his lips on her own, she couldn't resist engaging in the flirtatious exchange. "You can always make one."

He smiled at her wit. "You write speeches, don't you?"

"I'm assuming that's a rhetorical question." She had gotten over her distaste at him knowing so much about her.

"Do you still have my card?"

"I know how to reach you if I want you," she answered, thinking the disheveled look suited him well.

The overtones of her words had Darren feeling the rush again, but he figured there probably wasn't anything she could say that wouldn't turn him on at this point. "I have a job for you. Now, I work for Uncle Sam, so it doesn't pay great, but it's for a good cause."

Before she could say yes, which she had every intention of doing, a quick, hard knock on the door caught their attention. Darren held up his hand to Skye, she nodded, and he went to the door.

"What?" was all Sierra could say the second she saw Darren before looking at Skye with accusing eyes.

Skye had forgotten she was coming back. Although she still had the set of keys Sierra had given her, she was unable to find the codes and called the young woman to get them. Sierra wouldn't give anything until she agreed to let her come over and look at the contents together. She had gone to get lunch and returned almost an hour later with two paper bags with grease stains.

"Hello, Sierra." Darren kept the door open. He knew

his moment had passed and wasn't going to push it. There was no doubt that Skye would be calling him soon no matter what garbage the little intern would tell her.

Sierra ignored him as she entered. "Skye, for all you know that thug that body-checked you could be working for him. Now he knows where you're staying."

Skye didn't believe that; she couldn't. She was developing feelings for the man standing in her doorway and hoped she wouldn't be made a fool for it, or worse.

"I know this will upset you, Sierra," Darren said, "but I'm going to have to be leaving now."

He looked at Skye and found pleasure at the sight of her pressing her lips together to avoid a smile. That would be enough to hold him for now, but very soon he wanted those lips on his and that body against his again.

And he wanted to know what was on that computer.

Chapter 6

Skye wasn't much encouraged by what she was finding on Jeff's disk. The link to the *New York Times* article was about an investigation into Grafton Services, a professional services firm in North White Plains. The company was defined as performing miscellaneous business services and had apparently been under suspicion for some time. Only three years old, it was a multimillion-dollar corporation that apparently did most of its work for clients with Russian names that didn't seem to exist before hiring Grafton and disappeared very soon after paying Grafton large fees for services as yet defined.

The IRS had put its substantial foot down, stating only that there were tax evasion issues, but Skye knew it had to be more than that. A company in business for less than three years wouldn't be shut down for tax evasion unless it was doing something illegal. It was too soon. As unforgiving as the IRS was, it gave companies time to pay back taxes before shutting them down.

Trying to do her own research on Grafton, Skye realized that the private company took the term *private* very seriously. There was hardly any news except charitable contributions, the kind every company wants. She couldn't find any connection to Darren, and after checking opensecrets.com, a Web site that tracked all political contributions, Skye deduced that there was no financial contribution either.

So what was going on?

Skye got her answer in Jeff's other links. The head of Grafton was Andre Avegny, a man who had amassed millions with only a high school education. He was also rumored to have strong ties to the Fedulev family, part of the Russian mob active in the U.S. Jeff had linked several articles on Avegny, and Skye felt certain this man was at the center of what he suspected.

Another article mentioned that Avegny's cousin, Aton Avegny, had just been released on probation from jail for extortion, and was possibly going to have to return to Russia since his release in the U.S. was based on a position at Grafton. Avegny was a henchman for the Fedulev family.

She went to another link, a New York society magazine that covered a charity for breast cancer held at the Plaza Hotel on Fifth Avenue less than a year ago. For five hundred dollars a plate, the cream of the crop in New York society could mingle with an impressive list of television and movie actresses as well as female athletes.

Skye scanned the more than two pages of pictures of beautiful people wondering if any of them even cared about breast cancer and its affects on women, especially black women. Did they even know what they were there for or was it all about the chance to see and be seen, pat themselves on the back for their humanity and add the sum to their tax write-offs?

"Money is money," she said out loud. "Heartfelt or not, a good cause is a . . ."

Skye felt her heart jolt when she laid eyes on the very last picture on the bottom of the page. Darren was standing in the middle with an ear-to-ear smile, one arm around a man and the other around one of the most beautiful women Skye had ever seen. Skye wasn't jealous, but only because she knew she had no right to be. She had to work harder at fighting the negative emotions that were darkening her aura.

She couldn't help it and for a second, Skye forgot why she was doing this research in the first place. Who was this woman and was she still in his life? Why did she have to be so pretty, so classy, and demure looking?

Darren's kiss was still with her, on her mind constantly. There was something about its all-consuming nature that made her believe she was getting everything he had. The way he looked at her when he had given her that last chance to change her mind, Skye seemed assured there was no one else, but she had to know better. She was naïve when it came to those types of things, but Darren was a man, a politician at that. The combination created the perfect formula for man's greatest downfall: the need for more.

After all, he was from the capitalist privileged class. Everything they wanted already belonged to them, didn't it?

Skye bit her lower lip and allowed herself a second of regret before letting it go. She didn't have the luxury of caring about her romantic life right now. Encountering that attacker in Jeff's apartment had made her priorities clear. What Darren and Ms. America had going on would have to take a backseat. Who knew? She could be with the other man.

Looking at the caption beneath the picture, Skye was hopeful the woman had the same last name as the man on the other side of Darren, but she didn't and Skye completely forgot why that mattered when she read who that man actually was.

From left to right: philanthropist Elizabeth Sandon, Congressman Darren Birch, and financier Andre Avegny.

Skye took a deep breath. "That doesn't have to mean anything, does it?"

There was no guarantee that Darren even knew this man. She had been to plenty of these events. The cameraman says, "Picture" and whoever had gotten his attention would turn, place their arms around each other, and be all smiles. It was a proximity thing, she told herself. They didn't even have to know each other.

Skye decided that Jeff was seeing what he wanted to see and she wasn't going to fall that easily.

That was until she followed the next link showing a picture of Andre Avegny and Darren Birch standing outside the offices of Grafton Services. Both men were sharing the shears of an oversized pair of scissors and cutting the big, red ribbon for the grand opening of Grafton's business.

Skye pushed away from the desk and went to the window. She took in a clear view of the U.S. Capitol, across the street from her hotel. With a tug at her heart, she remembered standing at the steps with Jeff as he admired his future. She had focused on its majesty and had forgotten the brutal power those inside could sway if they wanted to. Darren had that power and more, but that didn't mean he would use it. Despite being on the wrong side of almost every issue and somewhat intimidating, Skye fed off the atmosphere immediately around a person. She had sensed Darren's atmosphere was clean.

Looking beyond the capitol, Skye watched people going on with their lives. They knew what she had been avoiding: life is about moving forward. She had to get back into the swing of things and join them, and that was only going to happen after she got to the truth about Jeff's death.

As she ejected the disk, Skye was clear about one thing. The truth about Darren's connection to Jeff's death, if there was one, wasn't going to come from looking at pictures and reading newspaper clippings from a safe distance. She had to jump into the mix and face it head-on. After all, that was her style.

Sitting across the desk from Darren, Franklin was reading the brochure in his hand intently. Darren watched as his face ran the gamut of expressions and felt impatience looming.

"Fielding Flagg is supposed to be top-notch?" Franklin asked, looking up.

Darren nodded. "It's the best facility out there."

"Then why didn't you pick this one before?" Franklin swallowed hard at Darren's angry stare.

"Beaven was also one of the best and it was close to Mom and Dad. That's why I sent you there. Clark Medical was a referral from someone I work with—"

"You don't have to go through the entire list." Franklin's tone was annoyed. "It was more of a joke."

"Sorry," Darren said. "I'm not getting the humor in your fourth trip to rehab."

Franklin had a strangely injured look in his eyes as he slapped the brochure back on the desk. "West Virginia. So I'll be what, one of three black people in the entire state?"

Darren sighed. "I can't take you, so I've hired a car."

"Too busy to send your big brother off?"

"This time." Darren wasn't really concerned with Franklin's feelings now. He had been too concerned and it had gotten him nothing but abuse and more headaches in return.

"This murder thing is really getting to you, isn't it?" Franklin didn't seem to need a reply he knew he wasn't going to get. "That White House throne is getting further and further out of reach."

"We're done here."

"Hey, I'm just playing with you."

"I'm not in the mood for your stupid, jealous games."

Franklin jerked to his feet, his jaw clenching tightly as his eyes narrowed. "I'll admit I've been jealous of you before, but trust me . . . I'm not now. You're about to lose everything just like I did."

"I'm not going to lose anything," Darren said.

"Don't be so sure, little brother." Franklin smirked. "You've got no alibi and a pretty evident motive. You're a fierce competitor, Darren. Everyone knows that."

"There was no competition." Darren stood up. "Jeff Preston never had a chance against me."

"That's a matter of opinion." As both men turned to her, Skye's face was expressionless, hiding the doubt she was feeling about coming here after walking in on this conversation.

"Skye." Darren dismissed his pleasure at seeing her with concern for how much of the conversation she had heard.

"Skye?" Franklin opened his arms wide with a smile. "Skye Crawford?"

Skye nodded hesitantly at the other man. He was older than Darren, a shade or two lighter. Both men had similar complimenting features, but Skye could tell that the older man's life had hurt his looks.

She accepted his hand, which he held out to her as he approached.

Darren came around his desk. "Skye, this is my brother, Franklin."

"I've heard all about you." A wry smile crept up the left side of Franklin's face.

"Have you?" Skye felt the tension as thick as molasses and knew this was more than an everyday argument between brothers.

"My brother has a thing for you," Franklin offered.

"Franklin was just leaving." Darren was too happy to see Skye to care that his brother was busting him out in front of her. "Weren't you?"

Franklin explored Skye with his eyes. "When is the car going to be here to take me away? I need to smoke one last joint first. You want to join me, Skye?"

Darren rolled his eyes as Skye turned to him with a confused, annoyed look on her face. This was just great.

Franklin's eyes widened as he placed a hand over his mouth. "He probably didn't want it to get out his brother is an alcoholic dope fiend. You wouldn't be press, would you?"

"I'm not." It was clear to Skye that Franklin's intent was to make her just as uncomfortable as he was making Darren. Something was very dysfunctional here.

"That's right." Franklin looked sideways as Darren approached. "She's the dead guy's girlfriend."

"Franklin!" Darren grabbed his brother by the arm and directed him out of the room.

Before the door slammed, Skye heard Franklin yell out, "She's better looking than Elizabeth!"

Skye didn't doubt he was talking about Elizabeth Sandon, the woman from the picture.

Darren turned to Skye, shaking his head. "I'm sorry. I'm really sorry."

"How does your brother know about me?"

"You didn't happen to see my elusive office manager, Mia, out there, did you?"

Skye wasn't falling for it this time. He always did this when he didn't want to answer a question. "What have you told him about me?"

"Nothing really," Darren said. "He reads the papers. He's going through some stuff and—"

"You don't have to explain him," she said. "He seems to be able to speak for himself just fine."

"Sensitivity isn't his strong point." Darren cleared his throat. "And I guess it wasn't mine today either. I didn't know you were standing—"

"Don't worry about me," Skye said coolly, surveying the office. "I'm not as sensitive as I may have appeared in the past. Jeff seemed certain you had no chance against him either. I wouldn't expect you to say anything less."

Darren smiled. "I'm surprised that you're here. Happy, but surprised."

"Why?" She took confident strides to the middle of the office, leaving Darren standing at the door.

"I don't know." Darren returned to his desk, leaning against the front as he watched her walk around. He took her distraction as an opportunity to get in a full view. She seemed to look better every time he saw her. "I'm sure Sierra made her Satan-Darren comparisons after I left yesterday."

Skye smiled casually, pointing to the sofa. "May I sit?"

"Please." Darren couldn't believe he was letting a woman fluster him. That hadn't happened since high school.

Skye was a little disconcerted as he joined her on the sofa. She had hoped he would sit at his desk and keep his distance so she could think clearly. Oh well, she thought. It wasn't like she could avoid being close to him if she was going to get what she wanted.

"Sierra didn't compare you to the devil," she said. "She thinks you're worse than him."

Darren laughed. "She's entitled to her opinion, which she no doubt shared with you."

"I don't need her opinion," Skye said. "I have my own."

He looked intently into her eyes and felt his confidence take hold. He had been right at the hotel. Things had changed between them and he was glad for it. "Then I can only hope you're here to finish what we started in your hotel room."

"That's out of the question," she answered, amused by the immediacy with which his face went flat.

Darren recovered quickly. "I'm sorry to hear that. I had thought . . . no, I was certain there was something there."

"There was," Skye said. "No denying that. It's just that it isn't appropriate for two people to carry on with each other when they're working together."

"I'm not sure I understand."

"Your job offer?" She moved closer, wishing despite herself that he would kiss her again. "If it's still on the table, I'll take it."

Darren leaned in, their faces only inches from each other. She was up to something, and for him, wondering what that was felt just as torturous as it was enticing. Those lips were going to be his again, office romance rules or not.

"Let's get started."

Darren was offered a prime seat at the window of B. Smith's Restaurant. Located in the former Presidential Room of the famous Union Station, the popular dining spot was nice enough to provide quality food and service while not being too high end. Darren knew Skye wouldn't be impressed if he had taken her somewhere too expensive. Here, they would eat good soul food while in nice, romantic surroundings.

Not that he needed the setting to get in the mood. Just one look at Skye as she walked into the restaurant took care of that.

It was his decision to select a restaurant less than two blocks from her hotel. It would be more convenient for her, and putting her at ease was important to him. Their plan was to go over the main points for the speech she would be writing for him, but Darren had much more than that on his mind. Thin spaghetti straps holding up a slinky velour hunter-green cocktail dress only made him more determined to mix business with pleasure.

He stood to meet her as the hostess directed her to his table. "Green is your color."

"I'm a Gemini," Skye offered, accepting the seat she was directed to. She waited for Darren to sit back down. "May is my month and green is my color."

"You believe that stuff?" Darren asked, reaching for the glass of wine in the chill bucket. "Ninety-eight Bordeaux?"

Skye nodded, pleased that he bothered to change since she had seen him earlier that day. It was probably inconvenient for him and the effort satisfied her. Green was her color and she wanted to look stunning. She wanted Darren Birch to tell her everything she wanted to know. It was underhanded, but she had to do right by Jeff. Besides, she couldn't go any further with Darren without knowing if he was the fine, upstanding public servant he appeared to be or complicit in a murder.

"Of course I do," she replied. "When were you born?"

"That stuff is ridiculous." He poured her glass of wine. "It's full of false assumptions and contradictions."

"The positions of the stars determine personality and spiritual nature."

"Sorry." Darren replaced the bottle. "I prefer to give God credit for that."

Skye tilted her head in a quick nod, her eyes squinting as she leaned forward. "You aren't one of those religious fanatics, are you?"

Darren took a sip of wine. "I'm pretty certain what I was thinking when I saw you walk into this restaurant with that dress on disqualified me from any religious status."

Skye's lips slid into a smile as she felt her cheeks get a little hot. "When were you born?"

Darren felt the sparks on all cylinders as Skye's left strap fell to the side. A flash of amusement hit his face as he leaned back. "Fine, I'll humor you. August twenty-seventh."

That flutter in her chest reminded Skye of silly schoolgirl crushes she had as a teenager, but there was something in the way he looked at her that made her want to jump the table and plant a big wet one on those thick lips.

"Virgo," she said, her raspy voice hitting a low tone. "I should have guessed."

Darren rolled his eyes. "I'll take the bait."

Skye read off the characteristics of Virgo. "Meticulous, reliable, practical, and diligent."

"Doesn't sound very exciting."

"You fancy yourself exciting?" Humor framed her expression.

Darren laughed in amusement. "I fancy myself much more than that."

"I forgot overcritical, harsh, perfectionist, and conservative."

"You made that up."

"Check for yourself." Skye reached for her menu, aware that his eyes were studying her. It was tantalizing and the idea that she was making this conservative Christian think such naughty thoughts made her feel very sexy.

Darren gestured for the waiter, who approached. They placed their orders, his the safe prime rib, hers the more adventurous special called Swamp Thang.

"I wasn't sure you'd come," Darren said after the waiter left.

"I wasn't either." She reached into her purse and pulled out her notepad and pen. "But I decided to believe you when you promised to be professional. Are you going to prove me wrong?"

You're damn right I am. Darren shook his head, reaching for the bottle. "I'm a man of my word. More?"

She nodded and watched him pour. "I should warn you. I can hold my liquor, so don't think you can drink me into your bed."

Skye was electrified by the lazy smile that was his response. He was so composed and unrevealing and it made her want to break his stride. She looked away, trying to keep her mind in one piece.

Darren watched as she opened her notebook, feeling a rush of heat run through him at the mixture of innocence and danger she gave off. He knew she wouldn't bother to correct the fallen strap because it wasn't a problem for her. Things out of place, loose straps falling down your shoulder were just all part of going with the flow. He envied her freedom and wanted her attention badly.

"You look incredible, Skye."

Skye kept her attention on her notebook. "Thank you, Congressman."

"Put the pad down," he directed with authority. "I want to get to know you first."

Skye looked up, studying that genial smile on his face. Conservative Christian image or not, she knew she couldn't afford to trust him. "Your interest is purely professional, right?"

"What do you think?"

"I think you already know a lot more about me than I ever would have told you to this point."

"You're bothered by that." He stated it more as an observation.

"Who wouldn't be?" Skye asked. "It gives you an advantage over me."

"I'm no genius, Skye, but I'm certain it would take a lot more than your basic stats to get an advantage over you."

She leaned back with a flirtatious grin. "You have something you want to ask me?"

"I have something I want to offer."

"This speechwriting job is more than enough, Congressman. Thank you."

"How much is that metro modern hotel you're staying at charging you a night?"

"Don't worry," Skye said. "I was going to bill you for the hotel stays starting tonight. It's about 165 a night."

"I know some place you can stay at no cost."

As fresh as he was being this evening, Skye was certain he hadn't meant what she thought he meant. "I'm listening."

"An apartment a few blocks from my own. A friend of my family has temporarily moved to Kentucky to help her father run for governor."

"A lady friend?"

"A lady friend who is into ladies, not men."

"I appreciate your offer." Skye paused as the waiter delivered their bread and salad. "But it sounds a little inappropriate. I mean, for me inappropriate is no problem, but I'm surprised at you. I take you for being in that let's-not-raise-any-eyebrows category of politicians."

"I'd say you were worth more than a raised eyebrow." He took pleasure in her engaging smile. "She is eager to have someone hold things down for her. A last-minute sublet fell through. You understand. I'm sure you have someone watching your place in Chicago?"

"My friend Monica is keeping an eye on things."

Skye hadn't seen it coming, but the flash was extremely bright and made her jerk and blink. The photographer had already turned and was heading out of the restaurant by the time her sight returned.

"What . . . what was that?"

Darren's expression was tight and strained. "I should have warned you about being in public with me."

"Now isn't too late."

"If you're an attractive woman," he said, "it's going to get your picture in the papers. It's the bachelor thing."

"Oh, really?" Skye wasn't too happy at the thought of being the new flavor of the week in the newspapers. "How long is the list of potentials they'll add me to?"

"There is no list," Darren assured her. "My reputation with women is respectable."

"What about Elizabeth?" Skye was intrigued by the uneasy look on his face. He was good, covering it up quickly with a casual smile, but she had taken him off guard. This woman was obviously somebody important.

"What about Elizabeth?"

"I'm prettier than her, according to your brother." Skye laughed a bit to lighten the mood, which had suddenly become quite tense. "You both know her apparently."

"My brother is right," Darren answered. "You're not eating your salad. Is something wrong? I'll send it back if—"

"Are you dating her?" Skye had no intention of falling for that again.

"No." At least that was the truth. "Elizabeth was someone I was . . . close to, but that's the past. She's not in my life anymore. No one is."

"Poor lonely baby," she said with a smirk. "We should get to work."

Darren was grateful to have survived that one. He wasn't done dealing with Elizabeth's betrayal, but he wasn't going to let her, or the memory of her, mess with his life anymore. "You've done the research?"

"I was on the Internet all afternoon. Barrio Futuro is a very small organization for its scope and effectiveness. They've done a very good job. I was thinking your speech should be about how the ties of the community have related to their inspiring growth and how more

funding of social programs can lead to small but powerful—"

"Skye," he interrupted. "I'm a Republican, remember? Barrio Futuro's success isn't about funding. It's
about the Christian values the community has held itself together with and the personal responsibility its
members teach the young men and women."

"We can include that," Skye said, "but you don't want
to shove values down their throats. These people know
they have values. They don't need you to give them
credit for it as if it took effort on their part."

"Maintaining strong values in this society does take
effort, and reinforcing those values is not the same as
shoving them down someone's throats." He mocked
her stubborn frown. "It is my speech you're writing, remember?"

"Whatever you say." Skye put her pad down and focused on her salad.

Darren knew he had taken a step backward. "I don't
want this to turn into a liberal, conservative cross talk."

"We would both do well to avoid labeling each other."

"That's fair," he said, "but if you were going to work
for Jeff, I'm assuming you shared some of his liberal
viewpoints. I just want it to be clear that I don't and I
don't want any of that in my speech."

"Any truth, you mean?"

"Who says it's truth? Just because you hear catch
phrases and sound bites spat at you everywhere you
turn doesn't make it truth."

"Neither does the fact that you don't." Skye put her
fork down, fired up enough to start something. "This is
the thing with you new, black Republicans. You're even
more closed-minded than your white counterparts."

"Look who's labeling now."

Skye huffed. "If the label fits, what else can I do?"

"I am open-minded," Darren argued. "But I'm not absentminded, and to believe most Democrat ideology, I would need to be."

"Are you calling me absentminded?" Skye asked. "I believe most of it."

"This speech isn't about what you believe. It's about what I believe. Can you grasp that?"

"I don't know, Congressman. I'm a Democrat and as you well know, we're all a little absentminded."

"Among other things." He could see he was boiling her blood and it excited him. He could feel his body reacting.

"Excuse me?" Skye hadn't noticed her voice was much louder now. "I will have you know that I have written speeches for Republicans and Democrats. I've even written a speech for a Libertarian."

He snorted arrogantly. "I'm sure that was hard."

"You sarcastic son of a . . ." Skye gasped at the smile on his face. He was playing with her! Toying with her and amusing himself with her frustration.

As the host approached the table, he cleared his throat and wrung his hands together. "I am so very sorry to . . . I'm going to have to ask you to keep your voice down."

Skye looked around, and to her astonishment, everyone was staring at them. She lowered her head, embarrassment lighting through her.

"I can find you a more private table," the host added nervously. "If that's—"

Darren held his hand up to stop him. "That won't be necessary. We apologize. Just friendly banter."

"Of course." The man seemed grateful and relieved to be done with the episode and rushed away.

"See what you've done?" Darren asked in a light tone.

Skye looked up at him, clueless as to how he could appear so oblivious of her utter humiliation. "This is your fault."

"It absolutely is not." It may have been a humiliating experience for her, but it had given him a second wind. He wanted this woman with an appetite to rival any he'd ever had. "My question to you is, how can a woman so absentminded be so incredibly alluring?"

He saw her left hand was flat on the table and reached across to place his gently on top.

Skye felt an arresting sensation run up her arm, and the hair on her skin stood up straight. If she didn't get this under control, something very dangerous was going to happen that night. Slowly, reluctantly, she slid her hand away.

"You see me as some kind of sport for you," she said matter-of-factly.

"I would never disrespect you like that," Darren answered. "I was just having fun. Disagreement doesn't have to be war."

Skye nodded in compliance. "That being said, it's probably safe if I just leave my opinions to myself."

"What would be the fun in that? Your beliefs are your fire and your bite, and I like it more than I could tell you. A beautiful woman tough enough to take an argument? We don't need to change a thing."

Skye sighed with a resigned smile. This fine brother definitely had her number.

* * *

The evening had moved with a tempered flow and was ending too soon for Skye. Despite the fact that she disagreed with almost everything he said, she was impressed with his conviction and very genuine concern. He wasn't someone who went after the position for the power and recognition; she could tell he would get that no matter what he had chosen to do.

Darren believed he was obligated to do good with his life because his life had been so good to him. With the exception of his brother and Elizabeth, of whom both he made it clear he wasn't going to talk about, he hadn't held back from her questions.

Skye stayed away from the subject of Jeff's murder for two reasons. She hadn't wanted to seem too eager and didn't want anything to dampen the mood. She was having a great time, something she hadn't had recently. She was living in the moment and it felt good.

It took only a second before they were standing on the sidewalk in front of Skye's hotel, and Darren wasn't willing to let the evening end there. He had spent the last three years of his life either absorbed in his work or dating women who cared about nothing more than the Washington game, and had forgotten how nice a simple evening with a woman who wasn't eager to get her picture in *Washington Life* magazine or afraid to raise her voice on a man who ruffled her feathers in public could be.

"I can walk you to your room," he said as they reached the revolving doors.

"I think I can manage from here." Skye didn't want him anywhere near her hotel room, because he was definitely going to get dragged inside. "Thank you for walk—"

She gasped as he took a step closer to her and gently

took hold of her arm. Skye was lit on fire by the look in his eyes. He was intense and determined and it turned her on like crazy.

"I want to kiss you, Skye." He was giving in to the tightening heat that was swarming around him in anticipation of the taste of her full, silky lips.

Skye couldn't speak but managed to shake her head. This couldn't be how it went. She would never know what to believe if she let herself fall for this man.

"I know it's unprofessional," he said. "And I've never been one to break the rules. Rules are there for a reason."

"Then what do you want?" she asked in an uneven voice.

"You." Darren's tone was deep and urgent. "I want you, Skye."

Skye was almost out of breath as she turned away. She was feeling dizzy, but tried to think straight. "We work together now, Darren. You know—"

"I'll fire you if you want," he offered with a tender smile.

Skye couldn't help but laugh and she didn't bother to resist when he pulled her to him and his lips descended on hers. She felt an erotic fervor crashing her senses and grabbed at his coat jacket as she met his kiss with all the pressure she could muster.

With a lustful need urging him on, Darren's hands explored her warm body, squeezing the soft flesh of her arm. He felt himself harden at the closeness of her body, the smell of her sweet perfume, and the little sounds she made that told him she wanted everything he was giving.

Skye begged for what little sanity she had left to help

her and pushed away. Her first push was ineffective against the force of his body and she tried again. This time, his lips separated from hers and in a barely audible voice, she said, "No."

Darren stopped and leaned away. He let her arm go as he tried to catch his breath. He had lost control, something he rarely ever did, but seemed to do repeatedly with her. He didn't just want a physical thing with Skye like he had with Elizabeth, and he had to keep that in mind.

Somehow.

"I . . . I should go. Good night, Skye."

As he turned to go, she reached out and grabbed his arm. He looked so disappointed when he turned back to her, Skye's heart did a little leap. "I'm not angry with you, Darren. Please don't be angry with me."

"I'm angry with myself," he said.

"Don't be." She removed her hand, uncertain if she could handle touching him and not falling back into a situation she wouldn't have the power to pull out of again. "I don't think either of us could have prevented that. It was sort of inevitable."

Darren's tension lightened. "Is this something about the stars again?"

"Exactly. It's the natural progression of warm spring nights, ninety-eight bordeaux, and . . ." She glanced down at her shoulder. "Runaway dress straps."

She winked and Darren knew he was down for the count. "Good to hear it wasn't just me."

"We just need to be careful," Skye warned. "You know that more than I do."

He knew exactly what she meant and she was right, but it just wasn't going to be easy with her. For a man who had been careful his entire life, he had never wanted to jump unfettered into anything until now.

"I can do careful," he said with a calm reassuring voice belying the tornado inside him. "But careful or not, Skye, you might find yourself in D.C. a lot longer than you planned."

As she sauntered into the hotel, Skye wasn't so sure he was wrong. Was she just some silly flower girl under the spell of his political charm and influence or was she really falling for a man that was falling for her? It was exciting to think about it and frightening in a way. Skye was more than eager to see how it would all turn out.

She was getting her free spirit back.

Darren wasn't getting a good vibe from Hammet Beslan, the man Grant had just introduced him to over lunch. He understood that Beslan was one of the major stakeholders benefiting from the sale of government land by the bill Grant was lobbying for. When Grant called and told him Beslan would be joining them, Darren had Lonnie Google the man and wasn't too happy with what he heard. He quickly deduced that Beslan was unhappy and Grant thought connecting him with a player on the Hill would calm him down a bit.

Darren didn't mind doing Grant the favor especially considering how stressed out the older man seemed, but something about Beslan, a second-generation Latvian with dark, hollow eyes and a thin frame, rubbed Darren the wrong way. He had the suspicious nature of a man that had friends on both sides of the law, and Darren was eager to end this conversation with no intention of meeting with the man ever again.

"Mr. Beslan." Darren placed his napkin on the table. "What relationship do you have with Sage Breen Corporation? You were a major partner there before it went bankrupt, right?"

Beslan smiled, although it was apparent that he was not pleased, and that suited Darren fine.

"Please, Congressman." Beslan nodded in some sort of deference. "Call me Hammet. I can understand a man in your position must be concerned about his . . . associations. You should know I severed my relationship with Sage over two years ago."

"That's what the paper said." Darren ignored the frown on Grant's face.

Beslan cleared his throat. "I'm not being dishonest with you."

"Of course not." Darren sat up. "But you understand my concern after hearing that many of the major partners in Sage are now silent partners in other firms."

Beslan was taken off guard and his frown gave him away. "Those are only rumors."

"Probably," Darren said reassuringly. "I'll look up my FBI contacts. They'll know."

Grant cleared his throat. "Darren, Hammet and I have talked about this. I was clear with him when I said that there was no room for impropriety if he wanted your ear. He assumed as much and exposed all of his information to me."

Darren nodded, temporarily satisfied. Grant knew politics even better than he did, and he understood when Darren demanded no risk in his relationships. Still, Beslan had that thin smile that Darren didn't trust. "That's good to hear."

An anxious Beslan sighed and returned to his steak just as his cell phone rang. He reached for it and smiled nervously. "My office, please excuse me."

Grant leaned into Darren. "Take it easy."

"I can't do that," Darren whispered. "You know that better than anyone. If my name is going to be on the bill, then I intend to know everything. Grant, I mean everything."

"That would require you to actually study it," Grant advised.

Darren's head tilted back a bit as both men eyed each other, but he decided the wise choice was not to respond. He was going to cut Grant some slack considering all of the personal problems the man had been through.

"Grant." Beslan held the phone to his chest as his brows centered in an uncertain frown. "Do you know a Michelle Parks from the *Washington Post?*"

Darren rolled his eyes at the mention of her name. "She's a glorified gossip columnist."

"What did she want?" Grant asked anxiously.

Beslan shrugged.

"You're not available," Grant said.

Beslan nodded and turned away. Darren waited until he was out of earshot before sharing his reservations.

Grant, always the understanding one, was prepared for everything. "Do you think I would put this bill in jeopardy? It means everything to me. My damn marriage is about to fall apart over all the work I'm putting into this. He's clean."

"I thought that was getting better."

Grant waved his hand away. "Forget it. You know how these things go. I'm not home enough."

"You'll be at the Futuro Barrio event next week, right?"

Grant nodded. "She's looking forward to it. I'm hoping it will get me off the sofa for one night at least. Who are you bringing? Elizabeth?"

"Hell no." Darren took a hearty sip of his cognac. "That woman was one of the worst choices I've ever made."

"She gave you what you wanted, didn't she?"

"That was the problem," Darren said. "I was only thinking with one head. I knew better than to think I could get away with that kind of irresponsible relationship."

"There's always a price to pay for selfishness."

"You're right." Darren just hadn't planned on that price being his becoming a murder suspect.

"So who?" Grant asked.

Darren's lips formed a fiendish smile. "Skye Crawford."

Grant was clearly confused. "You two are . . . what?"

"Don't ask me for a definition," Darren said. "I don't have any idea what we are. I just know what I want."

"That's gotten you into trouble before."

"No," Darren said. "I don't want with Skye what I wanted with Elizabeth. Skye is the whole package."

Grant chuckled to himself as he dug into his salmon steak.

"This is funny?" Darren asked. "What, you don't believe me?"

"I believe you," he said. "I just find it ironic how you bite my head off every time I mention marriage and here you are talking about the . . . what did you call it? The whole package?"

"You're getting ahead of me," Darren said.

"But you think she could be?"

A frown set into Darren's features. He was thinking of the kiss outside her hotel and how connected he had felt to her. But there was still that kiss in her hotel room, which although passionate enough to get a rise out of him just at the memory, stayed with him as well. She was trying to prevent him from seeing what was on her computer, and Darren got the distinct feeling whatever she was hiding wasn't personal, but political.

"I just don't know if I can trust her."

"What woman can you trust?" Grant slapped him on the back. "You shouldn't trust her. As a matter of fact, you can't afford to trust anyone right now. Not until all this nonsense passes by."

"Except you of course?" Darren asked.

"Well . . ." Grant opened his arms wide. "That goes without saying."

Chapter 7

As she arrived at the Café des Artists, the dining hall at the famous Corcoran Gallery downtown, Skye had barely gotten out the name of Valerie Salvatores before being directed to her table. Waiting for her was an attractive, forty-something Latina woman dressed in a sharp red business pantsuit who quickly ended her cell phone call and stood up to hug her.

"Skye," she said. "It's so nice to meet you."

Despite their relationship only consisting of a five-minute phone conversation, Skye wasn't surprised by the warm gesture. She had learned a lot about Latin culture from Monica and they were a hugging type of folks. When Skye sat down across from her, she already felt like they were friends.

"It's so nice of you to meet me here," Valerie said. "I'm on the campaign steering committee and we're working so hard on summer events. I really can't get away."

"Oh, no problem," Skye said. "The Corcoran is one

of my favorite art galleries. I've never been here, so I'm loving the new exhibits."

"You're an artist?"

Skye smiled. "What makes you ask that?"

"You have that way about you." Valerie gave her a quick once-over. "I know artists. I've spent my life around them."

"I'm a writer," Skye said. "But I do paint and sculpt in my spare time."

"A writer is an artist," Valerie said.

"Maybe a fiction writer, but . . ." Skye stopped herself. "Thanks. Yes, I am an artist."

"As I said." Valerie offered her some tarragon salad. "Please help me feel less guilty about this."

Skye handed Valerie a copy of the speech. "It's the second draft, so you can expect another before the event."

As Valerie looked it over, she nodded and smiled a few times. Skye wasn't nervous. After a block or two in the beginning, she had hit her stride and thought the speech was perfect.

"You write like a person who knows Barrio Futuro's vision very well," Valerie said, putting the speech down. "Did Darren tell you about us?"

"A little." Actually Skye hadn't spoken with him in a couple of days and it was starting to bother her that it mattered so much. They had only been able to play phone tag because between a group of visiting New York state legislators and a busload of Westchester high school students visiting, he had his hands full. She missed him and it was pretty pitiful.

"He's very proud of what you're doing," Skye added.

"That means a lot." Valerie sighed, placing her hand over her heart. "I just love Congressman Birch. Don't necessarily agree with all his politics, but I get that you don't either."

Skye was surprised. "Because of my speech? I tried to—"

"No." Valerie laughed. "The speech sounds exactly like Congressman Birch. I just get your vibe and I feel like you're planted on the left side of the aisle. How is that handsome conservative?"

Skye got a whiff of the change in Valerie's tone when she asked that last question. She was fishing. "I'm just his speechwriter."

"It's none of my business," Valerie said. "It's just that he's done such good things on the Hill. He could have lived so comfortably just focusing on his own district and their road complaints, but he's rolled his sleeves up on several projects like Barrio Futuro. He's just got that leadership pizzazz and that goes for miles in his business."

Skye soaked it up, not wanting to believe Darren was anything other than what everyone believed him to be, what she had seen him to be.

"He's never asked for anything in return. Not donations to his campaign or to talk him up to the press. Valerie tried to suppress a giggle. "I should stop. I'm making you uncomfortable."

"No, you're not."

"Look, I understand how it is in D.C. When you're dating someone high profile, you want to keep it under wraps for as long as possible. You must be disappointed."

Skye felt her pulse quicken. "Who told you we were dating?"

Valerie reached into her bag and pulled out a copy of the *Washington Post*, wrapping a few pages around, before showing it to Skye. Skye blinked, thinking maybe she had Darren on the brain and had seen wrong, but she hadn't. There it was, she and Darren sitting at their table at B. Smith's. She knew it was going to come out eventually, but after a couple of days her mind let it go.

"That was a business dinner," Skye said with an uncertain tone. "We were discussing this speech."

"It says you two got into a little tiff. Is that going to change things for the fund-raiser?"

"Why . . . what would it change?"

Valerie was eating heartily with one hand and talking with the other. "Well, Darren told me yesterday that you were going to be his date. I just thought—"

"He said what?" Skye's hands formed into fists under the table. He practically ignored her for two days and assumed that . . . "Did he really say that?"

Valerie was clearly uncomfortable now. "I'm not sure. I probably should have . . . Am I in trouble?"

Skye's brows arched. "Someone is."

"Why don't you ask him?" Darren had been pacing the living room of his loft for several minutes now. He knew he was yelling, but he didn't care. A phone call from Fielding Flagg Rehabilitation Center telling him Franklin was suspected of sneaking out was enough to make him lose it.

"Well, we have." The woman on the other end of the phone spoke so calmly and quietly that Darren could hardly hear her, and it was only making him angrier. "He said he hasn't."

"Then he hasn't," Darren said. "What are you bothering me for?"

"Because we have evidence to suggest otherwise, Congressman. We were hoping you could talk to him."

"Did you confront him with this?" Darren asked.

"Of course not."

"Of course not," Darren repeated mockingly as if it had been silly to ask.

"You know our policy of trust, Congressman. If he says no, we have to trust him."

"But you don't." There was a short silence on the other end and Darren sensed the woman was losing patience with him. "I'm paying you seven grand a week, Doctor. Did he leave or not?"

The doorbell, finally fixed, buzzed.

"Lonnie!" Darren yelled toward the kitchen. "Get the door!"

As Lonnie came running out of the kitchen mumbling something about not being paid to be a house servant, Darren returned his attention to the phone.

"We need you to ask him," she said. "If we do it . . . may I call him to the phone?"

"First, I need your advice." Darren was egging her on. "Is it okay that I cuss him out? Because I intend to if he gets on this phone any time soon."

"That isn't the strategy we would encourage."

"Then I think I'll call him after I've calmed down."

"Thank you, sir. Good evening."

"Good evening." Darren hung up, yearning for the days when you could slam a phone on its receiver to make your point. "Lonnie?"

Lonnie, on his way back to the kitchen, yelled back, "It's Skye Crawford."

Finally, some good news. "Then you need to be leaving as soon as possible."

"Five minutes!" Lonnie yelled again. After some intense after-hours work, Lonnie was making himself a sandwich before heading home.

A couple of minutes later, Skye walked through the open doors to Darren's condo. She envied anyone who lived loft style. She had never been able to afford one herself, but loved the wide-open space, earthy walls, and windows. It was an artist's dream to make a home a work of art in any form, style, and design wanted. Darren had obviously opted for the controlled, traditional bourgeois white, red, and black. Everything was expensive and matched perfectly. Skye thought it definitely needed some life added to it.

"Hello, Skye." Darren waved her over as he stood at the bar pouring two glasses of Chateau Lafitte. "I'm pleasantly surprised to see you here."

"Is that so?" All of the righteous anger Skye had was dealt a severe blow at the sight of him. He was wearing a short-sleeve navy polo that fell off his trim, muscular figure perfectly and tan flat-front pants that accentuated his flat stomach. The look softened him and made him much sexier than the dark conservative suits she had seen him in up until now.

"A drink?" He offered her a glass, but she shook her head. Something was wrong, but it didn't matter because he was glad to see her. Despite his frenzy over the past couple of days, he hadn't forgotten about her one second. "I have to drink alone?"

"It looks like it." Skye helped herself to his sofa taking note of its soft, luxurious feel before looking around. "You live very well, Congressman."

Darren cautiously joined her after putting both glasses down. "Thank you. I've tried to develop some taste during this life's journey."

"What about manners?"

"I would say impeccable," he offered, "but I have a feeling you're about to prove me wrong."

An Important Message From The ARABESQUE Publisher

Dear Arabesque Reader,

I invite you to join the club! The Arabesque book club delivers four novels each month right to your front door! It's easy, and you will never miss a romance by one of our award-winning authors!

With upcoming novels featuring strong, sexy women, and African-American heroes that are charming, loving and true… you won't want to miss a single release. Our authors fill each page with exceptional dialogue, exciting plot twists, and enough sizzling romance to keep you riveted until the satisfying end! To receive novels by bestselling authors such as Gwynne Forster, Janice Sims, Angela Winters and others, I encourage you to join now!

Read about the men we love… in the pages of Arabesque!

Linda Gill
PUBLISHER, ARABESQUE ROMANCE NOVELS

P.S. Watch out for the next Summer Series "Ports Of Call" that will take you to the exotic locales of Venice, Fiji, the Caribbean and Ghana! You won't need a passport to travel, just collect all four novels to enjoy romance around the world! For more details, visit us at www.BET.com.

ARABESQUE

SPECIAL OFFER!
4 BOOKS
FREE!

BET★ BOOKS

www.BET.com

A SPECIAL "THANK YOU" FROM ARABESQUE JUST FOR YOU!

Send this card back and you'll receive 4 FREE Arabesque Novels—a $25.96 value—absolutely FREE!

The introductory 4 Arabesque Romance books are yours FREE (plus $1.99 shipping & handling). If you wish to continue to receive 4 books every month, do nothing. Each month, we will send you 4 New Arabesque Romance Novels for your free examination. If you wish to keep them, pay just $18* (plus, $1.99 shipping & handling). If you decide not to continue, you owe nothing!

- Send no money now.
- Never an obligation.
- Books delivered to your door!

We hope that after receiving your FREE books you'll want to remain an Arabesque subscriber, but the choice is yours! So why not take advantage of this Arabesque offer, with no risk of any kind. You'll be glad you did!

In fact, we're so sure you will love your Arabesque novels, that we will send you an Arabesque Tote Bag FREE with your first paid shipment.

* PRICES SUBJECT TO CHANGE.

YOU'LL GET 4 SELECT ROMANCES PLUS THIS FABULOUS TOTE BAG!

ARABESQUE

Visit us at: www.BET.com

"Your feeling would be right." Skye held her resolve despite the intriguing dance in his eyes. He wouldn't find her so amusing in a second. "I had lunch with Valerie Salvatores today."

"Is something wrong with the speech?"

"No." Skye leaned back, crossing her long legs. "Absolutely not. The speech is great. Vintage Darren Birch, she said. She was so pleased with it, just as she is pleased with you."

"Of course," Darren said coyly, knowing the shoe was about to drop.

"She is so looking forward to seeing you . . . I mean us . . . at the ball next week."

Darren pressed his lips together and resigned himself to the tongue-lashing he was about to get. "It's not like it sounds. I was going to get around to asking you."

"When?" she asked. "The morning of? Or maybe a couple hours before? Why not? It isn't like I have anything to do. I'm just here for your pleasure."

"Funny choice of words," Darren said. "Because if that were true, you'd—"

"If you want to be walking five minutes from now," Skye warned, "you might not want to finish that sentence."

Darren swallowed. "I agree."

Noises from the kitchen got Skye's attention and she immediately thought of a woman. "Are you entertaining?"

"Would you care?"

She wanted to say no, but Skye's inability to lie made her look like a fool when she tried to. "I just think it's so ironic when you family values politicians say—"

"Hey," Darren protested. "I'm not married. That's not a mistress in my kitchen."

"No, but you offered me a glass of wine while some-one is—"

"I always offer my guests something to drink."

Skye's hand went to her hip. "Do you always make sexual innuendos to your guests as well?"

"Just the sexy ones." He slid a bit closer to her, feel-ing randy from her anger. "Are you jealous, Skye?"

"Of who?" Really, she wanted to know who.

"Lonnie."

"Lonnie," Skye repeated. "How very Barbie-like."

"Wow." Darren laughed with gusto. "Lonnie's a kind heart, but being a former college running back, he'll be very disappointed to be considered Barbie-like."

Skye realized his game and reached across to slap him, but Darren grabbed her wrist.

"Whoa," he warned, feeling the scorch of her skin against his as her anger turned him on.

"You're an ass." She pulled her hand away.

"If you'd just asked me," Darren said, "I would've told you it was one of my legislative assistants."

"Whatever." Skye thought she should have felt com-pletely humiliated but could only laugh. "That's beside the point. I came here because you had no right—"

"You're right," he interrupted. "I was wrong to as-sume you would come with me. Although you won't be-lieve me, I meant to ask you. It's just that so much has happened."

"Why wouldn't I believe you?" Skye asked.

Their eyes fastened to each other and Skye was struck by the imprint of reliance she felt. Was she imag-ining the trust his eyes conveyed? She knew she wanted to.

While never diverting his eyes from hers, Darren's

words came slow and deliberate. "You're under no obligation to join me, but I would be grateful if you would."

Even though she didn't want to say yes, there was no way she could say no. So instead, she said, "No funny business."

Darren frowned. "I'm not sure what you mean by that."

"You know damn well what I mean by that, Congressman."

Darren slid closer to her until their knees were touching. He knew he was playing with fire as his hand gently touched her thigh. It was worth it. He wanted to taste her energy, her life, all of her.

"I can promise no funny business," he said, "but I'll have my fingers crossed behind my back when I do. It's only honest to tell you."

"A politician admitting he'll be lying to you ahead of time." She tilted her head up, chin stubbornly forward. "How refreshingly honest."

Skye closed her eyes as his mouth came down on hers. The taste of his lips, the sensuous way in which they pressed against hers, made Skye's insides swirl with ecstasy. It was like everything good in one moment with a cherry on top.

The sweet delight of her lips had Darren in a euphoria that teased on the edge of indulgent insanity.

"I'm leaving!"

As she separated from Darren, Skye turned to the large figure walking toward them with hard, quick steps. She wasn't at all prepared for what she saw and had to blink to make sure she wasn't imagining it. He was large all right, large and familiar. Although she hadn't thought about the man watching her outside the police department during her last visit to D.C., she hadn't forgotten him and he was standing right before her.

"Skye." Darren stood up. "This is Lonnie Richardson."

Skye's temperature dropped fifty degrees and a chill ran up her spine. Standing up too quickly, she stumbled back into Darren's arm, but quickly pushed out of his grasp.

"Skye?" Darren watched as Skye's complexion turned a shade lighter and her eyes widened in distress.

"I . . . I have to go." Avoiding eye contact with Lonnie as she passed him, Skye rushed for the door.

"Skye." Darren hurried after her, grabbing her arm just as she reached the door. "What's wrong? Did I do something?"

She looked up at him, wanting to believe the look of wonder on his face. "I just . . . I have to go, Darren. I'll call you later."

He tried to hold on to her arm, but the force with which she jerked it away made it clear to him that he had to let her go. He fought the urge to go after her, knowing it would only make things worse. Instead, he turned back to Lonnie, who didn't seem as surprised as he was at Skye's peculiar behavior.

"What?"

Lonnie made a guilty sigh. "I think it's me."

"What's wrong with you?" Darren asked.

Lonnie sat down. "Can I at least eat my sandwich while I tell you?"

The Barrio Futuro fund-raising event was being held at the City Club of Washington at Franklin Square, a prominent business and social club elegantly furnished in modern elite style. The club's private events were usually reserved for those with connections and money, but Darren had used his connections to get a colossal-style discount on space and food. Charitable publicity was currency in Washington, D.C.

Darren had worked such miracles before, but nothing he had done in the past compared to the wrangling he had to do to get Skye to agree to attend the event with him. After five days of expensive flowers, phone calls, and humble voice-mail messages, he succeeded in convincing Skye that Lonnie's surveillance was nothing nefarious and it would never happen again. Standing in front of the building on I Street, Darren still wasn't sure she would come.

It was ironic for him. Here he was, standing outside in inclement weather hoping for a woman to show up for an evening he did everything short of begging her to attend. That was a first and overwhelmingly discouraging for a man considered a sought-after bachelor. Then again, Skye was the exception to all the rules, and as eager as he was to hold his ground, he imagined there wasn't much he wouldn't forgo for her. When the limousine he had sent for her pulled up and the driver opened the door, Darren corrected himself. There wasn't much he wouldn't forgo for her? No, when he saw her he knew there wasn't anything.

Skye looked stunning in a strapless, straight-lined, sage-green fitted silk chemise dress that trailed to her ankles with a sultry slit up her left thigh. Her dress wasn't too tight, but hugged her curves, making her look voluptuous yet unattainable. Seeing her created a rising storm inside Darren and he only hoped he could behave. His body certainly didn't want to.

Skye was more than pleased by the expression on

Darren's face, having spent the last two hours making sure she looked her best. After finally agreeing to join him, she pushed her apprehension aside and went full force. Now here she was standing inches from him and that warm, seductive smile on his face made her all but forget any concerns she had built over the past week.

"It's a good thing you came," Darren said, forcing his hands to his sides. *Take it slow, buddy.*

"Because you would have been alone?" Skye smiled flirtatiously.

"No," he answered. "Because if you hadn't, I would have had to come get you, and I get the feeling that would have ended ugly."

"For you," she said. "Very ugly."

As they both laughed, Skye's hand went to his arm without any thought on her part. She could feel his muscles underneath the tuxedo jacket and it sent a warm rush of blood to her head. She was tired of pretending, of being safe. She wanted to feel free again, free to express her feelings, free to react with honesty and not protection.

As he took her arm and led her inside, the blood rushed through her entire body and she hoped he would never let go.

As they entered the private dining hall, Skye immediately felt the eyes on her, on them. "People are staring at us."

He squeezed her upper arm for comfort, but the soft touch of her flesh distracted him. "We've talked about this, young lady. You have to keep up."

"Don't tease me," she said. "I know about the bachelor thing, but they're making me feel like there's a bug on my nose or something."

"Have you looked in a mirror?" he asked. "Trust me. If you had a bug on your nose, they wouldn't notice."

Skye beamed.

Darren greeted everyone quickly and politely as he directed her toward the front of the hall. "They're just eager to see the rumor in the flesh."

"Or maybe they were expecting someone else?" Skye looked up at him inquisitively.

He pressed his lips together as if he was amused, but he wasn't. Thoughts of Elizabeth, his big mistake, flashed before him and he worried about her name being mentioned tonight.

"Don't start with me, Skye. There is no one else in my life and I've made that clear."

"I know," she said. His change in demeanor hadn't escaped her. "They just make me nervous."

"Washington is like Hollywood," he explained. "See and be seen. Everyone has read about us in the papers and the blogs have been spreading rumors."

"What have they been saying?" Political Web logs, among the latest crazes in political commentary online, responded to news faster than the news did. Skye was an avid reader of the more liberal sites, but hadn't been able to keep up lately.

"I think we're engaged." Darren nodded as Grant waved them over to his table. "There is word that you and I were in a love triangle with Jeff."

"Darren, that's awful." Skye wasn't at all amused. "Don't they have respect for the dead?"

"The mourning period is very short in D.C. Especially when there is good gossip waiting to be spread."

When they reached the table, Skye took notice of the older white man who stood up, focusing on her with a wide smile across his face. The woman with him, an attractive black woman in a red designer suit slowly stood up, but the smile on her face was barely visible.

"Well," Grant said. "Here she is."

"Skye," Darren directed. "This is a good friend of mine, Grant Coleman, and this lovely woman is his wife, Joy. This is Skye Crawford."

"Well," Grant said approvingly, "aren't you just as pretty as a picture?"

"Thank you." Skye thought the man was going to rip her arm out of the socket with his vigorous handshake. "It's nice to meet both of you."

"No need for polite manners," Joy said, offering a seat next to her. "We're too close to Darren for that. You come sit next to me so I can give you all the dirt I have on the representative here."

Darren laughed, but not too heartily. He wasn't sure how much Grant told Joy about Elizabeth, and he knew that the rumors had reached her.

"Sit down, buddy." Grant winked his endorsement of Skye as he waved a waiter over. "Let's have a drink before this getup gets started."

Darren agreed, sharing a glance with Skye as they sat apart from each other. He wanted to be with her and felt, from the way she looked, that she wanted to be with him, but this was how social events in D.C. went. Darren wasn't sure when he'd be alone with Skye any time soon, but knew he was going to make the most of it when he got the chance.

Skye felt no shame in the fact that she just wasn't sophisticated enough not to be impressed. In just short of a half hour, it seemed as if all the people in the room made a trip to their table to greet Darren. They either wanted a picture taken with him or to tell him about the latest political talk show they had seen him on. The eager looks on their faces, seeming just happy to be noticed by him, intrigued Skye. He was warm and kind as if each short greeting brought him a unique pleasure. Everyone walked away with a smile on their face.

As Joy fed her story after story of every District elite in the hall, Skye felt more as though she were watching an episode of *As the World Turns* instead of a community fund-raiser in the nation's capital. The women were beautiful and confident. The men were classically handsome and held powerful postures. She recognized two presidential cabinet members, a female senator, and a few Latino community leaders nationally famous for their hard, thoughtful work.

Skye had attended countless fund-raisers and charity events in Chicago, with local celebrities and powerful people, but there was something different about the same event in Washington, D.C. She felt the power of national decision-making around her, and it was exciting to be a part of. The other difference was Darren, and nothing she had been a part of in Chicago compared to the way he radiated in the room. Skye was captivated.

When he approached the stage to applause, his charm and poise made her speech more spectacular than she even imagined. She wasn't just proud of herself, she was proud of him and she was falling hard. Every word was enhanced by his conviction and passion, and as the crowd stood and applauded his closing, Skye knew that this wasn't just political hype. Darren Birch was special and she wanted very much to be special to him.

*   *   *

Just as he approached her, Skye turned to Darren and the smile that came to her face got such a rise out of him. It wasn't just a physical thing. He had wanted her to be pleased. He cared what she thought. So much time had been wasted following the protocol of etiquette and failing each time because his attraction to her was too strong.

That was over. He wrapped his arm around her waist and pulled her to him. "Finally I have you to myself."

Skye let him lead her to the dance floor as the band played a merengue tune. "Are you sure? We're not going to be interrupted by some very perky, cute blonde congressional aide so delighted to see you again?"

Darren loved the spice of her biting words. "That wouldn't be jealousy I sense in your tone, Ms. Crawford."

"You just seem very popular tonight." She would have been a little envious of the countless women that had flocked to their table for his attention after the event ended if Darren hadn't made it obvious to everyone he only had eyes for her.

As they danced, their movements quickly became in sync as if they had been close like this forever. Darren felt a sense of fitting with Skye in more ways than one.

"Well," he said casually, "I am quite an incredible man. You have to see that by now."

Skye laughed, hitting him sharply in the chest. "You try to make a joke, but I can see that you really think you're quite something."

"Don't you?"

"Yes," she answered slowly. "I do."

Darren was unprepared for how deeply the softening of her smile and the tender tone of her raspy voice reached him. He stopped, pulling her to him, and leaned in to brush his cheek against hers. He heard her inhale and it turned him on.

He whispered into her ear, "I want to be alone with you."

Skye felt her knees getting weak again as his scent made her dizzy. "We—"

"Now," he urged. "Come with me."

He took her hand in his and Skye followed him without question onto the Atrium terrace overlooking the gardens and expansive trees. Standing at the edge, she felt anticipation tickle at her as she watched him in earnest. He had his head down, his eyes impatiently following the couple passing by.

When they were gone, Darren looked at Skye and she reached for him. Their lips connected in a hunger that erased the world around them in an instant. Their hands searched each other with the greed of lovers separated over time. Their lips wouldn't separate, preferring to suffocate rather than be apart for even a second.

He separated her soft lips and searched her mouth as he felt mania take him over. He could only hold her so tight, kiss her so deeply, and none of it was enough.

Skye held on tighter, just to keep from falling down. Her craving for him seeped into her soul and made her melt in his arms. His touch was masterful, yet tender, and it made her feel as if she were floating on air. Their clothes were nothing but a nuisance to her now, wanting desperately to feel his skin against her own raging-hot flesh.

They both gasped for air as their lips separated and Skye used her first breath to call out his name as his mouth pressed hard, gluttonous kisses as potent as lava on her neck and shoulder. His hands reached down, caressing her hips and traveling to her behind.

Skye was so caught up in the overwhelming sensation of his taking possession of her that she felt as if she had been tossed over a thirty-story building when he let go and stepped back from her.

Darren felt the haze of heat closing in on him and he knew he was on the verge of losing complete control in a way that words couldn't describe. He was going to embarrass himself and Skye and he wanted her so bad it began to seem worth it. That was why he knew he had to stop.

"This won't be practical," he said between heavy breaths.

Skye could barely hear above the thundering of her heart. "Only you would be thinking about practical right now."

"Someone has to be."

She stepped toward him, placing her hand flat on his chest. Feeling it moving up and down as his heart beat wildly made her want him even more. "Not right now, Darren. Just kiss me."

Darren rolled his eyes and removed her hand. "You're torturous, Skye. You have no idea how hard it is for me not to take you right here, right now."

"That's okay," she said. "If you go too far, I'll kick you in your groin."

Darren laughed, shaking his head. He turned, looking out over the gardens. "I live in D.C. and you live in Chicago. I travel to New York every other weekend. I spend all my district breaks there. We're complete opposites on the political spectrum, which wouldn't matter so much except politics is my life, my future."

"You really know how to charm a sister." With the fluttering in her belly, Skye didn't want to hear about their challenges. She just wanted his lips on hers. But this was a responsible and practical man standing beside her, a challenge in itself.

"It would be easy if we could just . . ." He looked at her, those tender eyes touching his soul. "But no, I don't want something casual with you. I want you."

"I'm right here." She reached out, placing her hand on his back.

"What about Jeff?"

Taken off guard by the question, Skye lowered her hand and took a step back. "What does Jeff have to do with this?"

"Do you think I had something to do with his death?"

Skye looked out over the terrace. "If I thought you had murdered anyone, let alone someone I had loved, do you think I would be here with you like this for even a second?"

Darren turned to her and ignored the voice that told him he wasn't sure he could trust her. "You can't say you don't have any reservations."

"You've given me reason to," she said. She caught his eye and blinked innocently. "Besides, what would be the point if all we could see was clear sailing ahead?"

Darren contemplated the prospect of falling in love with this unpredictable firestorm, and frankly, he had enough trouble to deal with. He straightened up and held his hand out to her. "Let's get back on the dance floor before we get into any more trouble."

Skye woke up with a smile on her face usually reserved for the mornings after she had had great sex. Although that hadn't happened last night, despite her desire for it to, she still felt that burst of energy and light. Last night, after Darren walked her to her room and kissed her passionately, Skye knew she was going to fall in love him, and although it should have made her apprehensive, it made her feel happy for the first time in a long time.

When a knock on the door came, she panicked. Her first thought was that it was Darren, and although she felt like a beautiful princess, she certainly didn't look like one.

She was rushing for the bathroom when the voice from the other side of the door inquired, "Ms. Crawford? I have a package for you."

It was a woman.

Skye didn't bother to hide her disappointment when she opened the door, and the young woman's eagerly pleasant expression made her feel bad for it.

"Ms. Crawford?" She was young, pretty, and too perky for this early on a Sunday morning.

Skye nodded.

"I'm Tara and you've got a gift!" She seemed as happy as if the gift were from her. "We were ordered to deliver it immediately."

Skye looked the empty-handed woman up and down. "Is it invisible?"

"Oh!" Tara jumped, her long hair bouncing up and down. She reached over her side and pulled an over-sized gift-wrapped box about four feet tall, two feet wide into view. It was decorated in a myriad of colors with a sparkling red bow on top. "This is it!"

"Oh my goodness." Skye stepped aside as Tara pushed the box in.

"It's not heavy," Tara said. She stood eagerly by the box, her hands clasped together. "Is it from your boyfriend?"

"I don't have a . . ." Skye laughed. "I think so, actually."

"You're gonna open it, aren't you?"

"Yes, I . . ." Skye reached for the package, but was beaten to the punch by Tara, who began ripping at the wrapping.

What was revealed touched Skye to her heart. As last night had progressed, she and Darren spent the time talking, trying to ignore the tension between them. Jokingly, she decided that since he knew so much already she might as well fill him in on the details.

"It looks expensive," Tara said.

"It's top of the line." Skye's hand came tenderly to her heart. "I told him I liked to paint."

"Awww," Tara said. "It's so sweet when they show you they actually listen."

The paint set included everything Skye could have thought of, and she was completely amazed. How could he possibly have known everything to get, and where on this earth had he gotten it in such short time? It was barely nine in the morning.

Alone again, Skye surveyed the set. Three pressed canvases on a five-foot wooden easel, a set of seven silk brushes, two liner brushes, a glass palette and two palette brushes, fifteen colors, mixing oil, and turpentine. When she had told him that her work was done, she remembered what Darren had said the night before. *I'll find a way to keep you here.*

When she reached for her ringing cell phone, Skye was in too much of a daze to check the name. She hadn't expected to hear Sierra's angry voice on the other end.

"You having fun?" she asked.

"Sierra?"

"I heard about your dream date last night."

"Word travels fast in this town." Skye thought for a second. "Exactly what are you doing here? I thought you were supposed to be in New York."

"I am. My parents don't know. They think I'm visiting my cousin at Howard. How could you, Skye?"

"Look, Sierra. I'm sorry if it bothers you that I'm spending time with Congressman Birch, but—"

"My question is, why doesn't it bother you?"

"Darren had nothing to do with Jeff's death."

"Why not?" she asked. "Because he's so fine? Yeah, only the ugly brothas commit crimes."

"Sierra, I wish I could explain to you—"

"I'll save you the work and do the explaining. While you've been out taking over chocolate city with the black George Bush, I've been investigating. I hacked into that journalist's computer. You know, the one who wrote the article on Wanda Bunning and her lying ass."

"That's illegal."

"So is murder."

Skye heard papers shuffling and her stomach began to tighten. "What do you want, Sierra?"

"First, I found out that this journalist has all kinds of doubts about that little trick's story. She typed up all her notes, including the place where she worked, a hair salon."

"I want to talk to her," Skye said, certain she could get the woman to tell her the truth. "Did she admit to you why she lied about Jeff?"

"She wasn't there when I went. She quit, but I found out that salon is on the black gold coast. You know, the area north of Rock Creek Park, where a lot of rich black folks live."

"I don't know D.C. that well."

"Well, you'll learn about that neighborhood soon enough if you keep dating that bourgeois front man."

Skye was already feeling protective of Darren as if he was her man. "He's just as eager to find out what happened to Jeff as we are. It means his reputation."

"Good luck clearing his reputation when it gets printed that one of Wanda Bunning's regular clients was Darren's last girlfriend before you stepped on the scene."

"Elizabeth Sandon?" Skye's entire body tensed as she almost dropped the phone. Her voice couldn't hide how shaken she was. "Wait a second. There has to be an explanation."

"Yeah, there is. It's a clear connection and now that I've anonymously sent the notes to Detective Ross, I'm sure it's going to be followed up on. I don't mean to hurt your feelings or anything, but I don't think they've broken up. I think all this, including you, is just a part of a big plan."

"No," was all Skye could say. She had some doubt, but she would never go that far. It was impossible. "No."

"Maybe if you keep saying that enough," Sierra said, "the evidence will disappear."

"It could be a coincidence." The uneasiness of Skye's voice reflected her confidence in her words.

Sierra's tone was cynical. "You tell yourself whatever you need to in order to hold on to your man. After all, what else matters?"

Skye blinked with a start as the phone clicked and the dial tone followed. Slowly, she put the phone down and looked over at the paint set sprawled across her bed. Five minutes ago she had gloried in a moment of happiness. Now all she wanted to do was cry.

Chapter 8

"You make me sick," was Lonnie's response to the wide smile on Darren's face as he entered his office.

"Come on." Darren leaned back in his chair, crossing his feet together on top of his desk. "I don't ask you for details about your hot dates."

"I'd offer them to you if I had any." Lonnie leaned over the table at the edge of the room, loosening his tie.

"Well, I'm a gentleman, so . . ."

"You work me like a slave, Congressman. I have no time for a social life. I live through you and other people who help me remember what it was like to actually touch a woman."

"Not a chance." Darren looked up at the clock on his wall. It was eleven. Two hours until he saw her.

It was Monday and he was anxious to see Skye again. Yesterday, she had left him a message while he was in church to thank him for the gift, but not much more. He tried to reach her to confirm their lunch today but didn't want to seem too eager. The truth was, even going a day without her seemed like too much.

"Then quit your smiling," Lonnie ordered. "It qualifies as torture."

"I'll tell you one thing." Darren waited as Lonnie leaned forward, eyes open wide. "I'm asking her to come home with me this weekend."

"Whoa." Lonnie ran his hand over his bald head and whistled. "So exactly who are you and what did you do with my representative?"

"It's a little out of character, but—"

"It's a lot out of character. What happened to the guy preaching about taking time, thinking things through, and following all the steps?"

Darren winked at him. "He met a girl."

"Congressman Birch." Mia's voice on the speaker broke the male bonding moment. "It's that reporter, Michelle Parks, from the *Post*. She wants to talk to you about Jeff Preston."

Darren rolled his eyes as Lonnie shook his head no. "No, I better take it. I want to do what I can to put an end to this."

"Yes," Mia responded. "And Skye unfortunately canceled your lunch."

Darren sat up, grabbing the phone. "What do you mean? When did she call?"

"Just a second ago."

"I told you to interrupt me if she calls."

"Yes, but . . ." There was an awkward pause. "She specifically asked me not to get you."

Darren contemplated the gesture and couldn't think of a good excuse or reason. It bothered him. "Mia, take a message from Ms. Parks and get me Skye's room at the George Hotel."

"Yes, sir."

"What was that about?" Lonnie asked.

Darren felt the tension creep through him. "I don't know but I'm going to find out."

Mia returned to the phone and the message wasn't good. "No one is answering. I have the concierge on the line. What do you want?"

Darren thought quickly about his strategy. "You have Skye's cell. Try her there."

When he was able to reach the concierge, Darren first thought to shamelessly use his name and the power that came along with it. He knew it was wrong, but he was impatient. He would try to avoid it, but if he didn't get answers soon, he would do it.

"Can I help you, Congressman?"

"My secretary told you who I was?"

"Yes, sir. What can I do for you?"

"I'm planning a romantic dinner for Ms. Crawford in room 382 this evening. Who do I talk to to set it up so that it's waiting for her when we arrive at six?"

"I'll appoint Tara, Congressman. She's my best."

"It's an early dinner, so I want to make sure that the room is clean and—"

"Of course," he said. "Hold on a . . . Oh, here we are. Well . . . I'm confused, sir."

"What's wrong?"

"Her room is checked for turnover by three today."

"Turnover." Darren was angry now. Was she playing games with him? "You mean she's checked out?"

"She hasn't yet, but noon is the deadline."

"Thank you."

Darren slammed the phone down and pushed away from his desk.

"Where are you going?" Lonnie asked.

Darren didn't answer. As he grabbed his keys off the edge of his desk and stormed out of his office, he was wondering what kind of drama cycle he had gotten himself into with this woman.

With one hand on the doorknob, Skye turned back to look at the paint set she had left on the bed with her note. The hotel promised it would all be sent back to Darren immediately. She knew she was being a coward by writing to him instead of telling him to his face she was going back home, but she couldn't. For a second there, she had allowed herself to let go, but the world was different now. There was a price for being carefree, for going with your heart, and she didn't have the money to pay it.

With a deep sigh, she turned back and opened the door. When she saw Darren standing there, she jumped back.

"Skye." His expression didn't hide his anger as he stood there, apparently arriving just in time.

Skye blinked once, then again. No, it was him. "Darren, what are you—"

"What are you doing?" he cut in. "Are you leaving?"

"Oh, Darren." Skye looked back at the note on the bed. "I was going to . . ."

"Leave," he said, trying to keep his temper under control. He was hurt by this, but too mad to acknowledge it. "Just skip out. After everything that happened Saturday night. That's just great."

"I'm sorry." Skye fought the urge to cry. "Last night was wonderful and the paint set is . . ."

"Apparently not impressive," he said. Damn, this stung. "What in the hell is going on?"

"I can't do this now." She couldn't even look at him, choosing instead to look at the floor. "I left you a note."

"A note?"

Skye pointed to the bed and gasped as Darren pushed the door open and stormed into the bedroom. He reached for the envelope.

"Hotel stationery," he said. "How intimate."

When he ripped up the envelope, Skye felt as if he were ripping at her and she couldn't believe how guilty she felt.

"Now," he said, approaching her, "you have to tell me whatever it was you were too spineless to before."

"Spineless?" Skye dropped her bag. "How dare you? You want to know what that letter said? I'll tell you. It's about Elizabeth."

"I've told you about her," Darren said apprehensively.

"You forgot to mention that she's a regular client of Wanda Bunning," Skye said. "Or didn't you think anyone would ever figure that out?"

"Who in the hell is Wanda Bunning?"

"Very sloppy of you, Darren. A man who is so meticulous and careful should remember that he shouldn't use his girlfriend's beautician to lie about an affair with his political opponent."

Skye felt her body begin to relax at getting the truth out. Darren just stared at her with nothing to say. He had been caught.

Darren's mind was racing to put this new news together and he felt a sense of dread in the pit of his stomach. He looked back at the bed and shook his head.

"This paint set cost a lot of money," he said. "Were you just going to leave it for—"

"Darren!" Skye's hands clenched into fists.

He looked at her with a casual confusion. "I'm sorry, did you expect a response? I don't make a habit of responding to baseless accusations of murder and cover-up."

"Don't give me your political bullshit," Skye shouted. "That girl never had anything to do with Jeff, and Detective Ross is going to find out exactly how she knew what she did, so you're right. Don't waste a carefully prepared speech on me. You should be saving it for her."

"Since you're here," he said carelessly, "will you write it for me?"

Skye was incredulous, but she couldn't think of anything to say. Was he insane?

"Skye." He stepped toward her but stopped as she took a step back. "Are you afraid of me?"

"The fact that you find this amusing makes me very afraid for you, not of you."

"Don't be." He hesitated before taking another step toward her. "I don't know what in the hell is going on here, but I will find out and explain it all to you."

"I think it explains itself." She couldn't figure out if this sudden calm was confidence or a ploy. She was more than confused now. "You're tied to her."

"I am *not* . . ." Darren took a deep breath, fighting the worry that threatened to make him say things he would regret. "I am not tied to that woman. I don't know who she is or where she comes from. I had nothing to do with Jeff's death or her lies."

"What about—"

"I don't know," he answered, "but I had no idea Elizabeth knew her. Elizabeth and I aren't together and I know she would never do something like that."

"Like what?"

"Like cover up a murder." Darren knew Elizabeth was hard, but this was too much. Besides, he was with her when Jeff was murdered. "There is an explanation for this, Skye. I swear to you. Someone is setting me up."

"But who?" she pleaded. "Why?"

"Someone wants it to look like I had a part in this to make it more likely that I murdered Jeff. They had to know the connection would be made at some point. When this comes out . . ." Darren turned away. The reality of the damage this could cause him made him vulnerable.

Suddenly overcome by emotion, Skye reached out to him, placing her hand gently on his back. His entire body was tight and tense, and this made her want to believe him. "If they wanted to make you out to be a murderer, why would they try to make a convincing case for suicide at first?"

"I don't know." Darren was calmed by the comfort of her touch. "Maybe because it would make me look even worse if I . . . either way, I murdered him. How could I look worse by trying to cover it up? It's not like it was an affair. It's murder."

He turned back to her, looking into her warm, caring eyes. "It's murder, Skye."

"What are you going to do?"

As his defenses built, Darren's face hardened. "It's not your concern. You have a nice flight."

In her shock, Skye hesitated, but quickly grabbed him before he could leave. "Where . . ."

"Someone has declared war on me," he answered. "Someone evil enough to commit murder. I don't have any time in my life for anyone who isn't on my side."

He reluctantly jerked his arm from her grip.

Skye felt her heart catch in her throat as she called out to him again. "Darren!"

He turned around. "Just go home, Skye."

"Don't tell me what to do!"

Skye watched in desperation as Darren made a grumbling sound under his breath, turned, and stormed out of her hotel room. She felt her stomach shaking, held captive by not knowing what to do.

"No," she said out loud as her head shot up, her shoulders straightening. She did know what to do, but before she could run after him, she was stopped in her tracks.

Darren had returned. This time, he seemed angrier than ever. The threatening look on his face, the darkening of his eyes turned Skye on more than anything had to this point. She felt suddenly breathless, riveted to her spot as her entire body began to throb.

He slammed the door behind him, not losing a step as he came for her, taking hold of her head with one hand and her waist with his other. With a heavy groan, he pulled her to him and his mouth descended on hers. His anger, his frustration and passion displayed themselves in cruel ravishment as his lips pressed harder and harder. He wanted her despite how much she had hurt him, and it made him only angrier with her and himself. The touch of her body against his, her lips responding to his own made him crazy and he no longer cared what made sense. There was only this woman.

Skye was grabbing at him, pulling at him desperately because their bodies touching just wasn't close enough. His lips, punishing and taking, sent waves of lightheaded pleasure through her. She took hold of his shirt, pulling him back toward the bed. Together, their lips never separating from each other, they crawled onto the bed. As she held his head with one hand, Skye pushed all of the paint supplies onto the floor. She felt her body pulsating and trembling in anticipation of tasting this man, having this man. Her emotions of anger, confusion, doubt, fear, and desire were swirling around her, leaving her senseless and completely open to the fury that engulfed her.

As they rolled over, Skye positioned herself on top of Darren and finally parted her lips from his. She kissed his perfect chin, and moved down to breathe a teasing kiss at his neck. The hair on his skin stood up as he reached for her lips. She denied them as she leaned back and straddled his waist. She could feel his reaction to her, and her body responded by writhing in a rhythm of its own making.

Quickly she removed her thin blouse, revealing her full, firm breasts and taut nipples. Darren's hands reached up hungrily for them and Skye's head fell back with a moan as he caressed and rubbed them, calling out her name. Reaching down, she hastened to remove his dress shirt and began kissing and biting at his chest, reveling in the frenzy she was causing for both of them.

Every inch of Darren's flesh prickled at her touch, and his desire skyrocketed out of control as her lips trailed down his chest, leaving circles of heat around each nipple with her tongue. She had ignited in him a wild, wanton need that he had never known but knew would be there forever for her. He was in a confused euphoria, helpless against the utter demolition of his brain by his body. His lust for her threatened his resolve to take his time, building with every touch, every kiss.

Unable to take the heavenly torture of her lips, Darren took hold of Skye and switched positions. He smiled as she laughed, but didn't hesitate to rip every piece of clothing off both of them. Before he tossed his pants to the floor, he reached for his wallet knowing if he didn't think of protection now he wouldn't have the mind to think of it later.

He explored her body with sweet diligence, giving no indication of where he would go next and feeding his own desire by not bothering to think himself. Her skin was sweet and warm and he felt her tremble underneath him, only making him hotter and more desperate to have her. As he devoured her body with his mouth, his tongue sent delicious sensation after sensation rippling through her.

He parted her legs, lifting them in the air. Skye let out whimpering sighs of pleasure as his lips gently kissed her inner thighs. Kneeling down, he moved his mouth to her center, and her eyes rolled back in her head as she screamed out his name. Her body was twisting and turning every which way as his mouth and fingers worked together to bring about an insanity that sent Skye into space.

"Please," she yelled again and again.

He obliged her, finally and slowly entering her. A carnal groan escaped him at the sweet, smooth, and tight hold she had on him, lifting him up and sending him out of his mind.

Skye savored the sweet pain as he entered her, feeling almost faint at the thought of drowning in him. There was only this man and as he came harder and faster, Skye felt as if she were circling in a train wreck, skidding like crazy around the world, lifting up in the air. She closed her eyes and arched her back, pushing her hands against the headboard. His mouth came down to her left breast and encompassed it. The agonizing vexation was unreal and built with every thrust, every moan, and every touch of his mouth.

When the fire hit her like a brick, bells ringing around her, Skye felt delirious and hysterical at the same time. She dug her nails into him, trying to brace herself for what was to come. The explosion made her body shake all over as she screamed out her pleasure over and over again.

Darren came only seconds later as she tightened her hold on him. In the hands of God, he left this world for only a brief moment, but it was enough to let him know that his life, his future was in this woman. There was only this woman.

They rested for a minute, in each other's arms. Their bodies were wet with sweat, the pounding of their blood through their veins was deafening. Skye closed her eyes, her hips still swaying in the afterglow of passion as it tickled at her senses.

As he reached for her again, Skye laughed at the thought of leaving D.C. This man was her home.

Darren heard his cell phone ringing again and opened his eyes. Looking outside, he saw it was dark and he wondered how long they had been making love. With a smile on his face, he turned to Skye and watched her as she slept peacefully. It was amazing how a woman could look so virginal and innocent as she slept and be such an incredibly hot, pleasing lover.

He had been selfish the first time, unable to be as patient as he wanted to, but hoped he made up for the second and third time. The sounds she made told him he had.

"Skye." He whispered her name as he nudged her.

He looked down at the seductive curve of her full hips and his hand went to rub her soft, round stomach.

Skye opened her eyes with a smile on her face. She looked up at Darren, feeling her body warm again at his touch. "I didn't know you traditional, conventional types could be so wild."

"We're the wildest kind." He leaned forward, kissing her tenderly on her lips. He went to her neck again, loving the give of her supple skin against the pressure of his mouth. "Let me show you again."

Skye laughed, pushing against his chest. "Take it easy, Congressman."

"Ohh." His hand went to her breast and his thumb pressed against her nipple. "I like it when you call me that."

"My mistake." Skye sat up in the bed, pushing his hands away. She reached down for the covers, pulling them up on her. "Let's take a little break."

"Okay." Darren lay back down, his fingers intertwined behind his head.

"It's that easy?" Skye asked.

"No." He looked up at her. "I just remembered I don't have another condom, so . . ."

"If you did?"

He slapped her thigh. "You'd be in trouble yet again, young lady."

Laughing, Skye looked down at him and the look of confidence and comfort in his smile frightened her. He knew she was falling for him and wasn't going to cut her any slack during the fall. She was going to be under his spell and he wouldn't show her mercy. Not that she wanted or needed any. There was no need for explaining. She was on his side and her heart told her this was the right place to be.

"I'm starving," Skye said. "I'll order room service. Do you want something?"

Darren reached for the remote control. He could see the red light on his cell phone sticking just out of the pants pocket on the floor. "A big fat juicy steak."

"Sounds good." Getting up, Skye traipsed lazily to the table to get the menu.

Darren, distracted by the natural, uninhibited sway of her hips, was jolted back to reality when he heard his name. The news flashed a picture of him and Jeff shaking hands, taken at a fund-raiser last year just days before the rumors of Jeff's run began to spread.

"This video," the background voice was saying, "of Mr. Preston was taken last year at a breast cancer foundation luncheon with the man he was supposed to be running against this year, Congressman Darren Birch."

Skye looked at Darren and felt pain at the misgiving expression on his face.

"Once again," the background voice continued, "the breaking news is that the murdered body of Wanda Bunning, a woman claiming to have an affair with Jeff Preston, was found in Rock Creek Park."

Skye gasped, dropping the menu to the floor. Darren turned to her, their eyes holding each other for a moment before Skye rushed to his arms.

"What is going on?" she asked.

"I don't know," Darren said, "but I'm going to find out and I'm going to fix this. I promise."

"They're going to find a way to pull you into this." Skye hated to think of all Darren could lose regardless of whether the truth of his innocence would come out. A taint was as good as the real thing.

"I can take it," Darren said, looking down at her. "As long as I know you're on my side."

"Don't even question it," Skye said. "You couldn't get rid of me now for anything in this world."

Skye felt the examining and inquisitive eyes following her as she traveled down the hallway of the offices of Dreyfuss Law. When she would turn to look at them, they would avert their glances and Skye couldn't help but feel ashamed. She knew what they were thinking. She showed up on the scene and their beloved Jeff was dead. At the least she was bad luck. At the most . . . with the recent press about her relationship with Darren, Skye could only imagine the things they were saying.

Finally, she reached Jeff's old office and saw Sierra sitting at his desk, typing away at his computer.

"You're late," Sierra said, without looking up.

Skye noticed that the office barely showed signs of life. It had been weeks since Jeff had left, and any hint of his existence was gone.

As if reading her mind, Sierra said, "We sent everything to his parents last week. George White in tax is moving in next week."

"Why did you ask me to come here?" Skye asked, closing the door behind her. "I'm clearly not welcome."

Ignoring the question, Sierra waved Skye over and she hurried around the desk.

Eying the computer, Skye was shocked at what she saw. "That's the district police—"

"Shhhhhh!" Sierra frowned at her. "This is why I asked you to come over here."

"How did you get into the police department's Web site?"

"A hacker never reveals her tricks." Her typing picked up a furious pace. "I got it."

"You've got what?" Skye lifted herself up and sat on the desk as Sierra turned the computer in her direction. "Is that—"

"Wanda Bunning." Sierra clicked on a few boxes. "She was shot twice in the chest."

Skye cringed. "Oh, Sierra. I didn't want to see this."

"Well, since your boyfriend might have something to do with it, maybe you should whether you want to or not."

"I told you over the phone," Skye insisted, "I'm not discussing Darren with you. He didn't have anything—"

"I heard the speech." Sierra rolled her eyes. "Look at this under witnesses."

"Someone saw this?"

Sierra shook her head. "Someone was seen with her in the area an hour before her body was found. It's still cold in the park during early mornings this time of year. Not too many people out for jogs, and those that are usually recognize each other."

Skye read the notes. "White male in gray . . ." Skye gasped, her hand coming to her mouth.

"Skye, what is it?"

Skye could hear her speedy heartbeat. "Gray sweatshirt and pants with red letters, possibly college insignia. It has to be him. Does it say Moscow State U anywhere?"

Sierra scrolled down the screen. "No. Just red letters."

"That's the man that was in Jeff's apartment. The one that knocked me down."

Sierra gasped, her hands gripping the edge of the desk. "The man looking for the disk?"

"Why would he kill Wanda Bunning?"

"Obvious," Sierra said. "Detective Ross got my info

and pressed hard on her. She was going to turn on Darren and Elizabeth."

Skye didn't bother to correct Sierra on that one. She was too confused herself. "What else is on there?"

Sierra clicked on another file. "They have some of the items found on her body here. A wallet with five hundred in cash."

Both women looked at each other before nodding.

"Someone was trying to get her out of town," Skye said. "That shouldn't surprise us. She was lying all along."

"But why kill her?" Sierra asked, returning her attention to the screen. "And why not take the money back after she was dead?"

"Probably didn't have time and didn't want to risk getting caught. Make the kill and get the hell out of there."

"You sound like a cop," Sierra said. "Okay, look. She had a plane ticket to Arizona. First class. Whoever this was, they were overdoing it."

Skye remembered the article mentioned an aunt in Arizona. Maybe it was a coincidence after all. "Can you find out who paid for that ticket?"

"Doubt it," Sierra said. "Probably cash or someone gave her the cash to buy it. Have you ever heard of Cashmere Scottsdale?"

"Like in the fabric?"

"No. I think it's an apartment building. It's the moniker found on her key chain. They don't have any notes on it, but I can try . . . Oh, shit!"

Skye jumped off the desk, stepping back as Sierra frantically clicked and typed away. "What? What just happened?"

"Someone is tracking me." Sierra was up on her feet

now, working at lightning speed. "They haven't found me yet, but they're trying to."

Skye's hands were clenched in fists as she watched Sierra type in a frenzy. "Can you get out?"

"I think . . ." Sierra's fingers were slowing down and a little smile creased her lips. "They don't know who they're messing with."

Skye let out a deep sigh as Sierra blanked the computer. "Don't be so cocky. That's a felony, isn't it?"

"I don't know." Sierra was breathing heavy as if she'd just run around the block.

"You should know the penalty of a crime before you commit it."

"Cashmere Scottsdale." Sierra showed none of the panic signs from just seconds ago. "I've got to look that up, but I'll go to my computer. This one is a little hot, you know what I mean? I'll understand if you don't want to get involved."

"Why? Because it's illegal?"

Sierra sent her a haughty nod. "Considering you're in the public eye now, you shouldn't be associated with this investigation."

"Neither should you." It hadn't skipped Skye's mind that the choices she made might affect Darren. He was already feeling the heat.

"You better be careful this weekend."

"I'm not in any danger." Skye told Sierra that she had accepted Darren's invitation home. She was scared to death. Not only was she going to meet his parents, she was going to stay with them. "At least not the danger you're talking about."

* * *

"Stop it. Stop it." Darren playfully leaned away from Skye as she tried to undo his top button. The flight attendant had already told her twice to buckle up and here she was sitting on his lap tempting him. "You have to sit down. There will be plenty—"

"Are you worried about looking unprofessional again?" Skye huffed. "You fired me, remember?"

Darren gave up, burying his face into her neck, letting her scent seduce him. "Yes, but I hired you again, remember?"

She tugged at his collar, delighting in her victory over his staunch insistence on propriety. "Then give me an order. I'll do whatever you . . ."

The stewardess returned to the main cabin with a dangerous glare that made Skye take her seat. She felt silly being so impressed with a private jet, something she would usually consider the waste of capitalist greed. The socialist inside her was enjoying the chocolate-covered strawberries and bypassing security lines too much.

"Fine," she said, "I need to write your speech about Wanda Bunning anyway, so I have to get into serious mode."

Darren didn't want to think about this even though he knew he should. There had been no formal investigation or allegation, but Wanda Bunning's death had reopened Jeff Preston's murder case and people were beginning to whisper his name again.

"If I answer to rumors," he said as the cabin phone rang, "I'm suggesting that they're legitimate."

"You know what damage letting rumors fester can do." Skye couldn't help but feel his hurt. He didn't deserve this, but was taking it with his head held high.

Darren took the phone off the receiver attached to the wall of the plane. "Yes, Lonnie."

Skye watched as angst morphed Darren's expression. She could tell it was bad news and worried that she had taken too long to respond to the rumors.

"What in the hell?" Darren shot up from his chair and kicked the table. "That's a lie. She hasn't been trying to reach me. You have to stop this, Lonnie. Don't let . . ."

The anguish on Darren's face when he looked at her made Skye afraid and she knew somehow she was involved. His eyes seemed to be apologizing.

"You have to stop her, Lonnie. Get the lawyers, whatever. Stop her." When Darren hung the phone up, Skye was right at his side. Looking at her worried frown, he knew he had to make things right. "I'm sorry, baby."

"What? What is it?"

"It's the press." Darren's hand went to her arms, holding them firmly as he looked steadily into her eyes. "They're going to run a story, a gossip story, about us."

"Everyone already knows about us." In the past week, rumors of their budding relationship had been printed in every social, news, and political publication and Web site available.

"No," he said. "Not that. They're going to run a story suggesting that you, not the campaign, were the reason I had Jeff killed."

Skye couldn't believe it. "They can't do that, can they?"

"I can try and stop them, but it's a tangled web. They work hard at not outrightly accusing me of anything."

"They have nothing!" Skye broke loose, turning away. With everything he was going through, now she was doing him damage. "They can't say that."

"They're also going to print the connection between Elizabeth and Wanda Bunning." Darren slumped into the chair. "And Franklin."

"Franklin?"

Darren nodded. "He's just been kicked out of the latest rehab facility I put him in. Apparently, he started a fight that turned into a riot and . . ."

Skye rushed to Darren, kneeling down and placing her hands on his knees. She looked up at him wishing she could remove the weariness that dragged underneath his eyes. "I have to leave."

"What?"

"I'm only hurting you, Darren." She held up her hand to halt his protest. "No, I don't want to hear it. Everything has gone to hell since I came to D.C., and me being in your life has been a wreck to your career."

"You can't blame yourself for this." Darren fought off the exhaustion that wanted to claim him. "It's this damn city. It eats people up. I won't let you—"

"Please don't fight me on this." It was already too painful to be this close to him and know she had to leave. "You and I both know I'm right."

"No." He reached down, taking her hands in his. "What I know is that I'm falling in love with you and I can't get through any of this if you're not with me."

Her heart leaped at the words, but not enough to cloud her judgment. She would be fine with rumors and innuendos, but Darren was different. His entire future depended on his reputation.

Darren pulled her to him, wrapping his arms around her. He wasn't certain of much at this moment, but he was sure of one thing. He would never let this woman go.

"It's a rough patch," he said. "I've come up against them several times before and I've always won. I'm innocent and that's all that matters."

As she felt herself melt into his arms Skye was taken over with a craving, an aching for this man. She had never experienced it before, a selfish desire to be connected to him. She was falling in love, but harder than she ever had before.

The emptiness of not being with him was too much to bear, and Skye knew in an instant that she wasn't strong enough to make the right choice. Maybe it was Jeff's death or losing her job. Maybe it was leaving home and venturing out into the world after being a lethargic soul for so long. Whatever the reason, Skye knew she couldn't leave.

"I have to be able to help you," she said.

"You are." He squeezed her tighter, letting the relief calm him. "This is helping me."

She closed her eyes at the touch of his lips tenderly kissing her forehead. She wasn't falling in love. She was in love and she had to do what she could to make sure Darren didn't regret asking her to stay.

As they reached the front door, Darren could see that Skye's tension was increasing.

"Honey, please breathe. I don't want you to pass out."

Skye smiled, but she couldn't help it. She had already been nervous about meeting Darren's parents because she wondered if they blamed her for this mess as much as she blamed herself. She knew that they were pillars of the Westchester community, and the idea of some little flower child from nowhere coming into their son's life and ruining his career couldn't make them as warm as Darren promised they would be.

The house was large, but its Colonial style design and warm fall colors were welcoming and unassuming. As he knocked on the door, Darren's other hand gripped Skye's tightly and she appreciated the gesture. She needed him.

"Trust me," he promised. "My parents are—"

The door flew open and Skye came face-to-face with a woman with wide-open arms. Lily Birch was a voluptuous, attractive woman with dark skin and a youthful glow of someone thirty years younger. She held none of the pretentiousness that Skye had feared.

"This is her?" she asked, looking Skye over with dancing eyes.

"Yes, Mom." Darren smiled proudly. "This is Skye. Skye, this is my mother, Lily Birch."

Skye held out her hand, but Lily ignored it. Instead, she grabbed her and hugged her tightly. "It's so nice to meet you. Do you know I spent an hour on the phone with this boy going on and on about you the other day?"

Skye blushed, looking at Darren, who was shaking his head. "I hope he was kind."

"Of course," Darren said. "Kind and clean. That's my style."

"Listen to him." Lily rolled her eyes before stepping back to look Skye up and down. "You're absolutely beautiful. You know, you remind me of myself in my younger, freer days before—"

"Mother?" Darren gestured toward the door.

"Of course." Lily grabbed Skye's hand and led her into the house.

Skye took in the tasteful decorations, an unusual mixture of suburban traditional and high-end Italian Tuscany. In an instant, she saw Ethan Allen, Bombay, Restoration Hardware, Williams Sonoma, with a little Crate & Barrel slipped in. Sleek, expensive antiques merged with modern accents. Price or brand dropping wasn't an issue, Skye could tell. It was all about look and feel. Whoever put this house together was creative and artistic.

Halfway through the living room, Lily stopped and the smile on her face faded. She looked from Skye to her son with a painful frown. "Darren, I . . . I wasn't able to warn you."

"What's wrong?" Darren asked.

"If it isn't boy wonder!"

Although she had only met him briefly, Skye immediately recognized Franklin as he paraded into the living room. Skye wasn't sure if that look of trouble was a constant on his face, but she hadn't seen any different.

"And with his princess," he added with inflection. "What a beautiful picture."

Darren took in his brother's disheveled appearance and prepared himself for a long day. He didn't want a scene in front of Skye or his mother. "What are you doing here?"

"It's my home too," Franklin spat back. "I have just as much a right to be here as you!"

Skye reached out and took Darren's hand in her own. She squeezed tight, hoping to calm him.

Lily cleared her throat. "Franklin and I were just talking about . . . well, that wasn't the right place for him. There has to be another."

"What's the point, Ma?" Franklin leaned against the

wall with a crooked smile on his lips. "I'm not the black sheep anymore. I mean, I may be a drunk, but at least I'm no murderer."

Darren ripped away from Skye and started for Franklin, whose eyes widened with fear. Just before he reached him, Gary rushed out of the kitchen and jumped between them. As angry as Darren was, he respected his father's authority too much to ignore what the gesture meant.

"That's enough," Gary told him sternly. "You too, Franklin. I warned you what would happen if you started something."

"You gonna put this on me?" Franklin whined. "After everything he has done?"

"You know Darren hasn't done anything wrong," Lily asserted.

Seeing the pain in her eyes, Darren went to his mother and wrapped his arm around her. He looked over at Skye and cringed at her expression. She looked as if she'd rather be anywhere in the world.

He mouthed a quick apology and Skye smiled in response. It was a weak smile because she was never good at hiding her emotions. Throughout her life she had considered it a sin to hide your feelings, but right now it would be a blessing if she knew how.

Before the wide-awake nightmare began, Skye had thought of Darren's life as a dream. Money, power, good looks, and prestige could only do so much. She could feel the tension and pain in the room and regretted the part she played in causing them.

With a charming smile and a face showing the foundations of Darren's features, Gary approached Skye offering his hand. "I didn't want to meet you like this."

"Skye," Darren said, "this is my father, Gary Birch."

"My wife has put together one hell of a weekend for you," Gary said. "She wants to show you off to all her girlfriends and whatnot. I hope you—"

"What in the hell is going on here?" Franklin asked out of the blue. Darren and Gary turned to him with warning stares, but he didn't seem to care. "Why is everyone treating her like she's the princess bride? This is all her fault."

"One more word," Darren threatened.

Franklin stood up straight, trying as dangerous a frown as he could. "Don't you talk to me like I'm the little brother here."

Gary made a grumbling sound and turned to his wife.

"Yes." Lily nervously grabbed Skye's hand again and was quickly leading her out of the living room. "Let me show you to your room. Let them . . . well, let's go."

Skye couldn't deny the relief she felt at the thought of getting out of there, but as she looked back at Darren, her heart ached for him. He had wanted a memorable weekend with his family, and Skye had no doubt it would be, but for all the wrong reasons, and she felt as if she was to blame.

Waiting until the women were out of earshot, Gary warned both his sons. "There isn't going to be any of that in this house. I swear to you, Franklin. You will regret it."

Darren backed away, trying to calm himself down. He had yet to tell his parents about the article that would be coming out in Sunday's paper, but the story would no doubt be picked up by the local media and weekend political talk shows. Add Franklin to the mix and the weekend mood had already been set.

Life with him in D.C. would be challenging enough for Skye. If this was how life away from the spotlight would be, he feared that her promise to stay by his side was going to be hard to keep.

Chapter 9

Despite the rocky beginning, the weekend in West-chester had taken a positive turn with a Friday night dinner at home sans Franklin. No one knew where he had gone and they were all too happy for the break to ask the question.

Skye for one was delighted he had made other plans. She wasn't sure she could handle another round of who's to blame. Happy to be with Darren again, she was able to let her guard down after a few moments at the table in the formal dining room, and things went smoothly from that moment on. Throughout the night, Lily and Skye held their own conversation while Darren spoke to his father. Every now and then, the topics would mix and they would all engage. Despite the distraction, every time Skye shared a private glance with Darren, they both held the same fear that things would certainly change once Darren told them about the article.

It was odd that in the absence of Franklin, while she

was sitting on the sofa alone with Darren, a thought would come to her that she didn't know what to do with.

Franklin had blamed this all on her. If Darren hadn't told his family about the article accusing him of killing Jeff over her, how did Franklin know? She thought of the animosity between brothers, and her mind began to wander into forbidden territory. She had to bite her tongue, not daring to tell Darren her thoughts and compound his worries. After all, it was one of those stupid ideas that her runaway imagination was prone to creating, which was why when she kissed him good night standing on his parents' doorstep her heart kept her mouth shut.

Still, the idea stayed with her during the night, and even now, as she sat across from Lily at a French bistro in Tarrytown for a late breakfast, she couldn't erase it from her mind. Skye had always believed that you just throw the truth out there no matter how painful. The truth always set you free and what was right was right. But watching Lily as she spoke of Franklin and the heartache he was causing her, Skye couldn't bring herself to add to the family's concerns.

After taking a sip of her coffee, Lily smiled and said, "You must hate me."

Skye was surprised. "Why would you say that?"

"For going on and on about one son and keeping you away from the other."

"No." Skye picked at her barely eaten plate. She had half expected a twenty-dollar omelet to taste different from all those three-dollar omelets she had eaten all her life, but it didn't and her appetite wasn't at its best. "He's at his district office anyway."

"From watching you last night, I could tell you two

don't like to be away from each other." Lily sighed, leaning back. "I remember that feeling."

"Remember?" Skye asked. "I thought I saw some sparks there between you and Mr. . . . I'm sorry . . . Gary."

"Gary is a wonderful man." Lilly shook her head and made a smacking sound with her lips. "It's me, really. I haven't been in a very romantic mood of late. Darren's problems in D.C. and this thing with Franklin are so upsetting."

"Darren seems committed to getting him in rehab."

"I know." Lilly nodded. "We won't give up on him. He's family. He's my baby, but the damage being done now between him and Darren will never be undone. They were once so close, Skye. This is killing Darren."

"I can see that." Reaching across the table, Skye placed her hand over Lily's. "I promise, I'll do what I can to make it better for him."

Lily smiled warmly. "You remind me of myself."

"You said that before." Skye was flattered. "How so?"

"When I was younger I was a free spirit. I felt first and rebelled against any convention in society that told me how I had to act, what I had to think, or what I should value. It was easy for me. My parents were wealthy and they indulged me despite how much they disapproved."

"My parents are just like me," Skye said. "They wouldn't have me any other way."

"Darren said you're an artist? I spent a summer in Rome painting and thinking I would be the female Michelangelo."

"What changed?"

Lily looked away for a moment with a tender sideways glance. "Life happens and . . . marrying Gary was right and it's the best decision I've ever made, but I let his social and professional status change me. I became a prominent man's wife, adjusting my behavior to what was expected. Then children came, responsibility and all the society stuff."

Skye knew what was going on. Lily was warning her. "Darren and I are aware of our differences."

"And I'm sure he told you how it won't be easy being with him." Lily laughed.

"Or for him to be with me," Skye said. "I'm taking it one day at a time."

"Good idea," Lily said. "Sounds like a plan. I, for one, am glad to know my son has a woman with a mind of her own by his side."

"I've got his back," Skye said with confidence.

"Tell me that after the match today."

"What match?"

"Didn't Darren tell you? We're all going to the charity golf tournament later this afternoon in Rye. It's a yearly event and all of Darren's friends will be there."

"I'm looking forward to it." Skye was lying. It wasn't because she thought of golf as the sporting equivalent of class segregation. She was feeling very protective of Darren and wanted to keep him away from possible prying eyes. "I thought we had work to do."

"That's later tonight," Lily said. "What you've got to survive is the attack of the bachelorettes."

"This doesn't sound good."

"It's never pretty, but so many of these little debs come to the country club in search of men, married or not, to latch on to. You've gotten one of the top five and the women there won't be happy about that."

"Well, they better get over it," Skye said, not pulling any punches. "I didn't take etiquette classes like they did. I know how to throw down."

As both women laughed, Skye got the feeling that she and Lily would be getting closer and closer. It had seemed funny that she thought Lily wouldn't accept her. That was one problem down. Skye couldn't wait to see Darren again and tell him about clicking with his mother. He needed and deserved some good news.

It was after ten and the strategy meeting was finally over. The team had spent the last four hours going over their response to the article coming out in tomorrow's paper. Skye was concerned about Darren, who had told his parents earlier that day, but he seemed in better spirits than anyone. He was a leader and his team of assistants, all six of them, fed off him. By the time the work session was over, doom and gloom attitudes became enthusiastic and hopeful and it was all because of him. With all that was on her mind, even Skye felt hopeful about their plan.

"I have to thank you." With his backpack securely over his right shoulder, Lonnie approached Skye while she attempted to clean up the dining room table in Darren's White Plains apartment.

"For what?" Skye asked.

"First of all, for giving me a second chance after that very awkward first meeting."

"I thought it was important to put that stuff behind us considering the bigger problems we're facing."

"And for keeping it live." He stepped aside as she placed pizza boxes on top of each other in the chair next to him.

"I didn't have much to say during the meeting," she said. "Darren did most—"

"Not the meeting," Lonnie said. "At the tournament.

You ruffled a couple of feathers with some of your . . . uh, politically diverse opinions."

"I was just speaking my mind. You don't think I was being rude, do you?"

"No way," he said, laughing. "That was what made it so great, the subtle way you slipped it in there."

"That buppie crowd needed a little mixing up."

"It's so funny that Darren would fall for someone like you."

"I expect you to explain that as a compliment." With a teasing smile, Skye leaned against the table, folding her arms across her chest.

"Just that . . ." Lonnie shrugged. "I think you and I probably agree on more things than you think. Maybe you can bring Darren around."

Skye laughed. "He's too stubborn and his convictions are too strong. That's why we both respect him so much, even those times we don't agree with him."

"You've got a point there." Lonnie took a deep breath. "Well, I'm just glad you're on board."

She patted him on the shoulder. "I'm glad to be on board."

After he had shown the last person out, Darren was eager to get back to Skye and seeing her waiting for him on his living room sofa with lazy, mischievous eyes made him downright horny.

"Now," he said, plopping down on the sofa next to her, "it's time to get down to real bidness."

With open arms, Skye received him as he leaned in and brought his lips to hers. In the past week, they had been making love nonstop and it was only getting better now that the beginning apprehension was gone. Now there was just exploration and discovery and it was all exciting and consuming.

Skye felt the passion kindling inside her and let her body act on its own. She felt transported into a paradise as his hands caressed her hips and his tongue played with her mouth. She let out an easy moan as he brought his tongue to her neck and brushed it gently against her skin.

As a floodtide of desire washed over him, Darren reached behind his back and took her hand in his. He guided it to his burning arousal, but was dismayed when she pulled away.

"Now," Darren pleaded in a low, breathy tone, "I want you to touch me."

"Darren." Barely able to catch her breath, Skye wriggled from underneath him. "I want this as much as you do, but your mother said she was waiting up for me."

"Let her wait." Sitting up, Darren leaned in again, determined to taste those lips again. "Trust me, she's used to waiting up late for her children to come home."

She turned her head to avoid his lips. "You know this isn't the same. It was your idea I stay at your parents' house. I was fine staying with you."

"It's an appearances thing." Darren picked her up and sat her in his lap. He nuzzled at her earlobe. "What is happening with this role reversal? I'm supposed to be the one following the rules."

"If it were just you and me, yeah, but your Mom."

"Sky, I want you here tonight."

She pushed his head back with her index finger. "She's waiting for me and it's late. You should drive me home."

"I'll do for you if you do for me." He was persistent against her frown. "Do you have any idea how hard it was to be this close to you and not completely lose control?"

"That's why I'm doing this," she said. "You and I both know if we start, we won't stop."

"I'll be quick this time." He rolled his eyes at the sound of his cell phone.

"In that case," Skye said as she stood up, "never mind."

"You just don't know, girl." Darren found his phone. "I can go long, but I'm good quick too."

Buttoning her shirt, Skye watched as Darren walked away talking on his phone. That walk, that butt; it all made her want to change her mind. When Lily said she was waiting up, Skye knew she meant it so the decision was already made no matter how hard it would be.

When he returned to her, she reached up and wrapped her arms around his neck. "Tomorrow after church we'll have some time together, right?"

"Sorry." He held up his phone. "That was our after church brunch at the country club."

"No, Darren."

"It's with Tommy Russo and his wife. He was a huge contributor to my last campaign."

"Because he donates money, you owe him?"

"I don't want to get into the politics of campaign fund-raising, but I need him for other reasons." He pinched her nose. "You'd actually be impressed with him."

"I'm listening."

"Mr. Russo is in real estate and in order to keep building his rich condos out here, he has to build a certain amount of low-income housing. I'm working with members of Congress to help move legislation that will allow him to build in the middle-class areas around New York."

"I thought New York only had rich or poor areas."

He smacked her lightly on the butt. "Don't start. It will allow a lot of people that work in those areas to live closer to their jobs."

"That is good news." Taking his hand, she began leading him to the front door.

Darren resisted, planting his feet. Maybe if he could impress her a little more . . . "He's doing it all over the country. He's got them in L.A., Miami, Scottsdale, and even your neck of the woods."

"Sounds good," she said. "Now come on."

"The only problem is his wife is a little . . ." Darren tilted his head. "Let's say she's a little rough around the edges. I should warn you."

"Meaning?"

"Well, her name first of all. It's Cashmere like in the fabric. Now, you know the only kind of people who name their daughter Cashmere are either rich as sin or ghetto as . . ." Darren was halted by the shocked look on Skye's face. "I'm sorry. Was I being a snob?"

Skye felt her stomach tighten and the hair on her arms stand up straight. "Does he . . . Is his company named after her?"

"His company is TR Limited," Darren answered. "He named it after himself."

"I just—"

"Oh, wait," Darren said. "He does name some of his properties after her, Cashmere Reno, Cashmere Austin. Kind of tacky, huh?"

Skye wished she hadn't remembered that Cashmere Scottsdale was the name on Wanda Bunning's key chain. This was no coincidence, but Skye's heart didn't have the strength, or maybe it was the courage, to speak up.

"What's wrong?" Darren reached out to her, but Skye backed away.

"Nothing," she said, looking away. "I'm just tired. Can you please take me home?"

She didn't give him a chance to respond as she hurried ahead of him and wondered what in God's name she was going to do.

Naomi pressed on the brakes and her car came to a stop at the large metal gate guarded by two men who looked as if they were guarding Fort Knox.

She looked at Skye, who was sitting in the passenger seat. "They look scary."

"It's an airport." Skye's stomach strained with anticipation of the inevitable confrontation awaiting her.

"Well," Naomi added, "they don't have to look so scary."

"I'm more afraid of him than either of them." Skye pointed ahead of them.

Standing on the tarmac, next to the private jet that would take them back to D.C., Darren targeted the Chevy they were sitting in. His look said everything.

Naomi shivered. "Is he trying to set us on fire using just the power of his mind?"

Skye smiled nervously. "If he could I think he might."

"We're only a little late."

Skye looked at her sister. "Naomi, you know that's not why he's angry."

Skye wasn't looking forward to facing Darren after the way she had been acting. Following a silent ride home Saturday night, he had leaned over to kiss her good night, but she pretended as if she hadn't noticed and hurried out of the car with a fleeting "good night."

Unable to sleep, she waited until the house was silent and made her way down the stairs to Gary's private office and accessed the Internet on his computer. It was true that Tommy Russo owned the Cashmere Scottsdale apartment community among many others. Only, Cashmere Scottsdale wasn't one of his low-income properties. The cheapest one-bedroom apartment went for over $1,500 and no one would believe that a part-time hairdresser could afford to live there. Maybe her aunt had money.

She was tempted to call Sierra and tell her what she'd found out, but she couldn't bring herself to do it. In her heart she wanted to believe that it was a coincidence even though common sense told her it clearly wasn't. She cursed common sense and reason, wishing she could stick with her heart, which told her there was some explanation. Her stomach was twisted so tight she hadn't been able to sleep at all and stayed up wondering what she should do.

Early the next morning, Skye called Naomi and asked her to come pick her up, promising to explain later. She knew she wouldn't be able to face Lily's kindness and Darren's affection without giving herself away. Running away wasn't the best solution, but she couldn't stay.

If Lily was disappointed when Naomi showed up, she didn't show it. She seemed to understand the logic in spending some time with family, especially where children were involved. Grateful to get his voice mail, Skye informed Darren of her new plans. She was sorry to miss church and brunch at the country club, but promised to be at the plane when it was time to go. She turned her cell phone off until moments before arriving at the airport. It had three messages and four missed calls, all from Darren.

"How are you going to explain not answering your cell all day?" Naomi asked as she pressed the button that popped the trunk.

"I left my phone at your house and we were running all day." Skye shrugged.

"You left it there on purpose."

"So? It's still the truth."

"You're really starting this relationship off right."

When Skye got out of the car, she waved to Darren, but he didn't respond. His hands stayed at his sides and his expression never changed.

"Here." Naomi handed over the suitcase. "Just tell him what you think."

"What if I'm wrong?" Skye said.

"You aren't. Remember what we found out today."

They had found out that Tommy Russo was a long-time supporter of all things Birch, whether it be Lily's charities, Gary's mergers, or Darren's campaigns. He was also a repeated sponsor of several charity events held for the Washington Ballet, where Elizabeth Sandon sat on the board.

"I don't think he had anything to do with it either." Naomi closed the trunk. "But something's going on and my bet is that his brother is behind it."

"It sounds awful," Skye said, "but I'm hoping it's the truth. As bad as that would be, it would explain a lot and clear Darren's name."

"So tell him." Naomi took her arm and squeezed affectionately. "And hey, stop going around hacking into computers."

Skye was able to find a smile and they hugged before she made her way to the plane. She was greeted by a male flight attendant who took her suitcase and hurried up the stairs. Despite the warm smile she greeted him with, Darren didn't waste any time in expressing his anger.

"What in the hell is going on with you?" Although he had softened at the sight of her, he wasn't about to hide his feelings. He felt rejected and feared his family situation with Franklin and the rumors had finally sunk in and she was pushing him away.

"It's nice to see you as well." Skye briefly touched his arm, unable to deny her heart its due. She wanted to wrap her arms around him, and it was his anger, not her own doubts, that kept her from doing so. "I'm sorry, I—"

"I've been trying to call you all day." He followed her up the steps to the plane. "I know you're upset with me about something, but this is not the way to handle it."

"I just needed time to spend with my—"

"Stop it."

Skye turned to Darren, feeling the force in his tone. She had pushed him as far as she could and he was warning her.

Inside the cabin, they both turned away from each other as the flight attendant came through to prepare it for them. They silently took seats across from each other and buckled up. Skye could tell the attendant was eager to get out of the cabin, refusing to make eye contact with either of them.

"I'm sorry, Darren." Skye waited eagerly for him to look at her. When he did, his expression seemed to soften and she was hopeful.

"We already agreed that you wouldn't have time this

trip for your sister because of the plans my parents had for us. We were coming back in two weeks and—"

"Naomi let it slip to my niece Nikki that I was here and she was so upset I hadn't dropped by."

"You're lying."

"Excuse me?"

"I can tell you're lying," he said curtly. "You're not good at it and your voice is cracking."

Skye looked away, taking a deep breath. "I'll apologize to your parents."

"I don't want your apology," he exclaimed. "I want an explanation."

"I told you—"

"The truth!" The second he said that, Darren wasn't so sure he wanted the truth. If it was what he suspected, it might be harder to take than a lie. "It's the article, right?"

Skye's eyebrows arched in surprise. In the midst of everything, she had forgotten that the dreaded article would be out in today's paper. "I'm so sorry, Darren. I left you to deal with it, with your parents, all on your own."

"I handled it." He wasn't sure what to think. She seemed so sincere and he wanted more than anything to believe he was wrong in thinking she was trying to distance herself from him.

"They probably think I was running away," Skye said. "What did they say?"

Darren shrugged. "Franklin certainly got a kick out of it."

Skye's senses sharpened at the mention of his brother's name.

Darren reached into his suitcase, pulled out the paper, and handed it to her across the table. "For him, the idea of destroying me is worth being called a deviant, violent alcoholic."

Skye stopped reading after the first few sentences. "Lily must be a mess."

"That's putting it lightly," Darren said. "We skipped church and I had to cancel the brunch with Tommy Russo. If it wasn't for the committee meeting tomorrow morning, I would have stayed."

Skye knew it probably wasn't the best time to bring this up, but it was the only window she would probably get away with. "Do you think it might hurt your chances with Tommy and the development?"

"It takes time to tell some of these things, but I think I can rely on Tommy."

"He's a good family friend, right?"

Darren leaned back in the chair, studying her foreboding expression carefully. "Why?"

"No reason." Skye sensed her window was closing. She needed to know if Franklin could be the connection between Darren and Tommy Russo without letting Darren know why she did. "It's just that if he's such a friend of yours, then it shouldn't matter what the press says about you and Franklin, right?"

"He runs a multibillion-dollar company. He's known both me and my brother for a long time, but he has to think about more than friendships." Darren unbuckled his belt and leaned forward. "Why are you asking me about Tommy Russo?"

"I wish you wouldn't be so angry at me. I am sorry."

Darren didn't want to hear any more apologies. "If you're not running away, then what? I thought I made it clear that I needed you."

Skye hesitated, stirring uneasily in her chair. "I know, Darren. I made a mistake. I guess I just got overwhelmed."

"This is about Saturday night." Darren's tone was more humble now.

Skye felt her chest tighten. "No, I—"

"I'm moving too fast," he said. "I know that."

At first realizing he hadn't caught on, Skye sighed but was quickly disheartened by the fact that he was blaming himself for her cold shoulder. "Trust me, Darren. I'm the queen of moving too fast. Jumping into things has always been my style. We've already slept together."

"Then what happened?"

"I told you."

"You haven't told me anything." Getting up, he sat on the table that separated them, leaning into her. "I wasn't thinking about sex when I said I was moving too fast. Visiting my parents this soon was probably not the best choice, but I know what I want. I want you and every fiber of my being tells me that you want me."

"I do." She placed a hand on his thigh, cursing herself for the dirty thoughts that entered her mind at the touch.

Her touch turned him on, reminding him of how much he missed making love to her. He had to fight his urge or this woman would control him completely. "If that's true, then I don't like the way you're showing it. Whatever your plan is, I'm not going to stand for games."

"I don't play games." Skye stood up, walking to the other side of the cabin. With her back to him, she hid how hurt she was because she knew she didn't have a right to that emotion. She cared about him so much and preferred he be angry with her rather than disappointed. "This is all new to me. You have to be patient."

"I have no intention of giving up on us," he answered. "I just need to know that you don't either."

Skye turned to him, feeling emotion well in her throat. "I don't, Darren. I promise you, I don't."

He watched her as she walked to the sofa in the back of the cabin and sat down. She looked near tears and it frightened him. He had thought she would be okay when he promised her he could handle the problems this article would bring. Maybe she didn't believe him. Maybe she didn't want to wait around and see if he could actually fix this like he said he would. Whatever it was, the look of apprehension and doubt in Skye's eyes led Darren to believe he had much bigger things to worry about than a little bad press.

"I don't know what you expect to get from me, Ms. Crawford." Detective Ross tossed a folder in the drawer of her desk and slammed it shut.

She wasn't trying to hide her annoyance with Skye's continued insistence that she get information on the investigation into Jeff's murder, but Skye wasn't giving up. She welcomed the challenge, considering that the alternative was to focus on what wasn't going well in her life, which was basically everything else.

After the short trip home, Skye had been prepared to give Darren reasons why he couldn't stay at the hotel with her. She would tell him anything other than the truth, which was that making love to him drove her crazy and she needed to think right now. It hurt her to think of turning him away, but hurt even more when she didn't have to.

He made no attempt to stay or even enter the hotel. The chauffeured town car stopped in front of the entrance and Darren was the perfect gentleman helping her out, but that was where it ended.

He said good night and kissed her softly, barely touching, on the cheek before getting back in the car. Skye was left standing outside watching the car drive away while the doorman called out to her. It was probably for the best. She was giving in to fear and doubt and being an indecisive wimp. Darren had no use for that in his life now, not with all he was going through.

She called Detective Ross first thing in the morning, but was promptly and politely turned down. Her second call, with Jeff's father on the other line giving the detective permission to treat her as a family member, was an effort the detective obviously didn't expect and she stubbornly agreed to spend a few minutes talking to Skye if she came down to the precinct.

"Mr. Preston distinctly gave you permission to—"

"I don't need their permission to do anything," Alice answered impatiently. "I don't care if you gave me DNA proof you're an actual blood relative or presented me with a marriage license that said you were the victim's wife. I don't have to tell you anything."

"I know you don't have to," Skye pleaded, "but I'm asking you to just out of some kindness you must have in your heart."

Alice squinted her eyes as if she wasn't sure whether or not she was being insulted. "This isn't about kindness. It's about procedure and I don't know what you and your boyfriend are trying, but you might want to get your timing straight before you decide to gang up on me."

"What are you talking about?"

"You know what I'm talking about," she answered.

"After your family bullying session call, the good congressman rang me up trying to use his pull with the chief of police to get information before you showed up here. What kind of fool do you two take me for?"

Skye swallowed hard. "What did . . . what did Darren say?"

Alice appeared angry now. "Don't play me. I'm not falling for your little clueless game. I'm not telling either of you anything about Jeff Preston or Wanda Bunning. Enough has gotten out already."

"Who are you blaming for that?"

"Careful, Ms. Crawford."

"How did the *Post* print the connection between Elizabeth and Wanda without your help?"

"I can't tell you," Alice said with a frustrated sigh. "I think we have someone on the inside. I heard it could be a hacker."

Skye cleared her throat, looking away. She hoped she didn't look as guilty as she felt. "I just want to know if the murders are connected."

"Why?"

"What do you mean why?" Skye asked. "I have a vested interest in this. I want to help anywhere I—"

"I know you have a vested interest," Alice said. "My question is, whom does that vested interest serve? Who are you looking to help? Jeff Preston or Darren Birch?"

"Both."

"Based on the evidence I have, that ain't gonna work." Detective Ross stood up.

Skye felt that now-too-familiar tightening in her chest. "Are you telling me you have evidence Darren killed Jeff?"

She placed a hand on her hip and looked down at

Skye like a mother waiting patiently for a child to get her act together. "This is not my job."

"What isn't your job?" Skye asked, standing.

"Making your decisions for you," she answered. "You don't know what to think or where to stand. You're fighting a battle between your mind and your . . ." She looked Skye up and down. "You know."

"I'm just looking for some answers," Skye insisted.

"So you can decide whether or not you can hold on to your prize catch?"

"I didn't come here to be insulted."

"No," Alice said. "You came here so I can give you a reason to stand by your man. Only, honey, I can't give you that."

"Darren is innocent," Skye said as much for herself as for anyone.

Alice's face held an accomplished smile. "Well, that wasn't so hard, was it? You've made your choice. Now I'd appreciate it if you left me alone. I have murder cases to solve."

As Alice began walking away, Skye yelled out, "What about Franklin?"

The look on the detective's face when she turned around confirmed for Skye that she had struck a nerve. "He is a suspect, isn't he?"

"Why?" Alice asked. "You in love with him too?"

"Darren's name is being dragged through the mud, Detective. If you have evidence that it was someone else, you should—"

"If you're about to tell me how to do my job," she warned, "I'd advise against it."

"He has a motive," Skye offered.

"You think so?" Alice's wide-eyed expression was

clearly cynical. "Thanks for the lesson in detective work. It was fun, but I think I've had enough of you for today."

Skye left the police precinct feeling that oh-so-uncomfortable mix of delight and sadness. She believed now more than ever that Franklin could be behind all of this, and that meant more pain for Darren personally and professionally. Then again, it also meant that he could be cleared, salvage his reputation, and still have a better future than he had now, and that had become what was most important to Skye.

It also meant she had some apologizing to do.

"I'm not hiding, Dad," Darren said. "That's not what I do."

"I'm not advising you to hide." The traffic around Gary as he spoke through his cell phone almost drowned out his voice. "I'm just saying you'll want to stay home for a while."

Darren was leaning against the window of his living room, looking at the covered pool in the courtyard area of his complex. The silence of working from home was what he needed today, but there was no way he could stay here.

"I stayed away today," he said, "because I didn't want my staff to deal with my mood. They're under enough pressure. I've gotten it under control and I'm going back in tomorrow. We have about eight votes on the floor."

"You can pass on naming a few post offices after dead people. The press is going to be calling you nonstop."

"They're calling me now."

"That's what you get for giving them your home

number. Trying to be accessible always bites you in the butt."

Darren hoped having a history of being accessible to the press would keep them from being so quick to judge and write rumors about him as if they were fact. "The press isn't my biggest problem."

"So why does that detective want to know about your relationship with Tommy Russo?"

"Obviously they believe he's connected to Jeff's death. Tommy is legit, right?"

"Of course he is," Gary insisted. "He's been a family friend forever. Just because he has an Italian last name doesn't give anyone the right to think he's crooked."

"Then why did Detective Ross want to know about my most recent conversations with him?" More important to Darren was why bringing up Russo was hitting at something on the tip of his tongue on a more personal level. "I canceled our brunch."

"He's not even your friend," Gary said. "He's really closer to Franklin than—"

Darren felt the tension thicken in the silence. "No, Dad. Franklin couldn't go that far."

"I don't . . ." There was a heavy sigh on the other end of the line.

Darren turned back to the phone, feeling a weight in the pit of his stomach. "I know he resents me, but he wouldn't murder someone. That's out of the question."

"I just remembered something." Another sigh.

Darren rushed to the phone and picked it up. He felt a sense of panic reach into him, familiar as he was with his father's sighs. This couldn't be good. "What's going on, Dad?"

"Yesterday," he said, "after you left, I thought I would catch up on e-mails so I went to my computer."

"And?"

"It was on. It was in safe mode, which happens sometimes when I try to turn it off and it doesn't turn all the way off for whatever reason. It just hibernates like it's off. I thought maybe I had left it on, but I remember your mother made me turn it off Friday afternoon when your car was coming up the driveway. She stood over me to make sure I wouldn't run back there and try and slip some work in while you were here."

"It didn't go into hibernation?"

"No. She checked to make sure. It was off."

"Was Franklin around on Saturday?"

"Gabrielle said he came by around dinner to get some things out of his old room. She had just finished cleaning up and was on her way home. He was just there for about ten minutes and didn't speak to anyone. Your mother and I were at the movies. With you and your meeting, we didn't—"

"Did Gabrielle see him go into your office?"

"No, but . . . whoever was in there had been researching Tommy Russo and his businesses. I checked my Internet browser by scrolling down the URL log."

Darren didn't get it. "Why would Franklin be researching Tommy? He knows more about Tommy than anyone."

"I know," Gary said, "but it can't be a coincidence that he would be looking up info on Tommy before Detective Ross asked you questions about him. Did she ask about Franklin's relationship with Tommy?"

Darren fell back onto the sofa as that thought on the tip of his tongue jumped up and slapped him in the face. He didn't think he could feel worse about what was happening between him and Skye than he had until now.

"What is it, Son?" Gary asked after a short silence.

"I think it was Skye," Darren said. "It was Skye looking on your computer. It isn't password protected, is it?"

"No, but . . . why would Skye . . ." Gary laughed. "I know what it was about. You probably told her you were having brunch and she did some research to come up with ideas for small talk."

"Skye isn't someone who needs to do research to come up with small talk." Darren was shaking his head. "Everything was fine between us, considering all that was going on. That is until I mentioned the brunch with Tommy. She went cold on me."

"Do you think she was just angry that she wasn't going to be alone with you?"

"That's what I thought at the time, but it got worse. Then, on the plane, she asked me about Tommy and Franklin. She wanted to know about their relationship."

"That doesn't sound good."

It didn't sound good at all, but Darren didn't want to believe that. "There has to be an explanation."

"She asked you questions about Russo the day before the police did? Maybe she's helping them."

"No!"

"Calm down, boy."

"I'm sorry, Dad, but . . ." Darren remembered the night Skye kissed him to keep him from finding out what was on her computer. He had selectively forgotten about it. "That's not possible."

"Anything is possible," Gary said. "Why did she say she was coming back to D.C. in the first place? She told you outright it was to get to the truth about Preston's murder. Then all of a sudden she just wants to be your woman."

"It didn't happen like that." At least Darren didn't

remember it happening like that. He had been too happy, too certain that he could trust her. "I don't know what to think. So much is happening and I don't have the luxury of taking a break from my life to try and figure it out."

"You don't have the luxury of letting your penis drag you to jail either."

"Dad."

"I'm serious, Darren. You said this woman turned the cold shoulder to you yesterday. Well, my advice is to let that shoulder stay turned. Stay away from her."

Darren's jaw tightened, feeling the tension eat at him. "I don't think I can do that."

"How do you figure?"

"It's not just about sex," Darren said. "I'm in love with her, and as angry as I am at the way she's been acting, I can't stand being away from her."

"You can't afford to be with her."

"I'll get to the truth." Darren wouldn't admit to his father that whatever the price was for being with Skye, he would have to risk paying it. Despite the fact that he was beginning to think he couldn't trust her, he was still in love with her.

After hanging up, Darren refused to think about the hurt Skye could cause him. He was already pretty miserable over the turn of events in their relationship. Now with this new twist, the water was even murkier and he had to see her. His pride urged him to stay away at least another day, but the dread of thinking she was out to get him was too much to mull over for another twenty-four hours.

The doorbell rang just as he grabbed his keys from the console. He had expected there would be reporters at his door and urged Sam to be extra vigilant.

"Congressman Birch?" Sam's voice was high pitched and uneven, making him sound twenty years younger than thirty-five.

"Who is it, Sam?"

"Ms. Skye Crawford."

Darren laughed even though he wasn't sure what for. "Send her up, Sam."

He tossed his keys back on the table, opened his front door, and headed straight for the bar to make himself a hard drink. It was barely one in the afternoon, a first for him.

Chapter 10

The second she saw him, Skye knew this was going to be harder than she thought. When she walked in, he was leaning against the bar, glass in hand and a scowl so deep he almost looked like another person. He was anguished and Skye was ripped apart because she knew she was mostly to blame.

"I'm surprised you let me up," she said, closing the door behind her.

Darren pushed the battling emotions down. He wasn't going to get through this if he let emotion play a part. "It's a day for surprises."

She approached him cautiously as everything about his posture advised her to keep her distance. "I wouldn't blame you if you hated me for the way I've been acting."

"What would you blame me for, Skye?"

Skye's stride was broken by his peculiar choice of words, but she recovered. "I wasn't angry with you, if that's what you mean."

"You were angry," he said. "Angry and cold after I told you how much I needed you."

Skye wouldn't make excuses. She was too guilty to try. "I haven't acted maturely in all of this, but I know now that the only way we can get to the truth is if we stick together. I won't let anything come between us again. You can count on me."

"Are you sure of that now?"

Darren gripped his glass tighter, hoping it would help him resist the urge to grab her and make love to her right there on the floor. It had been a huge mistake to let a woman with this much power over him into his life, but he hadn't let her into his life. He had pursued her and pushed her into his life, and as she stepped to within only inches from him, the promise of her eyes and the sweet parting of her lips made it quite certain he wasn't going to push her out for anything.

Skye leaned against him, pressing her hands against his chest. "I'm sorry, Darren. I've been a bitch and you have every right to hate me."

Darren's body was reacting to her touch at rapid speed. "I don't hate you, but I want some answers."

Unwilling to bring Franklin up just yet, she looked into his still-skeptical eyes. "I know I haven't been much of anything but a problem for you, but I need you to forgive me."

"Forgive you?" he asked.

"Even though I don't deserve it," she said, warming as his eyes softened and his face became a more familiar one, a gentle one. "I'm with you."

"Do you trust me?" he asked, hoping she wouldn't ask him the same question.

"Yes," she answered, finally happy to know she meant

it. She wanted to show him that she meant it. "I trust you and I love you."

Why did she have to say that? His resolve melted in the weakness of his desire for her. "I love you, Skye."

They made love on the carpet, beginning in a frenzy of ripping clothes off and drinking in each other as if dying of thirst, but ending as a tender, intimate connection of bodies, soothing, calming, and releasing each other from the bondage of uncertainty, insecurity, and fear. They both understood that from this moment on, it was all a formality. They were going to be together forever whether it was a good thing or not.

I love you with all that my heart has to offer and more. Those were the words that Darren had spoken to Skye when she awoke that morning in his arms, and they still warmed her to the tips of her toes as the night was coming to an end. With an almost senseless love, she watched him from a short distance as he engaged the crowd around him. They had all paid a good amount of money to hear him speak. It was a campaign fund-raising event in, of all places, Seattle. Apparently, people everywhere wanted Darren to succeed.

Skye knew he would soon notice she wasn't at his side and come looking for her, so she wanted to enjoy the moment while she had it. The last few weeks had been more like a fairy tale than anything else. Their relationship had flourished and it seemed the more they loved each other, the better their luck was.

Skye had always been afraid of that moment, when the chase was over and you both gave in, because sometimes it meant that a man would lose interest. More than sometimes it meant that she would lose interest. A man like Darren was used to the best of fresh kill and could be easily bored after the conquest was clearly his.

Only, the opposite had happened and Skye was swept off her feet by the new gestures of love he made every day. He seemed to be more and more interested in her life and especially in her opinions. He was an incredibly brilliant man and even though they argued about the issues nonstop, they always ended the argument with sex, which was only getting better as well. The buttoned-up congressman was actually a very naughty boy and Skye was grateful, because she couldn't think of being anything but naughty when his hands were on her.

She was still working at adjusting to life dating a high-profile politician. Everything had to look right and she was willing to do anything to make Darren happy. One thing that she was reluctant to change was their working relationship, but Darren didn't believe it was appropriate for him to pay her for any work now that it was clear they were romantically involved. Skye thought it was ridiculous mostly because it just was, but also because she enjoyed the time spent with him. With the session coming up on Memorial Holiday district break, some days the time they spent working together was all the time they had.

Skye's career was also benefiting from her relationship with Darren. After his well-publicized speech in response to the rumors printed in the newspaper, Darren's career took a turn for the better and many suggested it was due to the speech that the *Washington Post* had dubbed one of the most honest and affirming speeches heard on the Hill in years. Such accolades led to three freelance writing opportunities for Skye, two with high-ranking members of the State Department and another with Senator Marcus Hart. She knew that Darren had played a hand in getting her the work because he was insistent on keeping her in D.C., but she had earned it and made him and her clients proud. Now she had so much work she was turning clients down.

Darren was a take-control kind of man, and the stubborn feminist in her had to adjust to that as well, but he had made a lot of adjustments for her and she had to try and do the same. They argued over her moving into the apartment, which he had originally offered her a couple of months ago, but Darren had proven to be the more stubborn one and that argument ended quickly. Monica had already staked her claim on Skye's place in Chicago.

Skye had wanted to move in with Darren, but again came the issues of appearances and setting examples. Everything about Darren's life involved his future, and Skye was learning how hard a toll politics could take on a person's personal life.

The press was having a field day with the prep-school, Ivy League rich boy from the East and his wild child, footloose midwestern lover and all the baggage she carried with her from Chicago. Skye brushed it all off; she was too in love to care about how unlike the traditional political wife or girlfriend she was. She was too in love to let the occasional encounter with Elizabeth, who was clearly disgusted with her mere existence, get to her. Elizabeth, as well as any of the other Washington bachelorettes who were hoping to catch the grand prize, could hate her all they wanted to.

Hearing her cell phone broke Skye from her trance

and as she reluctantly tore her eyes away from her man, she had to smile at her good fortune. Of course, not everything was going well.

"I know where you are," the voice on the other end of the phone said.

"Monica?" Skye missed her best friend.

She had been able to go home last weekend to handle some business and get more of her things and was happy to introduce Monica to Darren. Monica's approval was always a good sign.

"You're at some swanky fund-raiser ball, right?"

"Not really a ball." Skye looked around the palatial estate they were in. "It's more like our get-togethers at my apartment, only in a ten-thousand-square-foot mansion with a bunch of millionaires."

"I'm so jealous. Every time I call you you're doing something exciting."

"It has been pretty whirlwind. I'm hoping it calms down when the session ends."

"Session?"

"Congress lets out for Memorial Day and then a few weeks in the summer."

Monica laughed. "Listen to you, sounding so . . . I don't know. Establishment."

"Don't say that. I'm already trying to recover from the fact that I'm in love with a Republican. To think I'm part of the problem is too much."

"I guess politics takes a backseat to some good a—"

"Have you been drinking?" Skye glanced down at her watch. "It's almost midnight in Chicago."

"Just got back from a nightmare date and I need to know where you keep your liquor."

"I don't."

"I knew there was something about you I didn't like. Maybe you'll fit in just fine with those conservatives."

"I was hoping you were calling to accept my invitation to come to D.C. for a weekend."

"So you do plan on staying longer?"

"I have a lot of work," Skye said. "You and the food are the only two things I miss."

"What about Wrigley Field, Navy Pier, Gino's East?"

"None of them compare to a warm, hard man."

"Tell me about it. Well, I guess it would be a waste of time for me to tell you that Jason called."

"My boss?" Skye asked. "My ex-boss, I mean."

"Yup, twice. He wants you back. Apparently, the rumors have spread that you're the next hottest thing in speechwriting."

"I've always been the hottest thing in speechwriting."

"That was your ass," she said. "Now it's being said about your skills. Well, he's been leaving you messages and he says he'll raise your salary by fifty percent."

Skye resisted the vile urge for security. "Forget it. I'm on a career roll, among other things, here."

"I read that the reporter who wrote that smear story printed a retraction."

"Yes, she did." Skye wasn't too comfortable talking about that.

She knew that Darren had used his influence to make that happen and she didn't like it. She was a big proponent of the First Amendment, and as much as she hated the printing of those lies, she had a strong feeling that the truth, or untruth, of the accusations wasn't why a retraction was printed.

"So all is happy again in district land?"

"Darren's name has been basically cleared and his

career appears to be right back on track, but everything isn't happy. Jeff's murder is still unsolved. I spoke with his mother yesterday and it's killing her. She needs the closure."

"What about the dead girl from the park?"

"Nothing panned out," Skye said. "It turns out her aunt admitted to sending her money to come stay with her."

"And she lived in a unit owned by Tommy Russo?" Monica asked. "You have to admit it was an incredible coincidence."

"I don't know. She's a nurse and she just married a young doctor. Russo has places everywhere."

There was a short pause before Monica said, "And that works for you?"

"What does that mean?" Skye asked.

"I guess it just seems like a lot of coincidence. Not about your boyfriend, but his brother."

Skye looked over at Darren, who was still charming a couple of elderly women. "Darren is so messed up about that. No one knows where Franklin is. He's just . . . missing."

"You don't think . . ."

"Dead? He left a message for his mother last weekend. It was cryptic. He was drunk but alive."

"And still a suspect."

"No one is talking." Skye was filled with compassion for Darren, who refused to believe that Franklin could be behind any of this. "After everything that Franklin has done to hurt him, embarrass him, Darren still wants to protect him."

Skye felt a nudge at her side and turned to see Grant offering her a glass of wine. She held up her finger for a moment. "Look, hon, I gotta go. I'll talk to you tomorrow."

"Hon?" Grant asked as he handed her the glass.

"It was a girlfriend," Skye said. "You were thinking another man?"

"I'm sorry," he said. "I'm just very protective of my guy."

"So I hear." Skye didn't know Grant very well, but he had been there for Darren and was mostly responsible for keeping these fund-raisers going while Darren had been absorbed in dealing with his controversies. "Darren is incredibly grateful."

"There isn't anything I wouldn't do for that kid." Grant handed his empty glass to a passing waiter, grabbing another. "I knew things would be just fine."

"So did Darren." Skye wondered how many drinks Grant had had. "I guess I was the weak one."

"I had my doubts about you," he admitted. "I'm just being honest, Skye. A lot of what I do depends on Darren's ability to influence legislation, and that is only as good as his reputation. You don't like being careful. You've got a bite to you and I thought you could hurt him."

"That makes two of us."

"I know better now," Grant said. "You're good for him."

"I'm great for him." Skye raised her glass to his and they toasted. "He's great for me."

"Are you ready for this?" he asked.

"This being . . ."

"Do you know why millionaires in Seattle are raising money for a junior congressman from New York? I mean, it's not like he can do anything for them, if in fact they ever needed anything."

"They like to support good candidates."

"Because they know this candidate is going to be on the national stage one day. Senator is next, then probably governor. My choice would be vice president, then president, but you know Darren. He'll probably shoot straight for the top first try."

Skye felt a little uneasy at the prediction, although she knew Darren would achieve no less if he wanted to. "I tend to live in the present, but I'm adjusting."

"We all have to," Grant said. "Even though I've given up any idea that Darren will find himself a Stepford wife, you're still a million times better than Elizabeth."

Skye tipped her head curiously. "From what I hear, everyone thought she was perfect for Darren."

"On the surface, but Darren isn't superficial enough to be satisfied with that. She was a cold woman at heart."

"I've noticed from the stares she's given me."

Grant laughed. "Like daggers for eyes she has. She probably thought she was going to be the wifey until you showed up."

"I don't see how," Skye said. "She was out of his life well before I showed up."

Grant looked at her, his mouth opening but no words coming out.

"What?" Skye asked, playing back her own words to see if she had said something wrong.

Grant looked away. "Nothing, I—"

"Talking about me?" Darren asked as he approached. He leaned forward, kissing Skye on the lips.

"Who else?" Skye wrapped her arms around him, feeling herself melt into the comfort of his touch.

"What's the tally?" Grant asked.

"Worry about that tomorrow." Darren patted Grant on the shoulder, sensing discomfort. "You okay, buddy?"

"I'm fine." Grant looked away. "You'd better stick by this one, Darren, before she goes home with someone else."

"Over my dead body." Darren grabbed Skye by the waist, pulling her to him. "What do you say? You wanna go home with me?"

"I'm ready when you are." Skye leaned up, kissing him again. "Let me say good night to the hostess."

Darren patted her on the back as she walked away, watching her until she was out of sight. That sassy walk of hers really did something to him.

Everything about her did something to him. Darren was more in love than he had ever been, and what had happened between him and Skye these past few weeks had forced any thoughts about not trusting her too far away to reclaim. He no longer believed Skye would hurt him. He couldn't bring himself to even contemplate that.

When Skye returned from the bathroom she was surprised to see Darren was no longer in bed. After a couple of hours of hot and heavy lovemaking that took place in his living room, the hallway, and ultimately his bedroom, she expected him to be halfway asleep. He would mumble at her insistence that they cuddle and talk, but would do it anyway. So, if he wasn't trying to get to sleep, where was he?

Forgoing a bathrobe, Skye walked through the spacious condo in search of sound and heard it in his office. When she entered, Darren was too caught up in his work to notice her, so she cleared her throat to get his attention.

"Hey, baby." Darren smiled as she stood in front of him in nothing but panties. "You staying?"

Skye was sort of surprised he asked her that. "I can leave if you want me to. I mean, if you're done with me."

Darren studied her for a second to see if she was serious or not. She could be a little testy about the living arrangements. If it was just up to him, he would have her living here, but there was more to it than that. "It's Saturday. I thought you said you had some errands to run."

Entering the modern minimalist-designed office, Skye moved a couple of books out of the way and sat on the edge of the old desk. "Do you want to come with?"

"I can't." He put the file down and powered up his laptop. "I have to push a bill at the committee meeting tomorrow. It's too much work."

"Which bill?" Skye had a bad vibe about his mood right now.

"The real estate bill I told you about." Darren thought that came out harsher than he had intended, and the expression on Skye's face confirmed that it had. "I'm sorry, I just . . ."

"Are you angry with me?"

"No, baby." He placed a hand on her thigh, feeling the heat from her skin. "It's this bill. I'm frustrated by it."

"I'm getting in your way," Skye said.

"I didn't say that." Darren was searching for another file, one he thought he had taken home with him. The thought that he might have left it at the office was making him angrier. "I have to call Lonnie."

"Can I help you with something?" Skye asked, wishing she didn't feel so rejected. She wanted to be with him all the time, but that was impossible, which was why mornings like this, when they were both together, meant so much to her. "Then we can go—"

"I can't go out with you today," he snapped. "I've made a commitment to Grant about this bill, and if I can't—"

"You don't need to explain." Skye hopped off the desk, feeling ashamed for seeming so needy. "Work comes first. I'll just get out of your hair."

"Skye!" When she turned to him, Darren spoke briskly. "Stop that, okay?"

"Not that I would take orders from you to stop anything," she said, "but what exactly are you ordering me to stop?"

"Making me feel guilty for not spending today with you," he answered. "I have to—"

"Enough." Skye didn't want to hear any more. "This is all a bit too humiliating for me."

"Why?"

"I'm not angry, Darren. Just work."

"Why are you humiliated?" he asked. "I'm just busy. What's the problem? Don't I do everything you want?"

"Everything I want?" Skye regretted ever walking into his office at this point. She knew they were going to fight and she didn't want to. "I knew it would come down to this. The apartment, the work, all of it was to appease me, right?"

Darren didn't have time for this. "You're being ridiculous. This isn't about what I've done for you. It's about—"

"Stop saying what you've done for me! I'm not your little charity case, and don't think you're so great that I can't stand to be away from you for one second."

He stared her down and could sense that she was about to cry. He had said enough. "I don't think of you as a charity case, Skye. I'm sorry you felt—"

"And don't talk to me with that calm, politician's voice!" Skye could see from the look on his face that he was about to shut down, turn away, and do that *I'm ignoring you* dance that even the most evolutionarily advanced men couldn't seem to escape. "I'm well aware that every moment can't be a honeymoon. I've been around these past two months, remember? I'm not the one that needed any handholding."

"Are you suggesting that I did?"

"No, I'm . . ." Skye wasn't sure what she was suggesting or thinking. "I just . . . Everything that has happened between us has laid waste to my feminist sensibilities. I've adjusted my life for you."

"Your feminist sensibilities are the problem," Darren said. "Not me."

"That's right," she responded. "I forget. Feminist ideology is a liberal concept. Therefore it has no basis in reality. I think we've had this fight."

"I'm not fighting, Skye." Darren returned to his work. "I've asked a lot of you, but I haven't forced you into it."

Skye placed her hands firmly on her hips, leaning back. "Then you won't mind if I give it back to you?"

Darren looked up. "Give what back?"

"Let's start with the apartment?"

Darren felt uneasiness creep up on him. "It was just a place to stay to get settled. They're coming back at the end of the summer anyway."

"Get settled for what?" Skye asked. "Until I found another place that suited you?"

Darren eyed her sternly. "Stop fishing for a fight, woman. If the compromises you've made bother you, then we can——"

"The compromises I've made aren't the only problem," Skye said. "It's the lack of compromises you've made. I've turned my life upside down for you and you balk at the idea of setting a file aside to run some errands with me."

"I don't have time for that right now!"

"You certainly had enough time to f——"

"Skye!" Darren stood up sharply.

Skye laughed sarcastically. "Is yelling out my name conservative-speak for me obediently shutting up and stop being a problem for you?"

"Go run your errands, Skye."

She ignored his warning stare. "Or else what? You'll tell me all the things you want to but don't think I can take? Go ahead. I'm not holding back, but then again I'm nowhere near as anal retentive as you."

"Don't accuse me of holding back," Darren said. "I'm not the one with secrets."

Skye hadn't expected that. "No, all your secrets are out in the open. Me, Franklin . . . we're all out there for everyone to see."

"Don't bring him into this."

"You're big on giving orders today, aren't you? Well, how about taking an order for once and kissing my ass?"

As she turned and headed out, Skye could hear another level of emotion and anger in his voice as he yelled after her, "I have made compromises."

She turned back to him, hit hard by the emotion on his face.

"I gave you everything I had," Darren said, "knowing that I couldn't trust you."

Skye's mouth opened wide, but nothing came out.

"I gave you everything I had knowing that you thought I was a murderer. I brought you into my life, into my parents' home even though I knew you were going behind my back."

"Behind your back?"

"I know what you were doing on my father's computer that first weekend we went home. You were researching Tommy Russo." He felt a wicked sense of satisfaction at the shock on her face. "It wasn't a coincidence that the police approached me right after that. The same day you said you—"

"You think I was helping the police get you?" Skye was thunderstruck.

"I didn't know what you were doing," Darren said. "You sure as hell weren't going to tell me, but I didn't care. I wanted you and it didn't matter."

"Darren." Skye was deflated. "All this time."

"So don't tell me I haven't made compromises."

As he sat back in his chair, Skye couldn't move. She watched him rummage restlessly through his files and papers before slamming his fingers down on the laptop keys. What had she started?

"I think . . ." She swallowed, her voice still shaky. "I think I better go."

Darren fought the sense of panic that threatened him at those words, but he held himself together. Without looking up, he asked. "Where?"

"I . . ." She realized what he was really asking and grabbed some piddling amount of relief from it. "Right now, I'm going to run errands."

"Okay." That was all he needed to hear.

A fight running as deep as this one within a realm of seeming serenity had jarred them both.

Darren understood that they needed some time apart, but there was no way on this earth he was going to let her go. As angry as he was at her, he couldn't stand to lose her.

When he heard the door to his condo slam close, Darren looked up from his work for the first time. He couldn't remember ever feeling this alone in his life.

"What do you mean you didn't present it?" Grant asked as he watched Darren lean over his desk.

"I'm sorry, Grant." Darren pushed his files away, leaned back in his chair, and faced his friend who was sitting on the sofa against the wall. He expected Grant to be angry and really had no excuse for him. "I just wasn't ready."

"We've been working on this for months now."

"Things have been happening," Darren said. "You know that."

"You told me you had this under control. You were having your kids doing the research. I answered every question, every doubt. What did I do wrong?"

Darren felt bad, but he couldn't feel worse. After his fight with Skye and her subsequent decision to move back to Chicago, he was a complete mess.

"It isn't you. It's just that I can't bring something to committee unless I already have an answer to all the possible questions. I can't risk looking incompetent or in the pocket of lobbyists."

Grant sighed, running his hand through his hair. "I know it's been hard on you, but you said you believed in this. When you believe in something, Darren, there isn't anything or anyone that can stop you."

"I do believe in this," Darren said. "I'm aware of the

jobs it will create, the vitality it will bring to this region. I just need to understand more about the investors and this tax issue."

"What tax issue?"

"I told you about that." Darren shuffled through papers trying to find the report Lonnie had written for him. "The taxes for businesses in the area are too high. The smaller companies will only be able to pay minimum wage for a lot of these jobs. My research says the property taxes will go up exponentially over—"

"You're concerned about that?" Grant asked. "With all the good these developments will bring, these people will be happy to pay taxes."

"I wouldn't go that far," Darren said.

"You Republicans." Grant waved his hand in the air. "You act like an itty-bitty tax is like a strain of Ebola."

"I'll bring it up at next month's meeting."

"That won't be soon enough," Grant said.

"Once I introduce it and refer it to committee," Darren said, "it's on the Congressional Record for everyone to see. Then the General Accounting Office will look over it with a fine-tooth comb. If there are any questions, you know it will—"

"I'm counting on you," Grant said. "A lot of people are. I know you and Skye are having problems, but—"

"We're having dinner tonight," Darren said.

Grant smiled. "Hey, that's great. I thought she was going back to Chicago."

"I talked her out of it." It was more like begged, but Darren had too much pride to admit that to anyone. "We talked for three hours. She told me everything about that disk. Remember I told you about it?"

"Yeah." Grant sat forward. "What did it say?"

"It was all about the Russian mob. I don't know

where in the hell Jeff was going with it, but I think he was trying to tie me to Andre Avegny."

"You barely know him," Grant argued.

"But you know what a few carefully placed pictures can do. It didn't matter because nothing ever came of it. The whole conversation was brutal. She was crying."

"When a woman's pissed off . . ."

"That's the problem," Darren said. "I could deal with a pissed-off woman. She wasn't angry, just resigned that this isn't the right time for us."

"That's not a good sign."

"There's nothing worse for a relationship than being resigned to its failure. It signals death and it's worse than breaking up no matter what anyone says."

"You convinced her to stay," Grant said. "You can close the deal, Darren. You always do."

Darren forced a smiled, but he wasn't so sure. "For the first time in my life, I'm up against something I don't think I can defeat."

"Some-*thing*?"

"My heart," Darren said. "I love this woman so damn much I'm willing to do anything to keep her here."

"And that's bad because . . ."

"Because I don't care whether she wants to stay or not," Darren said. "The entire time she was talking about how she was losing her sense of self and independence by being in D.C. and how she felt a couple of weeks away would be good for both of us, I didn't care. All I cared about was keeping her here and in my life. I pressured her, Grant. I used all the finesse I could, but basically I bullied her. "

"I'm sure you're exaggerating," Grant said. "You're not a bully, but you are a bit too moral for your own good. You convinced a woman to stay with you despite her doubts. It's the foundation of relationships and men do it all the time. As much as women like to claim they hold the relationships together, most times it's up to us to keep things together. You're doing what you have to."

Darren nodded, hoping that was true. After getting off the phone with Skye, he felt worse than he ever had in his life, and for the past couple of months, that was saying a lot. He could hear the affection in her voice and could feel the emotion through the phone. She told him she loved him, but went on about how she was on her way to getting herself back before she came to D.C. and the relationship derailed her. She needed to make that happen before she could commit to someone else.

Darren had always thought it was the man's job to put the brakes on commitment and a relationship moving too fast. He was learning a lot about going against convention with this unconventional woman, and it wasn't good.

He had things under control for now after convincing her to stay in D.C. for a few more days and have dinner with him. Although he felt he deserved that much, it was cruel for him to tell her so, but he did. If he was an understanding man, he would have given her the two weeks. After all, she said she loved him and that wouldn't change. But the thought that it might was too much for Darren. He imagined her going home and getting of taste of life away from the brutal spotlight of Capitol Hill and deciding it was better than anything he could offer her.

He wasn't going to lose this woman for anything.

"You can count on me," Darren said. "I can . . ."

He stopped, listening to the raised voices outside his

office. One voice he recognized clearly and cursed under his breath.

Franklin burst into his brother's office with both Lonnie and Mia right behind him, full of apologies.

"Look at them," Franklin teased as he laughed. "You've got them trained so well. They almost manhandled me. That big one almost got me down."

Darren was happy to see his brother alive, but could tell right away he had been drinking. "It's okay, guys."

Mia rolled her eyes and smacked her lips before abruptly turning and storming out, but Lonnie stood at the door a little longer, staring Franklin down.

"What?" Franklin asked him. "You want a piece of me? Trust me, kid. Your boss over here can't afford the press."

"You'd better be glad for that," Lonnie grumbled back.

"It's okay, Lonnie." Darren nodded for him to leave.

"You gonna let him threaten me?" Franklin asked. "Your brother?"

Darren kept his eyes on Franklin. "Grant, can you—"

"I'm way ahead of you." Grant was up, grabbing his briefcase. He avoided eye contact with Franklin as he passed him. "Call me today, Congressman. We need to discuss this."

"What's stuck up his ass?" Franklin asked after Grant was gone. "He's acting like I'm not even here."

"Maybe it's just wishful thinking," Darren answered.

Franklin pointed to his brother, squinting his eyes. "Little D was always the funny one."

"Where have you been?"

Franklin fell backward onto the sofa as if he didn't care how he landed. "He thinks he's better than me? I know better."

"Answer me!"

Franklin smiled wide. "You want something from me, I want something from you."

"You're not in a position to make deals, brother. The police are looking for you."

"Isn't that a bitch?" Franklin slapped his knee. "Turns out I'm a suspect in your murder."

"I didn't murder anyone and you know that."

"Maybe I do," he chimed. "Maybe I don't. Wouldn't you like to know?"

Darren stood up, rushing to stand over Franklin, who kept his eyes on the floor. "That's all over."

"Is it?"

Darren took a deep breath. "Unless you have something you want to tell me."

Franklin looked up with a satisfied smile. "And the truth is revealed."

Darren reached down and grabbed Franklin by the collar, pulling him up. "Tell me what you know about this!"

Franklin pushed away, falling back onto the sofa. Getting up on his own this time, he stepped a few feet to the side. "You better watch it. I could make things worse for you."

Darren came only inches from him. "Are you threatening me?"

Franklin backed away. "What I'm telling you, D, is that you've worked very hard over these past few weeks to clean up a reputation on life support. I can make it all for nothing or I can leave you alone."

"Let me guess," Darren said. "You want money."

"And you're going to give it to me." Franklin ran his fingers along the wall, stopping at a picture of Darren with their father. The smirk on his face faded. "Especially if you want Mommy and Daddy to still be grateful that they at least have you."

Darren wasn't going to give in. Turning away, he went to his desk and opened the top drawer. Pulling out a brochure, he turned back to Franklin. "There's a place in Wyoming. It's a good program and they won't let you leave."

Franklin laughed. "Is that all you have to offer? A prison alcohol program?"

"It's a longer program," Darren continued, "but you obviously need the extra time."

"The last place didn't let me leave either," Franklin said.

"The last place didn't want you to leave," Darren countered. "This place will prevent you from leaving."

"So it is a prison."

"They'll take you at any time," Darren said. "We can go today."

"You need to take me seriously, bro."

"This is not the day to test me," Darren said, having no compassion at this moment and feeling guilty for it. "Either we go or you get out."

"I'm not gonna beg," Franklin said. "I'm just going to give you one last chance. I need fifteen grand and I need it today."

Darren tossed the brochure on the floor and looked the brother he once admired directly in the eyes. "Get out of my office, Franklin, and don't come back."

Franklin's eyes widened and he swallowed hard. He seemed at a loss for words, and Darren knew that he would never expect his little brother to turn his back on him. That was then. Now, no matter how much he didn't want to believe it, he had to accept the idea that Franklin might have something to do with Jeff's and

Wanda Bunning's death. With that came his last bit of patience. It was all over.

Franklin's surprise quickly turned to anger as he seemed to realize there was no point in giving Darren yet another chance. "If that's how you want it, then that's how you'll get it. I just hope you've enjoyed your time with that hippie princess."

Hit with a massive surge of rage, Darren let out a groan as he charged his brother and slammed him against the wall. He pinned him down, staring at him with a violent anger. The smell of alcohol only fueled his fury.

"Don't you ever threaten Skye!"

"I wasn't threatening her!" Franklin looked genuinely scared but unable to stop.

Lonnie busted into the office. "Congressman?"

Seeing Lonnie allowed Darren to get control of himself, but he was still livid and refused to let Franklin go. "Get out, Lonnie!"

"I can't do that, sir." Lonnie stepped closer to them. "You can't do whatever it is you were planning to do, no matter how right you might be."

"I wasn't threatening her!" Franklin pushed off, looking like a bullied little boy. "I was threatening you, asshole."

Darren backed away. "What, you planning on killing me?"

Franklin smiled again, seeming to have himself together now. "No, little brother. I'm going to take a tip from your ex, Elizabeth. She said she didn't understand why people killed their exes because it would be so much more satisfying to hurt them and watch them suffer day after day."

"You talking to Elizabeth now?"

"What do you care?" Franklin asked with a smirk. "You're through with her."

"Get out of here." Darren turned his back to him, ashamed at having lost control of himself. He didn't want to set eyes on his brother again and was relieved when he was finally gone.

"Congressman." Lonnie treaded lightly.

Darren sat down at his desk. "Not now."

Lonnie stood still for a moment, staring at Darren for a while before nodding and backing out of the office.

Darren caught a glimpse of the clock on his wall. It was four in the afternoon. Three hours and he would see her. Skye was all he had to keep him sane, and even she was making him crazy.

Chapter 11

When Skye showed up at Darren's apartment, her stomach was dancing and her heart was beating faster than a speeding bullet. She didn't know what to do and wasn't sure what would happen. She had been on such an emotional roller coaster in the past few days and her confusion had laid waste to everything in its path, especially Darren.

She loved him, but she knew she hadn't been living in her best interests these past few months. She didn't doubt that Darren was good for her. She feared losing herself if she followed him everywhere. Wanting Darren to understand that when they spoke for the first time after their argument, was asking too much. His tone made it clear he didn't or didn't want to.

Darren was clearly her weakness, and sexually she was sure she wouldn't be able to resist him no matter what the gamut of emotions and thoughts swirling around her told her to do. Just in case she weakened, Skye purchased her plane ticket and she was leaving tomorrow morning. If she revealed this to Darren right away, it would be clear where she stood. Only the intense pleasure and tickle of desire she felt the second she saw him told her that she was a fool not to have thought of a plan B.

He heard her footsteps and looked up just as she walked in. It was then that he truly understood her fear. Seeing her again after just four days apart rang his bell and hit him like a brick. He realized that he had barely been able to breathe without her. The intensity of his emotional response to seeing her again helped him understand why she was so afraid of losing herself in him, because he was completely lost in her.

"You're early." Closing the gap between them, Darren flashed a harmless smile. He had to be careful and knew he would be tested. What happened here tonight meant more than he had a mind to comprehend. "I haven't finished setting the table."

As he got closer, Skye felt her insides tearing apart at the dark look on his face. His eyes were red and he looked tortured.

She dropped her purse and rushed to him. "What's happened?"

"Do I look that bad?" Darren asked.

"You look . . ." Skye went silent, realizing she was the cause of his pain. She hated herself for it.

"What happened?" he asked. "You happened. These past few days haven't been good for me. I'm secretly hoping you have had a hard time sleeping too."

"Of course I have." Ashamed, Skye turned away from him, her eyes setting on the table.

It was covered with a sage-green tablecloth; elegant blue and white China for two was set with four romantic ivory pillar candles in elaborate sterling silver holders inbetween.

"Don't be too impressed," Darren said. "The food is all catered. You've tasted my cooking before and I felt I didn't need any more strikes against me tonight."

"Darren, you have to know . . ." Looking at him again, she wanted to tell him about her flight, but she couldn't. He was in pain and how could she hurt him more? "I'm sorry these past few days have been hard on you."

Without thinking, Darren reached for her, taking her by the arm. The connection was like a scorching fire and he quickly let go. "I'm sorry."

"What for?" Skye looked up, confused.

"I didn't mean to touch you."

"I never said I didn't want you to touch me."

This was not the way Darren had wanted this to start. "It doesn't matter. Sit down and I'll make you a drink."

Skye reached for him as he started for the dining room. "I'm not angry with you. You have to understand that."

Turning back, he grabbed her arms and pulled her to him. Unable to stop himself, he kissed her hard and angry with all the need he could find. It was a punishing kiss as his fingers pressed against the soft flesh of her arms.

Skye fought the most carnal urges within her and pushed away. "Darren, we can't do that."

"I want you, Skye. I need you."

Skye turned away from him. "I can't think when you touch me."

"I don't want to think." Darren felt like a man on the edge. The full emotions from the day came back at him and he felt consumed in the anger. "I just want to be with you, inside you."

He grabbed her by the waist and pulled her to him. Their bodies slammed together and his mouth ravished her neck and the bare expanse of her chest just below. He was rough and raw, letting his mind escape into oblivion, the only place it would find peace. His body would find peace when he was inside the woman he loved.

Skye felt as if she were drowning at sea, unable to breathe. Engulfed in desire, she felt almost near tears as he ripped at her shirt and grabbed her breast. She let out a moan and leaned back as he lifted her higher and brought his mouth to her breast. Grabbing on to him, she dug her nails into his skin feeling as if she had gone crazy.

Hearing her call out his name over and over again sent Darren into a frenzy. He guided her to the floor, lifting her skirt to her belly. He kissed her stomach as his fingers laced the edges of her panties.

He had her panties halfway down her thighs when the doorbell rang. Skye heard it, but Darren hadn't. Reluctantly she reached down, grabbing her panties and pulling back. "Darren, someone is here."

The doorbell rang again and Darren cursed with a growl as loud as a lion's roar.

"Please." Skye wriggled out from underneath him and stumbled to her feet.

Standing up, Darren tried to push the fog from his mind and the heat of one thousand degrees from his body. "Skye, I know we're supposed to talk. It's just so hard and . . ."

He went to the door and pressed the button. "Sam."

"Congressman Birch, it's Detective Ross again."

Darren looked at Skye before saying, "Send her up."

"Why is she here?" She went to Darren, who was leaning against the door. "Is there something new?"

"I think she's here because of Franklin." Darren felt obligated to contact the detective after having seen his brother because he knew she was looking for him. Detective Ross was cold and indifferent on the phone when she thanked him and quickly hung up.

Skye gasped. "Is he . . ."

"No, he's fine. He showed up at my office wanting money today. I had to tell her."

"Of course you did." Skye didn't want to say more, remembering how angry her accusation had made him Saturday.

"Looks like you might be right," Darren said. "It's possible Franklin had something to do with the murders. At least he knows enough to raise suspicion."

"I hope you don't believe I'm happy about that."

"I was never under the impression."

She reached out, placing her hand gently on his cheek. "I love you, Darren. I would never want you hurt. I need you to believe that I'm not trying to hurt you with any of this. I feel so horrible for not trusting you, because you've never lied to me and—"

There was a knock on the door and they both looked at it as if it might open on its own. After a second, Darren reached for it with one hand while taking Skye's hand with the other.

Alice wasn't alone. She was with a tall, thin black man who looked to be in his early thirties. He had a long, dark look on his face and his ire was clearly for Darren.

"Congressman Birch." Alice tilted her head to the younger man. "This is Detective Aiken. We need to—"

"Come in, Detectives." Darren opened the door

wider and noticed the look of surprise on Alice's face when she saw Skye. "Ms. Crawford and I were having dinner."

Skye got an eerie feeling as both detectives eyed her as if she didn't belong there, and it made her anxious. She squeezed Darren's hand tighter.

"Ms. Crawford." Alice nodded to Skye, who nodded back, before turning to Darren. "Congressman, we need to speak with you alone."

"It's okay," Darren said. "Ms. Crawford can hear anything you have to tell me."

"I don't think that's a good idea," Detective Aiken said in a deep voice with a Caribbean accent.

"It's not against the law," Skye said, holding her chin high. "So I'm staying. If you're trying to protect me, don't bother. I know about Franklin."

Detectives Ross and Aiken shared glances and she shrugged her shoulders.

"What in the hell is going on here?" Darren watched as Detective Aiken reached into his jacket pocket. He was pulling out a pair of cuffs.

"Oh my God." Skye grabbed Darren. "What are you doing? Darren didn't kill anyone."

"This isn't about my brother?" Darren asked.

"No," Alice answered. "Detective Aiken here is from the Domestic Violence Unit. Congressman Birch, you're under arrest for assault and battery."

"Wait!" Darren let go of Skye and held his hand up to Aiken, who stopped in stride. "What did he tell you? That I beat him up? That's a lie, Detective. I grabbed him and shook him a bit to get him to make some sense, but—"

"Who is *he*?" Alice asked.

Darren paused. "Franklin. He's pressed charges against me because of our fight this afternoon."

"No, sir." Detective Aiken looked at Skye. "Please step aside, ma'am."

"No." Skye didn't move an inch.

"I can arrest you too," he said.

"You can try," she warned.

"This is grand," Detective Aiken said. "You won't be so quick to protect your boyfriend when you find out what he did."

"He didn't do anything!" Skye yelled.

"She's right," Darren said, although he guided Skye away from him. "Tell me what you're doing here."

With a smile, Aiken came face-to-face with him. "Darren Birch, you're under arrest for the assault and battery of Elizabeth Sandon."

Darren jerked out of his grasp. "You're crazy."

"Are you resisting arrest?" Detective Aiken looked ready for a fight.

Darren turned to Skye. "Skye, I—"

"I know," she answered. "This is a false arrest. Congressman Birch has nothing to do with that woman anymore. He hasn't for a very long time."

"How long did he tell you exactly?" Alice asked.

"Skye," Darren pleaded. "Please go into the bedroom. I need to speak with Detective Ross alone."

Skye just shook her head. "I'm not leaving you."

"Fine." Alice gestured for Detective Aiken to resume his arrest. "You're under arrest, sir, and I want to read you your rights."

Darren didn't resist this time. "Detective, whatever she has told you, it's a lie."

"I've seen the bruises," Detective Aiken said. "You smacked her around good."

"No." Darren looked at Skye, fearing that his whole world was falling apart. "She's lying."

"She said you came over to her place today afraid that your brother was going to tell us something that would place our suspicion back on you. You wanted her to lie again and go back on her alibi on the night of the murder."

"What?" Skye's head was spinning with bewilderment.

"That's right," Alice said. "The congressman here said he was with Ms. Sandon the night your friend was murdered."

"No, he didn't." Skye exchanged pleading glances between Alice and Darren. "It was over between them before I came to D.C. Tell her, Darren."

Darren looked away. "Skye, I need you to call Lonnie. Tell him about this. He'll know what to do. Then call my father."

"Darren." Skye reached for him, but Alice blocked her access. "Tell her you weren't with her."

"He doesn't need to tell me," Alice said. "Elizabeth already did and apparently, he beat the heck out of her, because she refused to say otherwise."

"I didn't touch her," Darren said.

"And you weren't with her on the night of Jeff Preston's death?" Alice asked.

Darren couldn't look at Skye even though he could feel her eyes on him. "I was, Detective. I swear to you I was with her that night."

Skye's hand went to her chest as she took a step back. "Darren?"

"Let's go." Detective Aiken pushed Darren along.

When Darren turned to Skye, the look on her face broke him in two. "Skye, it isn't what you think. That was the last night I was with her. I can . . ."

Skye turned away, unable to look at him.

Darren felt as if he had just been stabbed in the chest and as he was led out of his home, Detective's Aiken's words seemed a million miles away. Despite the situation he was in now, Darren wasn't thinking about his legal problems. He was only thinking of losing Skye, which would prove to be more than he could take.

Skye felt all eyes on her as she made her way up the steps to the police station. She was embarrassed even though she had done nothing wrong. She knew what they were all thinking, and in a way, their pity for her was worse than animosity.

"Skye?"

Turning, Skye was happy to spot Lonnie sitting on a wooden bench along the wall. She joined him and they somberly smiled at each other without speaking.

Skye had done what Darren asked her and called Lonnie the second she got her bearings. It had taken a few minutes to digest and she began to cry as she explained the situation to him. All he could do was apologize and promise he would take care of things before hastily getting off the phone.

Skye took a moment to blow out the candles on the dining room table before leaving. She sat in her rental car for an hour wondering what to do. She was tempted to call Monica or Naomi, but couldn't stand the thought of explaining it. She worked it through in her mind as best she could. Despite telling her that his relationship with Elizabeth had been over well before he began pursuing her, Darren had been in her bed at least the day after they met, which was only a week or so before he began pursuing her.

Skye knew that didn't have to mean he had continued his affair with Elizabeth after he began seeing her and every bone in her body told her that he hadn't. Those weren't his values, his morals. But what could she believe and whom could she trust? She fought with every inch of will she had not to give in to despair knowing that she only had herself to rely on right now.

For once her heart and her mind were in agreement. They both told her she should get on that plane to Chicago tomorrow and never look back. It was her soul that was the lone voice of dissent as it reminded her of the tortured look on Darren's face that reached too deep inside her to ever forget. It told her she would never forgive herself if she ran on Darren at his lowest moment whether he deserved it or not.

They were connected and that was what it came down to. It didn't mean that they would be together and Skye believed that a continued affair with Elizabeth would mean they wouldn't. However, that connection demanded she stay and see this through not just for herself, but for Jeff. She knew she was strong enough to get through and still held some hope that the ending would work in her favor.

What Skye needed more than anything was solace, but doubted she would find it since what she was going after was the truth, the truth leading her right to the police station and Darren.

"I didn't expect you here," Lonnie said after a while.

"That makes two of us."

"How are you holding up?"

Skye realized she must look a mess. "I'm going to be fine. How is Darren?"

"I haven't spoken to him yet, but Malcolm . . . that's

his lawyer. Malcolm said he'd have him out in a second about a half hour ago."

"He's good to have someone as loyal as you."

Lonnie shrugged. "I'd do just about anything for Darren. He's the best man I've ever known."

As she looked at the pitiable look on his face, Skye thought of all the other hearts that were aching over Darren.

"You know it's all a lie, don't you?" he asked.

Skye threw up her hands in indecision. "I'm not sure what I know, Lonnie. Darren told me Elizabeth had been out of his life well before I showed up in D.C."

Lonnie took a deep breath. "Well . . . you know how you women can be."

"Don't say that we force you to lie."

"You can make us feel like we have to." Lonnie shook his head. "But that's not the point. The point is Darren loves you. I know that much."

"That's not what I'm questioning," Skye said.

"Ms. Crawford! Ms. Crawford!"

Skye looked up to see a woman in a striped brown and beige business suit rushing toward her. Standing over her, the woman thrust a minirecorder in Skye's face.

"Janice Ellins. Channel Seven News. Has the congressman ever abused you?"

Skye gasped as Lonnie jumped up and stood between her and the woman.

"Get the hell out of here!"

The woman was noticeably intimidated by the towering, threatening figure in front of her, and her voice shook as she responded. "The public has a right to know if its elected officials—"

"Leave her alone!"

The reporter turned with excited eyes as Darren came toward her. She reached her microphone out to him. "Congressman Birch, can you comment on the charges against you?"

With a controlled aggression, Darren turned to Alice, who was standing near him. "Can you get them out of here?"

"I'm way ahead of you." Alice started for the reporter.

Skye shot up from the bench as the room disappeared around Darren. He looked terrible and she could only feel pain for him. She didn't believe there was anything that would make her not love this man, and that wasn't necessarily a good thing.

The relief he felt at seeing her couldn't be described in words. The sight of her alleviated his pain and ignited his determination to get through all that had been placed on him.

"I didn't think you'd be here." He spoke with a quiet, tender tone. "But I can't tell you how happy I am that you are."

"Don't speak so soon," she said.

Darren took her hands in his and looked around. "Come with me."

He led her to an empty, dimly lit interrogation room away from everyone. He directed her to a chair and grabbed one for himself. God was planting an unexpected gift in his hands and Darren wasn't about to risk wasting it.

"Let me say first, I didn't lay a hand—"

"I know you didn't hit her," Skye said. "You would never do something like that. What I want to know is why you lied to me about her."

Darren shook his head in shame. "I know I told you it had been a long time since I'd seen Elizabeth. The truth is I was with her the night Jeff died, but I broke up with her that night and it didn't go well."

"She's your alibi?"

"Yes, but she's refusing to admit I was with her in order to get back at me for ending things."

Skye didn't have room for the relief she wanted to feel. "What are your feelings for her, Darren? I deserve to know."

"Our relationship was mutually convenient," he said. "I'm ashamed to say I never loved Elizabeth and she never loved me."

"Then why is she so angry with you?"

"She wanted to marry me." Darren could see the confusion in Skye's eyes deepen. "It's hard to understand, but power and influence are more of a reason to get married than love to a lot of people in certain circles."

"But not you."

Darren shook his head. "I didn't love her and I knew it was wrong for us to be in this cold arrangement of sex and formal events. It was immoral and selfish. I never expected it to turn into this. I never expected to fall in love with you."

He held his hands out to her and Skye hesitated before responding with her own.

"She isn't in my life at all," Darren assured her. "Except for a few threatening calls she made to me in the week after I ended it, I haven't heard from her. I've seen her at social events we've gone to together, but we haven't spoken."

"Then why is she doing this now?" Skye asked. "Do you think she wants something from you?"

"Dormant revenge," he suggested uncertainly. "Maybe the publicity around my relationship with you has made her angrier. I think Franklin might—"

"Franklin." Skye leaned back. "Of course. She must be in on it with him."

Darren frowned. "The murders? No."

Skye knew Darren didn't want to hear her accuse Franklin, but they had passed the point of sparing hurt feelings. "Wanda Bunning was her stylist, remember?"

Darren tried hard to concentrate and think beyond everything and get his mind back on the murders. "Since killing Jeff didn't do the job, now she's framing me for abuse."

"Seems like a step in a backward direction," Skye said, "but not really. The murder case is still open. This will just disparage your reputation more and make people more likely to believe you did murder Jeff."

Something about that didn't feel right to Darren. "I've got to talk to her. I need to know what she's up to."

"You can't," Skye said. "You won't get near her and you shouldn't try."

"Why not? She's ruined my career, everything. I've got nothing to lose."

"You could go to jail."

"What do I care? I've lost everything already."

Skye squeezed his hands tightly and her eyes held all the compassion in the world for him. "You've got me, Darren. You haven't lost anything."

"I know I don't deserve you," Darren said. "But God, I need you."

"If you think I'm leaving now," said Skye, "after all this back and forth I've pulled on you, you're crazy. I love you, Darren, and I'm here to stay."

"I could end up dragging you down into hell with me."

"And back up again." She smiled. "Let's face it. A man like you never stays down long."

"Politics has destroyed the best of men, something I'm clearly not."

"You are," she argued. "And don't worry about me. I can play just as ugly as anyone else when it comes to saving the man I love."

Darren wasn't certain he liked the sound of that. "Now, be cautious, Skye. Let's take it easy."

"Be cautious? Take it easy?" Skye shook her head. "Sorry, Daddy, that's just not my style."

Espionage was not Skye's game. At first, the thought was exciting. She would follow Elizabeth around and get some good dirt on her. It was risky and dangerous, promising a good adrenaline rush. Only the reality was anything but. It was boring and tiring, and after three days Skye hadn't gotten anything she could take back to Detective Ross.

She didn't have much time left. Darren was dead set against her investigative endeavor and was losing patience. He had only agreed to it because he was at risk of losing everything and Skye stubbornly refused to be told what not to do. The press hadn't been as brutal as Skye was certain Elizabeth wanted. It was a confusing situation as Elizabeth seemed to disappear from the planet for the week after the news hit. She refused to speak to the media or anyone else. She had also refused to press charges.

The night he was arrested, Skye and Darren worked

into the night drafting a statement to release to the press categorically denying anything to do with the assault. The press, with the exception of some of the gossip columnists, seemed to want to give him the benefit of the doubt. The idea of a woman scorned getting revenge was more appealing than a promising son gone bad.

Not that she needed anything to make her love Darren more, Skye was still impressed with Darren's resolve and composure. It encouraged her to continue to hold her head high as she stood by him at every turn. His staff never relented in their support of him despite the whispers going on all over the Hill. Grant had pressed Darren to continue to deny the charges to drum it into the minds of the press, and Skye partially agreed, but Darren was insistent that once was enough. Any more would make him seem afraid and he wouldn't dare do that.

Skye had kept her distance when she sensed Darren needed it and had been there for him every second she could. That was until Elizabeth reappeared on the scene three days ago. Since then, Skye had been relentless in following her, searching and hoping for a clue. She promised Darren she wouldn't approach Elizabeth, both of them knowing only more damage could come from that.

Elizabeth shopped all day. Whether it was the Fashion Centre in Pentagon City, the Galleria in Tyson's Corner, or Georgetown Mall, the woman spent all her time trying on and purchasing expensive clothes and accessories. She wore sunglasses and hats with her long hair tied back to avoid attention. Besides a few exclusive clubs, Skye stayed on Elizabeth the whole time. She had no idea what she was going to see, but she knew she would get something.

Skye was playing it close as she entered the Topaz Bar just a few feet behind Elizabeth. Wearing a first-rate wig and glasses herself, she was convincingly hidden. Considering her picture had been in the papers just as often as Elizabeth's in the past few days, the fact that no one seemed to give her a second look was a sign that her disguise was working.

As Skye headed for the bar in the hip, modern restaurant on N Street, Elizabeth made her way directly to a table against the wall. Skye slowly turned to look after sitting down and took in a view of the young man waiting for her. He was tall, ordinary looking with a horrible dye job, skin that appeared to have never seen the sun, and a face that was no more than twenty-one.

Skye noticed first that there was no gesture of affection between the two of them. No smiles or signs of friendliness. She believed she might finally be getting something.

"What can I get you?" the bartender asked.

"Amaretto sour."

Skye turned away from the bartender just in time to watch the young man slide a thin envelope across the table. It was an unusual shape, more square than rectangular. Elizabeth placed her hand over his and slid it toward herself, placing it in her lap. She lowered her head and her shoulders fell.

Who was this person! Skye had brought a camera for something just like this, but there was no way she would get away with the flash in here.

Skye had time to take one sip of her drink when the young man stood up from the table. Without any gesture of good-bye to Elizabeth, he turned and headed out of the restaurant. Skye fumbled in her purse, pulling out a ten-dollar bill to leave on the table.

When she reached the sidewalk, she was relieved to find him standing on the curb, waiting for a cab.

With her head down, she walked past him, pretending to be interested in the *Washington Post* copy in the newspaper stand behind him while she grabbed her camera. Keeping her hand inside her purse, she pressed the power button on. He wasn't paying any attention to her as he spoke in a harsh, rushed tone on his cell phone.

"Don't worry about it," he said with a deep Russian accent. "She took it. She will be gone soon. Yes . . . I mean no, she did not ask. I would not worry, sir."

Skye listened intently as she planned to get a picture of him just before he stepped into the cab he was hailing down. That way, if he spotted her, she could hopefully get away.

"I am on my way, coming back to the office," he continued. "Will you . . . Okay, then. I will see you at the Pollies."

As a cab pulled up to the corner, Skye quickly stepped to the other side of the young man and pulled her camera out. She was ready to take a picture when the door to the restaurant flew open and Elizabeth stepped out and looked directly at her.

Startled, Skye let her hold on her camera loosen and it fell out of her hands. She stared at Elizabeth, who, after only a second, looked beyond Skye into the street.

She hadn't noticed her.

Skye reached down for her camera, but when she stood back up, the man was already in the cab with his back to her. She didn't care. She just wanted to get out of Elizabeth's line of sight. She turned her back to Elizabeth, walking toward the window of the restaurant, where she watched through the reflection.

Elizabeth stood at the curb, but did not raise her hand for a cab. When she stepped out into the street, a blue sedan pulled up and Skye leaned closer to the reflection to see whom she was meeting with now.

When Elizabeth opened the car, Skye's mouth fell to the ground. She swung around, not thinking or concerned with being noticed. She had to make sure she was really seeing what she thought she was.

In the driver's seat, Franklin smiled at Elizabeth as she got in. Elizabeth handed him the envelope with a force that showed her anger, and Franklin's smile faded. Elizabeth shut the passenger-side door and the car sped off.

Skye was frozen in place, worrying about what Darren would say when she told him about this, as if he needed to be hurt any more than he already had been by his own flesh and blood.

Skye didn't bother to try and catch a cab to follow them. She had learned enough for one day.

Grant closed the door behind him as he entered Darren's office with a solemn look on his face. "How you holding up, man?"

Darren nodded, leaning back in his chair. "As well as can be expected."

Grant smiled, sitting across from him. "Good old Congressman Birch. Always a chin up. I gotta tell you, man. I would be down for the count after all of this."

"I feel like I'm close sometimes," Darren said. "But I've got a great woman on my side and friends like you."

"I'll do whatever I can for you."

"I know." Darren felt guilty for even accepting the offer. "I'm sorry I failed you on the bill. I just have to change my priorities based on what's happening."

Darren could see the disappointment flash across

Grant's face as he looked away. He was letting his friend down, and as much as Grant said he understood, Darren knew he was upset. Despite that, Grant continued to be his friend.

"I'll find a way to make it work," Grant said with a big, heavy sigh. "I have to."

"Grant, you know this happens a lot. Bills get pushed back. If things change for me, I might be able to push it to committee after the summer district break."

Grant shrugged as if he didn't want to talk about it, and Darren decided to let it go.

"You'll be happy to get back to New York," Grant said in a way that wasn't clearly a question or a statement.

Darren nodded. "I need to get Skye out of this mess. She's been strong for me, but I have the feeling if I don't get her out of this fishbowl, she'll blow."

"So you two are solid?" Grant asked. "Even after Elizabeth?"

"I'm the luckiest man in the world," Darren said. "She believes me. She's got my back. I'm so hap—" Darren stopped, remembering Grant's situation. "I'm sorry."

"Don't apologize. My marriage is falling apart, but I don't begrudge you any happiness. You need it. Anyone else, I would tell them to shut up."

"Are you back at the hotel?"

"I'll be there for two more weeks, but I can't afford to stay there. Every penny I have is going toward keeping the house and my company going."

"Do you need money?" Darren saw the hurt pride of the man standing in front of him. "I'm sorry. I don't mean to insult you, but . . ."

Grant stood up and walked to the window. Stuffing his hands in his pockets, he looked vacantly at the people making their way past Cannon House to the capitol.

"I've got a place. When my intern goes back to Moscow this summer, I'm staying at his place."

Darren didn't want to think of what an apartment an intern could afford looked like. Especially compared to what Grant was used to. He worried about his friend.

"I know what you're thinking," Grant said. "But he's got rich parents. They rented him a place at the Metropolitan Apartments."

"Sounds nice," Grant said. "You've at least got the award to be happy about. How did it go last night?"

With his back to Darren, he hunched his shoulders. "Bittersweet. Yes, I won political consultant of the year, but that was for last year. I could just read the minds of everyone in that dining hall. *Look at how low he's gone.* I've pitched my whole future on this bill. That was only one of many mistakes I've made this year."

Darren stood up and walked to the edge of his desk. He was cautious not to approach Grant. He could tell his pride had been injured, and the last thing he needed was pity. "You're still standing. I'm still standing. We're survivors."

Grant turned back to him. "My problems aren't as bad as yours, Darren. I couldn't take what you're going through. I know you're getting the cold shoulder around the Hill. We're being frank, right?"

"Of course."

Grant seemed hesitant. "Well . . . have you considered . . ."

"No," Darren said adamantly. "I'm not stepping down. I haven't been charged with anything."

"You know Steed Gringham is—"

"It's not going to happen." Darren was aware that Steed Gringham, a former New York State senator, had been in D.C. for a few days now suggesting to several local papers that Darren step down. "He wants my seat. He was too chicken to run against me, but he hopes to pick up the scraps I leave behind."

" 'Cause he knew that's the only way he'd have a chance," Grant said. "But he's not a bad guy. He's friends with the governor, and if it comes down to his appointment, he'll give Gringham the seat."

"Don't waste your time," Darren said, returning to his seat. "I'm not stepping down. This will all be resolved soon."

Grant grumbled.

Darren could see he was doubtful. "Seriously, Grant. We've made some progress."

"Who is we exactly? You said the police are shutting you out."

"Skye has made some progress."

"I thought you weren't going to let her investigate."

"I wasn't, but . . . the truth is, I need her. I've got the weight of the world on my shoulders just keeping things going here. What she's found is significant and I couldn't have stopped her anyway."

"Why don't you let me help her?" Grant asked. "I'll call her. I mean, she shouldn't be doing this alone."

"We might not need to do any more," Darren said. "We spent last night with Detective Ross, and for the first time since I met that woman she didn't look at me as if I was the dirt of the earth."

"Because?" Grant looked intrigued.

"Franklin is still in town and he's involved with Elizabeth."

"You mean?" Grant's eyes widened. "Are you kidding me?"

"I don't know if it's sexual or anything like that." Darren didn't want to even put that in his mind. He wasn't jealous or anything like that. It was just a disgusting thought. "But they're collaborating on something and I'm sure it leads to Jeff and Wanda Bunning's murder."

"How did Skye find this out?"

"She followed her yesterday." Darren could see Grant's reservation. "I know it's nothing she should be doing, but I had to compromise. In the end, it worked out. She missed out on one potential clue, but connecting Elizabeth with Franklin will turn into something."

"Maybe now she can be pressured into telling the truth for once." Grant was rubbing his chin looking at the floor. "What was the other clue?"

"Elizabeth met someone for lunch right before Franklin picked her up. He was a Russian guy. Skye gave Detective Ross a description, and the more she shared, the more she thought she'd seen the guy before."

"And?"

"He gave Elizabeth an envelope and she wasn't happy about it. Neither was Franklin when Elizabeth handed the envelope to him."

"What can we do to make sure the cops catch up with her before she leaves town again?" Grant asked.

Darren could see anxiety all over Grant's face. "Grant, I know what you're thinking. I don't want you to do anything. Stay away from Elizabeth."

Grant winked, before he looked down at his watch. "I have to get going. I have a lunch meeting at Kincaid's."

"With who?" Darren was actually glad he was leaving. Between the awkward moment about the money and Grant's curiosity with Elizabeth, he was getting uncomfortable with the conversation.

"Just a friend." Grant cleared his throat and started for the door. "Call me if you need anything."

"I will."

Chapter 12

When Skye slid into Darren's bed, he turned off the computer on his lap and put it aside. She looked completely edible in a blood-red nightie with black lace along the edges. The neck went all the way to her belly button, and the inside curve of her firm breasts was calling to him.

He reached for her, but she laughed, pulling away.

"Not the reaction I expected," he said. "Come over here, girl."

Skye frowned, wondering how this man could think of nothing but sex with everything swirling around them. "Take a break, lover boy."

"A break?" He glanced back at the clock on the nightstand. "It's been since this morning. Fourteen hours is enough of a break for me."

"What about what we talked about?"

Darren leaned back against his pillow. "Is this about living with my parents while we're in New York? I don't want it any more than you do, but with everything going on . . ."

"I'm not talking about New York." Although that argument wasn't over, Skye had bigger things on her mind. "I'm talking about Elizabeth. She's vanished from the face of the earth."

"We don't know that."

"She hasn't been brought into the police station. She's not at her condo in Dupont Circle. I've been calling everyone I can think of, and nothing."

"Not nothing," he said. "Now the world knows you're trying to track down the woman that accused your lover of beating her up."

Skye got angry. "So I'm the bad guy now?"

"No, baby."

Darren reached for her again, wanting to return to the comfort of her soft skin, lay his face between those welcoming breasts, and taste the sweetness of her lips. It was his only escape from the world.

"Just don't worry," he said. "Now that she's gone, Detective Ross is more suspicious than ever. The police can find her. She's not an anonymous person and she's too high maintenance to stay in hiding for long."

"That package wasn't money," Skye said. "So if she's going into hiding, she'll have to get some."

"She has a lot of her own," Darren offered. "She's in the alimony business."

"Yes, but when she goes after it, they'll grab her."

"Now that that's settled," Darren said, "back to business."

He brought his lips to hers, but she turned her head and he got a mouthful of hair.

"What now?" Darren asked.

"This is nice," Skye said as she looked up at him. She

was crazy in love with this man. "You and me in bed, talking like a normal couple."

"Nothing about us is normal," Darren said. "I wish it was, but it isn't. And bed isn't for talking, Skye. It's for—"

She pressed her finger to his mouth. "You're starting to sound like me."

He grabbed her hand, kissing her palm. "My mother warned me about naughty girls like you. You're a bad influence. Got me cussing and—"

"Your mother!" Skye couldn't help herself. As distracting as Darren was, their problems wouldn't let her rest. "Have you told your parents about Franklin?"

The mention of his brother's name was enough to cool Darren down. "I had to. I need their help finding him."

Skye felt a stab at her heart for Lily. "They've got to be devastated."

"Yes, but they're strong. They understand what has to happen."

"They won't try to protect him?"

"No. They know what's right."

She gently rubbed his cheek with a tender smile. "That's where you got it from."

"So what in the hell went wrong with my brother?"

"That's not for you to figure out. You've got enough to think about. I just wish I could help you more."

"You've done all you can."

"I should have gotten the license plate of Franklin's car." She sighed regretfully. "I should have taken a picture of that guy. The more I see his face in my mind, the more I think I've seen him before."

"I've had Lonnie all over it. I don't know anyone named Polly connected to Elizabeth or Franklin."

"I've asked Sierra," Skye added. "Jeff doesn't know anyone named Polly either."

"Is there anyone at Jeff's firm with a Russian accent?"

Skye nodded. "She's a woman and somewhere near sixty-five."

Skye scratched her **head**, feeling something knocking at the back of her **brain.** Suddenly, she felt a chill run through her and **she shot up** in the bed.

"What?" Darren asked, concerned.

"It was him." She fought for her voice, trying to make sense of the image in her mind while pushing it away at the same time. "The man that Elizabeth . . . It was him."

Darren grabbed Skye by the arms and turned her to face him. "Skye, calm down and tell me who he is."

"The man who knocked me down in Jeff's apartment," she announced. "It was him."

"I thought you never saw his face."

"All I remembered was the Moscow State U sweatshirt, but now that I've seen him, I remember that hair. It's a sandy blond, brownish red mixture, the horrible dye job. It was him."

"Are you sure?" Darren asked.

"It was him," Skye said with shuttering certainty. "His build, that hair. He has a Russian accent. The sweatshirt said Moscow State U."

Darren held her shivering body. "It's going to be okay, baby. This is good news."

As he rocked her in his arms, Darren began putting pieces together that he didn't want to fit. He hoped a good night's sleep would help him think more clearly in the morning, but if he kept on the trail he was, he knew he wouldn't be getting any sleep.

"Skye?" he asked just above a whisper. "Where does . . . where did Jeff live before he died?"

Skye looked up at him, confused. She tried to rack her brain, but was drawing a blank. "I just can't think of—"

"The Metropolitan Apartments?"

Skye nodded. "Why?"

"Nothing," he lied. "Just want to remember where you first saw the man so I can tell Detective Ross."

"We should call her."

"Not tonight," Darren said. "We'll call her in the morning. Try to sleep, baby."

Skye would try to sleep, but images attacked her throughout the night. She felt safe in Darren's arms but knew she couldn't stay there forever. She was scared to death that they wouldn't get to the truth and Darren's life would be ruined. She couldn't bear the thought of him losing his dream just because of a jealous brother and a vengeful ex-girlfriend. There had been too much lost already with Jeff and Wanda.

Would there be more?

Skye reached over and picked her cell phone up off the floor as she opened the door to her temporary apartment.

"I'm so sorry, Valerie," she said. "I dropped the phone. Apparently doing more than one thing at a time is too much for me."

Valerie Salvatores laughed. "Have you ever heard of headsets? Everyone is using them."

"Yes, and they look absolutely crazy walking around like they're talking to themselves."

"You know they're the law in D.C. when you're driving."

"I'm not driving. I just walked here. Darren's place is only a few blocks away."

"So you've been staying there?"

"Don't spread the word, please." She tossed her keys on the console.

"Oh, please, girl. I wouldn't give those gossip columnists anything. Like you two need something else to be concerned about."

"Thanks." Skye tossed her purse on the kitchen counter and opened the refrigerator. "I haven't been here in a week. I'm sure the press release draft is in the living room. I'll get them and be right over, all right?"

"Sure. I'll see you when you get here."

Skye tossed the phone on the kitchen counter and grabbed a cola. She needed her morning caffeine and Darren didn't do the coffee thing. She had been slow to get up after an uneasy night, and now, because she had forgotten her work at her temporary apartment, she was going to be late for her appointment at Barrio Futuro.

She wasn't going to be negative about it. She was going to roll with it like she always did, trying not to be nervous about the way Darren had been acting last night and again this morning. She had unnerved him with her recollection and felt bad for that. Twice during the night she had woken up to find him wide awake. Skye asked to talk about it, but he said he was only thinking and didn't want to talk.

When morning came, she was prepared to reschedule her appointment with the State Department to go to the station and tell Detective Ross what she remembered, but Darren decided against it. His reaction to her insistence was so forceful that she gave in, mostly because she was just confused.

When she asked to have lunch with him, he told her he was working from home that day and they would go to the police when she got back in the afternoon. Skye didn't like the authoritative tone of his voice, but something about the look in his eyes told her his anger wasn't about being in control or giving orders. He was processing something and it had to do with the dire situation they were finding themselves in.

She felt useless and in the way, so she obliged and retreated to the shower. When she returned, he was getting dressed and Skye had to fight the urge to ask where he was going. If she had to be free, she had to let him be free, and he obviously wanted some time alone. So she left it alone and tried to put it out of her mind.

She tried not to think of it during a morning meeting, but she was noticeably distracted. She put her phone on vibrate hoping for a call from Darren, but nothing came. She was certain he would be home when she got back, but he wasn't, and she didn't have time to wait before her appointment with Valerie considering she had to stop by the apartment to get the draft of the press release they were working on.

Retreating to the living room, Skye headed right for the work area in the far left corner. When she reached it, she heard her cell phone ringing in the kitchen, but just as she was going to turn to get it, something pulled at her gut and a bad feeling rushed over her.

Looking at the state the desk was in, she knew she hadn't left this mess.

Papers were everywhere and some sheets were torn and crumpled. Looking around, Skye could see for the first time that the place was something just short of a mess. Pillows were on the floor and there was a plate of half-eaten sandwiches on the coffee table. Someone had been here!

Someone could still be here!

With her adrenaline rushing, Skye turned toward the kitchen to get her purse and get out. It was then that she saw him and let out a scream.

"I guess you caught me." Franklin stood in the passageway, blocking her way into the kitchen with an amused looked on his face. "Hello, hippie princess."

Skye swallowed hard. He was drunk and his eyes were bloodshot red. "Franklin, what are you—"

"I've been staying here for a few days." He leaned against the wall, talking as if they were having a friendly, casual conversation. "I figured since you weren't, I might as well. I copied this key from Darren about a year ago. He had no idea. For a smart guy, he's pretty clueless."

"He's looking for you." Skye was trying to calm her spirit, thinking of what to do.

"Isn't everybody?" he asked sarcastically.

"What were you . . ." She gestured toward the desk.

"I was trying to find out what you're up to," he answered. "You and that jackass brother of mine."

"We're not up to anything," she said. "We just want—"

"Where is she?" he asked with a hard, aggressive tone.

"Who?"

"You know who!" He took a couple of hard steps toward her, his face contorted in impatient anger. "Elizabeth! Where is she?"

"You're the one having an affair with her," Skye said. "Why don't you know?"

Franklin took a while to bounce back from his surprise. "I knew it. How did you get her to leave? It wasn't money, 'cause she don't need it."

"I don't know what you're talking about."

"Then he did it!" Franklin's hands formed into fists at his sides. "D did it! She must have broken down and told him everything."

"Darren hasn't spoken to Elizabeth. If you—"

"Shut up," he warned. "You sound like those damn nurses at the rehab D is always sending me to."

"He sends you there because he wants to help you," Skye said. "He still does. Even after everything you've done. He knows and he wants to help you."

Franklin's red eyes began to well up with tears as he pressed his lips together to suppress his emotions. "I just thought . . . I don't know what I thought. I'm just so sick of him getting away with murder while I can't do nothin' right."

Skye wondered if Franklin had actually convinced himself that Darren was responsible for the murders. "You can do something right this time."

"It just looked like he was gonna skate and . . ." Franklin was shaking his head vigorously. "Even after I leaked to the press that he killed Jeff over you, nothing was working. I couldn't take it. My own parents stopped talking to me and he's . . ."

"Why should he be in trouble?" Skye asked. "He didn't do anything, Franklin. You know that."

"Then what do I hear?" Franklin asked with a bitter laugh, ignoring everything Skye said. "I'm a damn suspect. Hell no if I'm going down for this."

"People are dead, Franklin."

"I know," he said. "And he's getting away. I didn't know what to do, but then Elizabeth came up with the idea. I went by her place to see if she wanted to help me get revenge against Darren. I knew she was still bitter over his dumping her for you."

"He didn't—"

"We were drinking and things got out of hand." Franklin smiled, shaking his head. "She came up with the idea. I didn't want to do it, but she said it had to be me because if she did it . . . you know, forensics and stuff. They figure out everything."

Skye ignored the confusion of his words. Things didn't match up, but all that she heard was his confession and she couldn't get past her anger. "Why did you have to kill him?"

Franklin frowned and stumbled a bit. "What . . . I . . . No, I didn't . . ."

"Is that the only way you could think to hurt Darren? By killing another man? Jeff Preston didn't do anything to you."

Franklin stood there staring at her without a word, and every second of silence only made her angrier.

"Tell me, Franklin! I deserve an answer. Jeff's parents deserve an answer."

"Whoa! Whoa!" Franklin backed up. "Are you crazy? I didn't kill anyone. Darren killed those—"

"No one is going to buy that anymore, Franklin. You killed them, you and Elizabeth."

A look of panic hit Franklin's ragged face, and Skye realized she had hit a nerve, apparently the last one Franklin had left.

She could hear his breathing pick up, and the hair on the back of her neck stood on end as her intuition warned her to brace herself.

"Hell no!" he yelled. "You two aren't getting away with this!"

The first time he lunged for her, Skye screamed and jumped to the side just out of his grasp. When she tried to run he reached back and grabbed the hem of her shirt, pulling her back.

"Get back here," he grumbled.

She slammed against him and the smell of alcohol made Skye want to throw up. She pushed harder and harder, but he didn't budge. "Franklin, please."

"Please what?" He was laughing now as he tightened his grip on her. "Please let you destroy what is left of my life just to get rid of me?"

Skye was too busy struggling to get away to care about what he had to say. "Let me go!"

"I guess rehab didn't work anymore," he went on. "Now I need to go to jail?"

"Darren will never forgive you if you hurt me."

"Forgive me? You two are a piece of work. If you think you're going off into the sunset while I rot—"

Franklin groaned and hunched over as Skye's knee made contact with his groin. He reached for her, but she eluded his grasp by an inch. She ran out of the living room, grabbed her keys on the console, and kept running out of the apartment. Her stomach was as tight as a knot, but her adrenaline was too high to contemplate that just a moment ago she could have been killed.

She had to get to Darren. He was only a few blocks away, but an inch seemed like a mile. She regretted having left her phone behind, but couldn't have risked it. Calling the police, asking for help was out of the question. She had to get to Darren before anyone else found out.

*   *   *

"Don't push me, Congressman." Detective Ross rolled her eyes before turning her back to Darren to close the file drawer.

"Really, Detective." Darren sat down at the old, wooden table in the center of whatever dark, intimidating room he had followed Detective Ross into. "If you were in my situation, would you do any less?"

She turned back to him with a hand on her hip and a sassy lift of her brow. "I wouldn't let myself get into a situation like you've . . . found yourself in."

"You need to hear what I'm saying," Darren insisted.

It was with a heavy heart that he made his way down to the police station after jogging until he almost fell on his face. He hadn't slept a wink last night, trying to fight past that block in his brain that refused to let him put the pieces together. He knew they were there, but refused to accept them. The despair was enough to make the relief irrelevant.

Even when he had arrived at the station, he spent an inordinate amount of time inquiring about progress on the search for his brother and Elizabeth.

"Where is your woman?" Alice asked. "She's always standing doe-eyed by your side. It's a pretty picture. You know the contrast of—"

"She couldn't make it." The truth was Darren didn't want her to come down. It was hard enough to deal with this himself; he didn't want to have to handle explaining it to Skye as well as the police. This was all yet another bad thing he had brought into her life. "I'm not talking about Skye anymore. I'm talking about the man who attacked her, the man Elizabeth had lunch with."

Alice leaned back against the file drawers. "You're

not talking at all, Congressman. You're thinking out loud and you're not making sense. Besides, you shouldn't be here without your lawyer."

"I don't need a lawyer," Darren said. "I know who's behind this. I can't say why, but I know."

"Your brother?" she asked. "We've already talked about him and I'm not telling you any more."

"I don't know where my brother fits in, but I have a feeling he isn't behind the murders."

"Wishful thinking, maybe?"

"I believe the man behind the murders is Grant Cramer."

Alice's mouth fell open as he finally got her full attention.

"Yes," Darren affirmed. "That Grant Cramer. The one you interviewed while you were investigating me."

"The one who spoke so highly of you I thought he might be your father?"

Darren smiled at the thought, although he didn't know why. "I need you to promise you won't go arresting him yet. Not until I can figure out why."

"First of all, we don't arrest based on the word of concerned friends. If you want to share your . . . thoughts, I'm listening, but I won't promise to act on them and I sure as hell won't tell you if I do."

"If you look at your records, the man who attacked Skye had a sweatshirt on, with Moscow State U written in red letters, similar to the one seen on the man spotted with Wanda Bunning before she was murdered. She recognized the hair and heard his Russian accent."

"We've been through that," Alice said, but without the annoyed tone she usually used.

Darren went through the steps and clues as he had

come to realize them. "Grant, I made some calls this morning. Cramer's assistant is Andre Avegny's nephew and he lives in Krylatskoe, a suburb of Moscow. He didn't go to Moscow State, but it's like any city here where people buy their local university sweats."

"That's good circumstantial," Alice said. "Might be enough to bring him in, but not keep him."

Darren smiled. "Well, maybe this will help you. He's going back home for the summer, and Grant, whose wife kicked him out earlier this year, is taking his apartment, which is on the eighth floor of the Metropolitan Apartments building."

Alice's face went flat. "That's Preston's building."

"The exact building where you suspected that the murderer used some magic tricks to avoid being seen on the security cameras."

Alice frowned, looking away. "He didn't need to use the entrance if he never had to leave."

"Exactly," Darren said regretfully.

Alice held a contentious finger up. "But we canvassed that building and there was no connection to you or—"

"You weren't looking for a connection with Grant. And even if you were, you would have found the apartment belongs to a Russian couple that didn't have anything to do with anybody."

"So who is Polly?" Alice asked.

"There is no Polly," Darren said. "I didn't figure that out until this morning, but Skye didn't hear him say Polly. She heard him say Pollies. That night was the award ceremony for the political consulting industry."

"The Pollies." Alice nodded as if the pieces were falling together. "For lobbyists and their kind."

"Grant received the Political Consultant of the Year award."

"Why?" Alice's guard was down as she seemed more concerned with figuring things out than keeping Darren at a professional distance. "What's the motive?"

"I don't know," Darren said. With a heavy sigh he added, "But I think it's about me."

"Did he think Preston was going to beat you?"

"He can't possibly have thought that," Darren answered. "But some time ago, Skye was . . . I think she was investigating me and she had some information that Jeff left behind."

Alice was suddenly angry. "She lied to me, didn't she? I asked her if she found anything that day and she said no. I should have searched her ass."

"Detective, let's not—"

"Let's not nothing," she snapped. "If I might have had that information, I could have made progress on this case and Wanda Bunning might not be dead. Unless you don't think she's still involved."

"She is," Darren said. "She's involved, as are Franklin and Elizabeth somehow. But I don't think what Skye found could help you. It was a lot of nothing and it was mostly about me."

"Damn." Alice walked past Darren to the small window providing the only light in the dark room. She stared out in a mental escape.

Darren gave her a moment before going on. "I've asked Grant to meet me at my apartment to discuss possibly stepping down from office. I'm going to confront him about this."

She turned back to him with a look of disgust on her face. "What are you, crazy?"

"I think all of this has turned me a little crazy, yes."

"If what you're saying is true and—"

"It's all true and easily verifiable."

"Fine," she said. "Then, if that's the case, you're putting yourself in danger by confronting him."

"I know what I'm doing," Darren said confidently. "I know this man and I'm not afraid."

"What difference does that make? He can still shoot you whether you're afraid he will or not."

"I don't think he wants to hurt me."

"He tried to frame you!"

Darren paused for a second. "I don't think . . . That's not what's important. I want you to wire me, Detective Ross."

"I would think if you learned anything it's that you don't know him. You especially don't know how he'll react when cornered."

"I'm doing this, Detective." Darren stood up, tightening his tie. "I wanted to do this along with you, but I can't force you to get involved any more than you can force me to stop. Grant will be showing up in less than an hour. I'm getting to the bottom of this one way or another."

"Trying to be a hero for your girlfriend?" Alice asked. "Or is she in on this too?"

"She's not and I'm keeping her out until . . ." It hit him like a brick.

"Until you mess things up so much that there's no chance of building a case?"

Darren reached into his jacket pocket for his phone and dialed furiously.

"What is it?" Alice seemed genuinely intrigued.

"Skye," he said. "I told Grant she recognized her attacker before I suspected him."

Her cell phone was ringing but there was no answer. "Is she at your place?"

Darren shook his head, dialing his apartment. "I made sure that she wouldn't be there. She had to work with a client on the Hill."

"Then she should be safe," Detective Ross said. "Unless she shows up at your place before you do."

"I'm not willing to take the chance," Darren said. "My gut instinct tells me I'll regret it for the rest of my life if I do. Either you're with me or not."

"I can stop you, you know."

"Or you can help me." Out of ideas, Darren called Skye's phone again. As it rang, he eyed Detective Ross plainly. "You can give me that hard look all you want, Detective. You know I'm not guilty of any of this and you know whatever is going on, it's going to be on the front cover. Don't be the detective that didn't see the signs."

"You son of a bitch!"

Darren was taken aback by the harsh words that growled at him over the phone. "Who is . . . Franklin?"

"I know what you're up to!"

Darren felt a rush of panic hit him, followed quickly by anger. "Why do you have Skye's phone?"

"You're not going to frame me for these murders! I'll go to the police. I'll do whatever."

Darren mouthed his brother's name to Detective Ross and she took a step closer. He had her, he knew, but that wasn't important now. "No one is going to frame you, Franklin. Is Skye with you? How do you—"

"She's gone, but I'll get her. I'll get you too."

"If you hurt her, I'll—"

"If I hurt her?" Franklin laughed. "After everything you two are doing to me?"

Darren gripped the phone hard. "I'll kill you, Franklin."

He heard a quick sigh before, like a scolded child, Franklin offered, "I'm at her apartment. She ran out of here. I didn't do anything. She's probably going to you, but—"

"She's going right to him," Darren said to Detective Ross.

He hung up and flew out of the police department not caring whether or not she was behind him.

Having done everything to keep it together on the way over, Skye fell apart the second she arrived at Darren's condo. Throwing the door open, she stumbled inside, almost falling over herself. With tears streaming down her face she yelled for Darren.

Running into the living room where she heard a voice, she was shocked to come face-to-face with Grant. He had been talking on his cell phone but was obviously jolted by her scream and seemed just as surprised to see her as she was him.

"I'll call you back," he said quickly before hanging up and tossing his phone on the sofa. He rushed to her.

"What's wrong?" He reached for her, but Skye backed away.

"Where is Darren?" she asked.

"He's on his way." Grant eyed her curiously. "You're crying. What—"

"I'm sorry." Skye turned away from him, wiping at her tears. She knew how close Grant was to Darren, but she couldn't tell him what had just happened. It was too personal. "When will Darren be here? I need to talk to him."

"I'm early." Grant glanced at his watch. "He'll be here in a half hour. Call his cell."

"No." Skye turned back to him, trying to put on the best face she could. "I . . . I need to talk to him face-to-face."

"I know," Grant said. "Phones are so cold when you're talking about something personal. Are you upset that he's stepping down?"

Skye's eyes widened in surprise. "What? Darren isn't . . . Where would you get that idea?"

Grant shook his head. "I'm not getting into this. I already stuck my foot in my mouth with that whole Elizabeth thing. You can talk to him."

"I'm asking you," she directed harshly.

Grant hesitated in response to her aggression before explaining. "I heard it from Darren. He called me this morning. We talked about it the other day and apparently he's decided it's the right choice."

"I don't know what you think he said," Skye offered, "but he would never step down."

Feeling her knees get a little weak, she sat down on the sofa. She was running Franklin's words through her mind, and something wasn't right.

"Skye, all I can tell you is that he called me this morning and specifically said he was considering it. That's why I'm over here. He didn't want anyone at his office to catch on."

Skye thought of how distant Darren had been that morning and it hit her suddenly that this could be the reason why. "I thought it was me."

Grant sat next to her, ignoring his ringing cell phone. "It's about everything, Skye."

"But why?" Skye turned to him. "Because he was afraid for my safety?"

"What are you in danger of?"

"I told him last night that I remembered that man I saw with . . ." Skye waved her hand away. "It's hard to explain."

"'I know," Grant said. "He told me about you following Elizabeth."

"Well, I recognized the man she was having lunch with. He's the same man who attacked me when I was at Jeff's apartment getting the disk."

"What disk?"

"A disk with information Jeff thought he could use against Darren. Something he thought he could send him to jail for."

"Damn it." Grant clenched a fist and hit his thigh. "I knew that asshole had something."

"Don't call him that!"

Grant seemed a little shaken by Skye's angry retort. "I'm . . . I'm sorry. You have to know that—"

"Jeff wasn't perfect, but he was a good person and he didn't deserve to die." Skye was too tired to bother crying anymore. She fell back against the pillows wishing that Grant would leave and Darren would get here.

"What did the disk say?" Grant asked.

"I don't remember." Growing uncomfortable with Grant's attention, Skye stood up and walked to the window. "Nothing makes sense now. Why would it scare him that I recognized that man? I thought it was good news. We're supposed to go to the cops this afternoon, but—"

"What did he say about the man?"

With her back still to him, Skye tried to remember, but she could only feel pressure at her temples. "Why would he tell you he was reconsidering stepping down before he told me?"

"What did Darren say about the man you saw with Elizabeth?"

The insistence in his tone caught Skye's attention, and when she turned around, seeing him standing as tight and tense as a log, she got the same vibe she'd had when she saw the unkempt desk at the apartment.

"What did he say?" Grant asked again.

"He didn't say anything," she answered cautiously. "He just asked me the name of Jeff's apartment and zoned out. What is wrong with you, Grant?"

Grant pulled at his chin, mumbling something to himself, and Skye felt a chill run down her spine.

"Maybe that's what it is," Skye said. "He's figured something out and wants to talk to you because you're one of the few people he can trust, one of the few who stuck by his side."

"Trust." Grant laughed.

"It has to be that," she said hopefully. "Trust me, considering stepping down is not on the table. I can't tell you why he would suggest it was, but I know. Maybe he just didn't want to tell you the real reason he's asked you over here so you wouldn't tell anyone or . . ."

Grant was still mumbling, only faster now, and Skye was growing more and more concerned.

She fought the urge to go to him, because although she cared for this man, something told her to keep her distance. He seemed to be getting more and more agitated with every second.

"I know this is upsetting," she said, "but we'll find out who that man is and we'll get to the bottom of everything."

"Then it will all be over," he said calmly. "Damn it!"

"That's a good thing," she said. "Darren will be cleared."

"You don't understand." He dropped his hands to his sides and moaned. "Why did you have to come to D.C., Skye?"

She didn't know how to answer. As hurt as she was that he would be blaming all of this on her, Grant looked on the verge of a breakdown and she didn't want to make a bad situation worse. She'd had enough of that today.

Grant threw his hands in the air before burying his face inside them. He was shaking his head rapidly from side to side, and Skye was mesmerized. She was unable to move until the phone rang and she went for it.

Before she could reach it, Grant jumped in front of her with a tortured look on his face.

"No," was all he said.

"Get out of my way, Grant." Skye was going with her intuition and it told her she was about to see a repeat of what had happened with Franklin only minutes ago, and she wasn't sure she could handle that.

"I have to think," Grant said, stepping in front of her again as she made a second try for the phone.

Skye decided then that she could handle it; she would have to. She just didn't understand why. "Whatever is wrong, Grant, you know Darren can help you."

He stared at her with doubtful eyes. "I have every right to hate you, Skye."

Skye stepped back. Had he just threatened her?

"If you hadn't come to D.C.," he continued, "no one would have doubted Jeff's death was a suicide. I have every right to hate you, but I don't. You're too good and Darren loves you, so I couldn't hate you."

Skye's confusion about what Franklin had said and what Grant was saying now disappeared. It was suddenly painfully and frighteningly clear to her what was going on.

"Oh God, Grant. Darren cares about you so much."

"Skye," Grant pleaded. "You have to understand that I care about Darren the way I would if I had a son. He's the only man I've met in the last twenty years I can respect."

Skye took another step backward. "Why would you frame him?"

"I didn't," he said angrily. "It was supposed to be a suicide! You made it more than that."

Skye just shook her head, wanting to hear the truth but wishing it wasn't at the same time.

"It's because of my bill." His face turned beet red. "That damn bill I need to get passed. If I don't get that money and that deal for Fedulev, I'm a dead man. I owe them more money than I could make in a lifetime. This is the only way—"

"This is about a debt?" Skye asked.

"Not just a debt," he corrected. "A debt to Fedulev."

Skye shrugged in confusion.

"The Russian mob, Skye."

"Oh, Grant," she said. "Your gambling is the cause of this?"

"I've already lost my marriage over this," he said. "I'm fighting for my life now."

Skye didn't bother to hide her rage for fear of anything. "You didn't kill Jeff to keep him from beating Darren. You killed him because the dirt he had wasn't going to lead him to Darren. It was going to lead him to you."

"You can't possibly understand the situation," Grant said. "If Jeff had confronted Darren with that information, Darren would have investigated. No matter how much I may mean to him, he wouldn't look past the law for me. Everything would be over and I'm not talking about jail."

"You were going to use Darren to get this bill passed and make sure the contracts went to your mob friends to clean your debt with them."

"I made certain to keep Darren out of it so he wouldn't be touched."

"He's sponsoring the bill, Grant. There's no way he wouldn't be touched. It would have ruined his reputation, his career, and possibly sent him to jail. It would have destroyed him."

"If I had to, I would testify that—"

"No one will believe you," Skye said. "No one believes a criminal."

"You have to help me, Skye." He stretched his arms out to her, his hands open wide.

"Are you crazy? People are dead because of you. Jeff and that innocent girl."

"That wasn't my idea," Grant said with a menacing frown. "Fedulev threw her at me. He wanted to bring the focus back to suicide because he was afraid Darren wouldn't be able to get the bill in if he was suspected of murder. He's the father of that baby she aborted, and those cash deposits in her account are from him."

"But how did she know about Jeff's—"

"Fedulev's men broke into the ME's office and took the pictures of Preston's body. That's how she knew about his anatomy. I had no idea she did Elizabeth's hair. It was one of those crazy coincidences that I wish I had known about. The connection counteracted everything I was trying to use her for."

Skye jumped back as Grant took another step closer. His eyes were begging for understanding. "I'm telling you this, Skye, because I need you to understand. I need you and Darren to understand what is at stake. You can't go to the police. I wanted to pay Preston off. It was Fedulev who had him killed."

"You were a part of it," she said in a tone that gave away the coldness of her heart to his efforts. "You can't blame anyone for what you've done to them both."

"That girl," he said. "I just wanted her to go away. I warned her and she said she would call her aunt and get out of here. Fedulev had her killed before she could leave. I didn't want anyone to die. I just wanted to get Fedulev off my back without destroying Darren's future."

"Stop acting as if you care about him."

"I do care about him," he urged. "I'm the one that has been trying to keep this together. I'm the one who made Elizabeth leave town after she and Franklin pulled that stunt. I don't know where in the hell that came from."

"She's not in on this with you?" Skye asked. "Franklin either?"

"No." He started toward her. "Skye, please—"

"Don't touch her!"

Darren rushed into the room, starting for Grant.

Skye backed into the window to avoid Grant, who was backing toward her. When he bumped against her, she pushed away.

"Darren?" Grant looked more and more unhinged

with every second. "I would never hurt her. I care about her because of you."

Darren's eyes blazed with the fury of anger he felt at the sight of him near her. "Skye, did he touch you?"

Skye shook her head. "He killed Jeff and Wanda."

"I know," Darren said, turning back to Grant.

Grant recovered quickly and cleared his throat. "All isn't lost, Darren. If we work together . . ."

"Why would I work with you?" Darren asked. "Look at what you've done to me."

"This was never about hurting you," Grant said, pointing to Skye. "She's the reason it got this far. There was no—"

Grant gasped out loud, looking around frantically. Skye didn't have time to react when he reached for her and grabbed her with one arm and wrapped the other one around her neck.

"No!" Darren lunged for him.

"I'll kill her!" Grant yelled.

Skye realized he wasn't yelling at Darren. It was then she saw Detective Ross standing at the door with her gun cocked.

"Let her go," Alice yelled across the room. "Mr. Cramer, let her go."

"I can snap her neck," Grant said, squeezing tighter. "Darren, you know I can. I did it for my country not too long ago."

"Grant, you know if you hurt her, I'll kill you. You won't give me any other choice." For the first time in his life, Darren saw that he could take someone's life. He would kill Grant if he hurt Skye, and his desire not to do that made him calm down.

"Now you know how I feel," Grant said. "I just wanted to make sure the bill passed."

"By hurting me?" Darren asked, hoping he could distract Grant long enough to benefit Detective Ross. He wanted to lose it, but he couldn't. Grant was right; he could snap her neck before Darren could reach him.

"That wasn't my intention," Grant said. "All that mess with Elizabeth, I had nothing to do with it. I thought we still had a chance until she came forward with those charges."

"You paid her."

"I didn't pay her. I blackmailed her. I took pictures of her and your brother and another man having sex. I made her get out of town to help you."

"Then why did you want me to step down?"

"Gringham is on my side. If he replaces you, he can help me lobby the bill during the district break and get it back in play when the session resumes. I'm sorry this happened to you, but I had to get that bill passed."

"Well, you're not getting anything passed now," Skye said. "It's all over."

"Skye." Darren shook his head. Her feistiness was not going to help the situation. "So you traded in our friendship for money?"

"For my life, Darren." He let out a heavy, painful sigh. "I owe Fedulev almost one million dollars. When he found out about the opportunity with the land, he upped my interest to fifty percent and called his loan in immediately. I had to help him with this or I was going to die and God only knows what might have happened to my family."

"We can protect you," Alice said. She was now inside

the room with a clear view of Grant. "We can't get you off, but we can protect you from Fedulev."

Grant sighed, shaking his head. "No. I can't live with this. I can't let my wife live with this. You have to help me, Darren. I never wanted to hurt you. I care about you like a son."

"I can't help you anymore," Darren said. "Just let her go."

Skye pulled away, but Grant tightened his grip on her neck and the constriction was choking her.

"No." There wasn't any anger in Darren's voice this time, only desperation and pleading. "Please, Grant."

"You're turning your back on me," Grant said. "I've got nothing to lose."

"But I do," Darren said. "I love her, Grant. I love her more than I could prove if I tried every day for a thousand years."

Darren wasn't looking at Grant anymore. His eyes connected with Skye as the idea of losing her broke down everything inside him. His life, his future ceased to exist at the thought.

"She's the air that I breathe," he said. "The reason why for everything. She owns my heart and my soul. If she can't be my wife and the mother of my children, you have to kill me too. Please, Grant . . . if you care at all about me whether I can help you or not, please give her back to me."

Darren stretched his arms out and Skye didn't wait for Grant to loosen his grip on her. Darren's words were all the strength she needed to pull away, and his eyes told her nothing or no one could stop her. She ran to him, burying her face in his chest as he swept her into his arms.

Darren leaned down, kissing the top of her head tenderly as he gripped her with all the force he had. The world around them disappeared; no one else existed. It was in each other's arms they knew that everything, even with the hell storm coming their way, would be all right as long as they stayed together. Forever.

Epilogue

"Come on!" Lonnie waved to Darren and Skye from halfway down the steps of the stage. "Your parents are almost finished."

Darren couldn't take his lips off Skye's as she tugged at his coat jacket. A knock on the head got his attention.

"Hey!" He turned around to see Sierra standing behind him, frowning.

"You heard him," she said. "You've got another sixty years to be kissing on her."

"Won't be enough time for me," Skye said.

Darren took her hand. "Fine. We can't put this off any longer."

"Shame on you for wanting to." Sierra squeezed past them and joined Lonnie down the stairs.

"You good?" Darren asked.

Skye nodded. "Couldn't be better. How about you?"

"I'm a king with you at my side." As they reached the

bottom of the steps, he wrapped his arms around her again. "I couldn't have gotten here without you."

"It's been crazy," Skye said. "I wouldn't have it any other way."

That wasn't exactly true. The last six months hadn't been easy on anyone. As a matter of fact, it had been pretty brutal and painful, but Skye kept her optimism and the light at the end of the tunnel grew closer and closer. It all culminated into tonight.

After Grant's arrest, the press coverage was insane, but Darren didn't run away. Even as the scandal spread and everyone involved was arrested on various charges, Darren answered every question and faced every accusation with his head held high.

Skye never left his side. When the truth came out and his heart was aching over the man he thought was his friend and the brother he loved dearly, she soothed it. While such a trial could tear most new relationships apart, it only brought them closer together. Their love gave Darren the strength to stay in the race, and it paid off.

It helped that Grant testified to Darren's innocence in all his plans and Franklin admitted to the con he planned with Elizabeth after entering rehab again. Elizabeth admitted nothing, but decided to leave Washington, D.C., considering that the entire social establishment had completely rejected her after Franklin's disclosure.

The Congressional Black Caucus, and its leader, Senator Hart, made a formal statement of support for Darren. Others in the House and the Senate followed suit. The Hart stamp of approval seemed to be the snowball rolling down the hill as more community, business, and national support streamed in.

Darren had become the survivor who stood by his principles under attack from all sides, and his promise only seemed brighter in the end. Once a favorite in New York and D.C., he was now the politician all of America loved, and those dying rumors of the Senate, the governor's office, and the White House came roaring back to life.

After what he had been through, the press said, what could stop him?

Certainly not a relationship with an unconventional, opinionated, and liberal spitfire with absolutely no desire to be a society darling. Darren had given his heart away the night he faced down Grant in his apartment, but made it formal during a warm August evening in a Bali hut standing over the piercing blue ocean. He asked Skye to marry him and she could barely wait for him to finish before screaming yes a dozen times.

They still fought on all the issues and stubbornly refused to concede a political point, but none of that mattered. What had begun as a Capitol affair had turned into the love of their lifetime, and what made them different only made them more intriguing and challenging to each other. They accepted their differences, found comfort in each other's flaws, and could barely wait to spend a lifetime together.

Darren's smile faded. "Honestly, Skye. If you hadn't been with me—"

Skye pressed her finger against his lips. "There was nowhere else I could possibly have been. I belong with you, at your side."

"That's oddly traditional of you."

Darren knew when he finally found the person God meant for him, he would be happier than he had ever been, but he never expected this. The feeling of strength, belonging, and pride a man could get from being with a woman he could rely on no matter what, when, or why, a woman he knew would never let him down, always love him, forgive him, and fight for him, was beyond words.

"Your conservative ways are rubbing off on me."

"I guess I can say the same about your liberal ways," he said. "I've sure thrown caution to the wind these past six months and faced disaster head-on, chest open and ready to receive the blows. No plans, no designs, just going with my heart and your hand in mine."

"It worked," Skye said with a wince. "Although I have to tell you, voting Republican today was as far as I'm willing to go."

"Hey!" Lonnie gestured for their attention before pointing to the other side of the blue curtain where cameras were flashing and people cheering.

"Your congressman Darren Birch!" Gary's deep, vibrant voice was drowned out by the wild cheers and applause.

Lonnie was waving wildly for them to go out onto the stage full of campaign workers and supporters from all over who had come to celebrate his victory on this November 4.

Darren nodded, turning to Skye. He squeezed her hand and pecked her nose with his finger. "You ready?"

"Ready?" she asked. "What would be the fun in that?"

"I love you, Skye."

"I love you too."

Skye had never meant any words more in her life. Her joy made her feel brighter than all the lights that faced them as they walked onto the stage to the crowd full of cheers and admiration for their young, charming, and hopeful representative.

"But I have to tell you," she said, barely audible above the crowd.

"What?"

"I'm not changing my last name."

He squinted, loving that stubborn press of her luscious lips. "We'll see about that."

More Arabesque Romances by
Donna Hill

More Sizzling Romance From
Francine Craft

__Betrayed by Love	1-58314-152-9	$5.99US/$7.99CAN
__Devoted	0-7860-0094-5	$4.99US/$5.99CAN
__Forever Love	1-58314-194-4	$5.99US/$7.99CAN
__Haunted Heart	1-58314-301-7	$5.99US/$7.99CAN
__Lyrics of Love	0-7860-0531-9	$4.99US/$6.50CAN
__Star-Crossed	1-58314-099-9	$5.99US/$7.99CAN
__Still in Love	1-58314-005-0	$4.99US/$6.50CAN
__What Matters Most	1-58314-195-2	$5.99US/$7.99CAN
__Born to Love You	1-58314-302-5	$5.99US/$7.99CAN

Available Wherever Books Are Sold!

Visit our website at **www.BET.com.**